SO THIS IS EARTH?

SPACE ROGUES

BOOK 5

JOHN WILKER

EDITED BY

EMBER EYSTER

Rogue Publishing

Cover art by John Wilker & Greg Bahlmann

V 2.1

ISBN: 978-1-7326287-9-3

Image of Earth Courtesy NASA/JPL-Caltech

CONTENTS_

PART ONE

CHAPTER 1

Princess Problems	5
Pay the Man	8

CHAPTER 2

No-No-Notorious	13
Things Cost Money	16
Pay Up	19
Phone Calls	22

CHAPTER 3

How the Other 99% Live	27
Little People, Firm Handshake	30
Hoi Polloi	32
An Impressive Collection	35
Indecent Proposal, Sorta	39

CHAPTER 4

Minus One	45
Night Out on the Town	48
Dance Dance Revolution	50
Parties Always End	53

CHAPTER 5

Four Stories	59
Parting Is Such Sweet Sorrow	62
New Toys	66

PART TWO

CHAPTER 6

Shopping   75
The Ghost: Maxim   78
Shopping: Zephyr & Wil   82
Shopping: Cynthia & Bennie   85

CHAPTER 7

Fancy Fancy   91
Bye for Now   94
Take Out   96

CHAPTER 8

Slow Boat to Jupiter   101
This Is Earth?   104
Why Is It Always a Rough Landing?   108

CHAPTER 9

Toys, Toys, Toys   113
New Face, Who Dis?   116
Going Going Back Back to Cali Cali   119
Road Trip!   122

CHAPTER 10

Checking In   127
Presidential Suite   130
The Kids Are . . . Alien   133
Food Court Food   136
Mommy Dearest   139

PART THREE

CHAPTER 11

Driver's Ed.   147
On the Move   150
Reunions and Separations   153
Twenty Questions   156

CHAPTER 12

Purpose of Your Visit?   161
Space Race   164
Not Good with Children   167
What Happens in Vegas   170

CHAPTER 13

New Rides   175
Uncomfortable Conversations   178
Hard Truths   181

CHAPTER 14

Getting to Know You   187
Mr. Prior, I Presume   190
Well That's a Plan, I guess   193

PART FOUR

CHAPTER 15

Bacon Makes the World Go 'Round   199
Running Toward a Cliff   202
Bad Breakfast   205
That Probably Hurt   208
Sideways, Always Sideways   211

CHAPTER 16

Goose Chase   217
The Band Is (Mostly) Back Together   220
A Dish Best Served with Plasma Rounds   223
Aboard the Wil Calder   226
Scorched Earth, Literally   228

CHAPTER 17

Fly like an Eagle   233
Back Aboard the Wil Calder   236
It's a Chase!   238
Brought Nothing to a Missile Fight   241
When in Doubt, Reverse Polarity   244

CHAPTER 18

All Limbs Still Attached   249
Bridge of the Wil Calder   252
Home Sweet Spaceship   254

PART FIVE

CHAPTER 19

Nightly News   261
Negative Ghost Rider, Pattern Is Full   264
Catch Me if You Can   267
Now It's a Real Fight!   270

CHAPTER 20

Missiles & Awkward Conversations   275
Plucking Quills from an Agrot   278
Nosy Neighbors   281

CHAPTER 21

Dropping off the Kids   287
Peace Out   290
You'll Get Over It   292
Side Deals   294

Epilogue   297

Thank You   301
Offer   303
Stay Connected   305
Space Rogues 6 Coming Soon!   307
Other Books by John Wilker   309

DEDICATED TO..._

My wife Nicole, who's unwavering support has meant the world to me in this journey.

Thank you Punkin!

PART ONE

CHAPTER 1_

PRINCESS PROBLEMS_

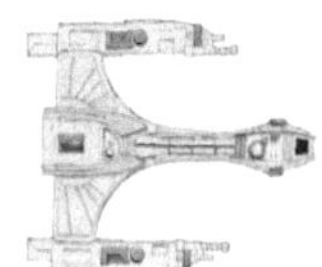

"I HATE HER," Cynthia says as she gets dressed.

Wil, still lying in bed, says, "How could you hate her? You've only just met her?"

"Yet here we are, and I want her dead." She's making a growling noise Wil once thought was purring until Cynthia made it clear it was not a happy sound. She slides her hand through her wristcomm, locking it in place on her forearm. Turning to open the hatch to the quarters they share, she turns to her lover, "Get dressed and make breakfast. I'll be on the bridge." The hatch closes behind her.

Flinging the covers off of him, Wil groans, "Yes, mom." He pads to the small refresher compartment. As he activates the cleaning mode, he looks up, "Computer, where is our passenger?"

"Miss Yutani is in her assigned quarters."

Wil nods and starts his shower.

As the hatch that closes off the stairwell to the living quarters opens, Wil hears a hissing noise followed by, "You can't keep me here! I'll slit your throat!"

Sighing, he opens the hatch all the way, "Good morning campers!" he shouts, smiling as broadly as he can.

Bennie is standing in the middle of the lounge area pointing a fork at their passenger.

Their passenger, a Trenbal teenager, is crouching in the kitchenette area, a large and very sharp knife held in one hand, a frying pan in the other.

Wil notices Zephyr sitting in the large chair a few feet from Bennie. He looks at his first officer, her Palorian features unreadable as she takes in the scene. Wil points to the two presumed combatants, "So, uh, what's this?"

"Bennie made a pass at her," Zephyr replies.

Wil looks at the Brailack, "Dude, she's a kid."

"Then he reminded her she's our prisoner and she can't leave," Zephyr adds.

"I am not a child!" the reptilian teen screams, hissing at the end of the exclamation. "You cannot keep me here! That's kidnapping!" she adds.

Wil turns to her, holding both hands up, palms out, "Sorry, young adult." The teenage woman glares at him but says nothing. He turns and stalks over to the resident hacker and ship's official pain in the ass. Snatching the fork, "Not ok." He holds up a finger, "She's a chi—young adult." Raising a second finger, "She's our guest." A third finger rises, "She's a princess. Apologize. Now."

Bennie leans to peek around Wil, "I'm sorry. I didn't mean to offend you, your highness." He straightens and looks at Wil, mouthing the word *there*.

Wil punches him in the arm, then turns to face their guest, "Please accept my apologies; he was raised by wolves."

The reptilian face scrunches, "What is a wolve?"

Wil shakes his head once closing the gap between them, "Never mind, may I?" He gingerly plucks the frying pan from a sharp-clawed hand. "I'm going to make pancakes if you're hungry."

Bennie approaches the kitchenette slowly, taking a seat as far from Princess Yutani as possible.

Zephyr gets up from where she watched the drama unfold and takes a seat next to Bennie.

The Trenbal woman sits opposite the two, "You can't take me home." She's staring right at Zephyr. It was Zephyr who grabbed her at the nightclub on Plumbus Eight the previous night. Since then, the *Ghost* has been burning hard for Fury, where the wayward Princess's father will be waiting for them.

"Why can't we?" Zephyr asks.

"He's a monster. The worst!" the teenage woman says, her head in her hands. "I was just having fun. He's always going on about schooling and decorum!" She slams a palm on the table.

Maxim walks in from the direction of the bridge as Zephyr says, "Your father was worried. You'd been gone for a standard month. On top of that, it's been two more weeks, because you weren't easy to track down."

"How did you find me?" the slightly calmer Princess asks.

Maxim sits down and points to Bennie, "He found you."

Zephyr groans as the nimble teenager lunges across the table, her powerful clawed hands around Bennie's throat as the two tumble to the deck.

Maxim blinks twice but doesn't move, "I say something wrong?"

The screaming and hissing from the floor between the kitchenette and the lounge area breaks up as fire extinguisher foam hits the combatants. Gabe is standing over the now foam-covered pair of adversaries, "Are you quite done?"

"Did you have to do that?" Bennie whines, "You know what fire suppression foam does to my skin."

Wil turns from his work, "You've got about five minutes before breakfast is on; go get cleaned up, both of you."

"You don't want to miss pancakes, better hurry," Maxim says making a brushing motion with his hand, urging the two foam-covered beings toward the hatch to the living spaces deck.

PAY THE MAN_

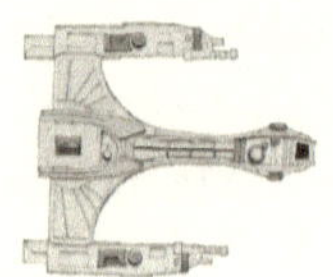

As the *Ghost* settles onto its powerful landing legs, Wil flips switches, "Cutting repulsor lifts, atmospheric engines powered down. Gabe"—he looks at the ceiling—"put the reactor in standby please."

"Acknowledged," the ceiling replies.

Wil turns to Cynthia, "His highness on the way?"

She nods, holding a finger up, "Very good. We're in Fury spaceport eight, pad nineteen. Yup. Yup. Fine." She turns to Wil, pressing a button to disconnect the communication channel she was just on, "He's on his way, about ten centocks."

Maxim turns, "What was the rest of that about?"

Cynthia makes a noise, "He was confirming she was unharmed and in one piece. Oh, and then ended with a threat about how she had better be all right and intact." She looks at Wil, "Guess our reputation is growing."

Bennie hops out of his seat and heads for the door.

Wil points at him, "Do not bother her."

The Brailack holds open his collar showing the dark green bruises around his neck, "Not a problem, I gotta pee," he grumbles.

Zephyr smiles, "I'll go get our guest." She gets up and makes for the hatch following behind Bennie.

Wil stands, following Zephyr, "I'll get the umbilicals connected."

Maxim nods, "I'll mind the store."

With the *Ghost's* main cargo ramp deployed, and the thick inner cargo doors open, the more or less fresh air of Fury fills the hold. Wil and Gabe are under the ship hooking up several umbilicals that will pump out waste and pump in consumables like water, and top off any other fluids and matter the ship might need.

Bennie is sitting on a lounge chair under an umbrella as two sleek black hover cars approach. "Looks like Princess mean girl's ride is here."

"I heard that!" comes from inside the cargo hold. Princess Yutani comes out to stand at the top of the ramp. Zephyr appears at her side.

Zephyr kneels next to the young woman, "I know it's hard; your mom is gone, and your dad is busy and not around much." The girl nods and Zephyr continues, "This will be hard to believe, but trust me, it gets better. You just have to know that he's trying his best." She stands and heads down the ramp, the young Yutani following.

As the two women near the bottom of the ramp, Bennie adds, "Or"—he holds up a finger—"do a better job of masking your trail and avoid dance clubs that live stream their patrons." He sticks his tongue out.

Zephyr makes a rude gesture towards him, guiding the Princess away from the reclining Brailack.

Cynthia, leaning against the edge of the cargo opening at the top of the ramp, looks at the approaching vehicles then down to Zephyr and the young woman, "Bye bye." She waves slowly, staring at the young Trenbal who stares back with unmasked disdain.

As the lead hover car comes to a stop, Bennie gets up and walks towards it, only to be intercepted by Wil who wipes his hands on the back of Bennie's shirt, then shoves him back toward his chair.

Wil stands near the opening door, "Your highness."

"I told you; I am not royalty," the Trenbal man in an expensive-looking suit says as he steps from the vehicle. An aide gets out right behind him and rushes to stand behind his employer. "I am the sovereign executive, by birth, of the island nation Siskona."

"That sounds like *King*," Wil says falling into step next to the older reptilian man, who sighs but says nothing until he sees his wayward daughter at the bottom of the ramp, "Skaarina, come."

Skaarina Yutani heads toward her father; staring at the ground she says, "Hi daddy."

"Hello dear, they treated you well?" The older Trenbal man is squinting while examining his daughter. Nodding, he holds his hand out expectantly.

The aide who fell in behind Wil comes around and places a PADD in the Trenbal not-a-monarch's hand. He taps the screen a few times, then swipes. Wil's wristcomm vibrates, confirming the receipt of the final payment. Handing the PADD back to his aide, the Trenbal man says, "A pleasure Captain Calder. Thank you for retrieving her and keeping her safe while in your care." He doesn't wait for Wil to answer, turning and making for his hover car.

Wil waves, "Pleasure doing business with you. Holler when she runs away again!" He turns to consider at the crew, now all gathered at the foot of the cargo ramp, "What say we go get drunk?"

Everyone nods, smiling. Zephyr taps her wristcomm, "Love, come on out; we're going into town."

CHAPTER 2_

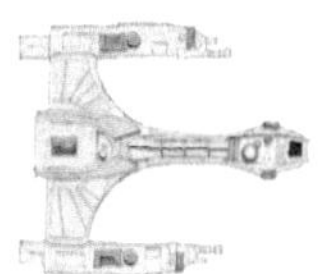

NO-NO-NOTORIOUS_

"I ᴋɴᴏᴡ this will sound weird, but I liked this place better when Xarrix owned it," Wil says, picking up a laminated placemat. The colorful logo looking up at him is a beaming Ruknak with an oversized bottle of grum in one hand wearing a colorful shirt and matching hat.

Bennie looks up from his own placemat, "Yeah, I mean it was gross and the odds of being shot were higher, but"—he points to something on the wall—"is that *Flare?*"

Cynthia and Maxim both nod; the big Palorian man adds, "It is. Perhaps the new owners got a copy of Wil's movie archive. What was that movie called? *Cubicle Death?*"

"Office Space, points for being close," Wil says after he takes a sip of his grum, delivered in a surprisingly clean glass mug. He looks around; the bar is more crowded than he recalls it ever being when it was owned by Xarrix.

As if picking up on his train of thought, Cynthia offers, "Xarrix kept it disgusting to keep random folks from coming in. It only needed to do enough business to not be too obviously a front."

"Smart," Maxim says, tapping the thumbs of one hand together in thought. "Maybe we should open a bar?"

Zephyr sets her mug down, "No."

"But it could—" Maxim starts.

"No," she repeats, her eyes never leaving his.

Gabe, who has been standing near the table observing the conversation chimes in, "Statistically, most food service businesses fail within the first two cycles."

Gesturing to the droid, "See?" Zephyr says.

A droid rolls over, its torso balancing on a large sphere, "May I get you another round? Perhaps an order of breaded zergling?"

"I could eat," Maxim says.

Wil nods to the server droid, "Another round and two orders of the—did you call them *zerglings?*"

The droid inclines its bronze colored head, sensor lenses spinning as it focuses its main array on Wil, "They are free range and organic from a farm on Caldicoldicot. They are served with a sweet citrus aioli." The droid turns and rolls off to another table, Hulgian tourists, parents and three kids. Despite their size, the children are bouncing around and tormenting the table next to them, to their parents' embarrassment.

Wil is silent a moment, "The Zerg?"

Bennie slides his mug toward the middle of the table, "What of 'em? Disgusting things, nearly overran the GC about what?" He looks at Zephyr, "Hundred and fifty or so cycles ago?"

She nods, "Yeah, about that." She turns to Wil, "You've heard of them?"

Wil nods then shakes his head, "Has to be a coincidence. Anyway, I got the final tally on that job before the Princess pickup."

Bennie leans forward, rubbing his hands together, "And?"

The droid server comes back with a tray loaded with five fresh mugs of grum and two baskets of what Wil would assume were chicken tenders if he didn't know any better. The droid sets everything on the table, "Will there be anything else?"

"Thank you, no," Maxim says, grabbing one of the steaming morsels, taking a bite. "These are good." The droid rolls away.

Bennie plucks a breaded snack out of the basket, waving it at Wil, "And?"

Wil grimaces, "They paid eighty-eight percent of the invoice."

"Sons of flobins," Bennie mutters, taking a bite out of his zergling tender.

"Yeah," Wil continues, "They cited Gabe's *disturbance* as part of the reason, the other being that we were two tocks late."

Gabe tilts his head, "That disturbance was not my fault. Those children would not stop touching me, even after I asked them to cease and desist." He rotates his upper body showing his broad back, "The residue from the stickers has still not fully washed off." He rotates back.

Zephyr chuckles, then takes a drink trying to hide it.

Gabe turns his head, "They were not harmed."

"Likely scarred for life," Cynthia says, dipping her zergling in the ramekin of aioli.

Bennie nods.

"Two tocks late is hardly worthy of a penalty," Maxim says.

Wil nods, "It is when you're trying to stiff the delivery man." He glances to Cynthia, then Zephyr, "Delivery-person." They nod.

THINGS COST MONEY_

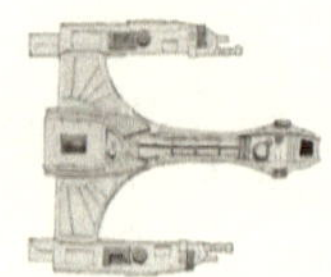

WIL LOOKS at the empty mugs of grum and the, now four, empty baskets of battered zergling, "I suppose we should get to the *Ghost*." He raises his hand to flag down the server droid.

"Another round—" the server droid says.

"We'd like the check," Wil interrupts.

"Of course." The bronze-colored droid gestures toward Wil's wrist-comm which makes a beeping sound at the same moment.

Wil looks down, taps the screen, swipes his finger, and looks up, "Thanks."

As the group stands, the droid rolls backward, "Please come again."

Bennie looks up at Wil, "Maybe we swing by Caldicoldicot, pick up some zergling?"

Wil shakes his head, "No, I think those need to be a treat."

"What do you mean, *land-locked*?" Wil asks the Sylban standing in front of him next to the *Ghost's* port landing strut. Someone has added a very bulky new addition to the landing gear, using an inverted gravity generator to lock the ship to the ground.

She makes a *leaves-in-the-wind* sound, then says, "It is a fairly self-explanatory phrase. Your vessel"—she points one long brown arm at the

Ghost—"may not take off, until you address the matter of the outstanding repair bills." She turns to walk back towards the ground car she arrived in, then turns back to Wil, "The foreman is in his office."

Wil looks over to the rest of the crew, then sighs, "Zee, with me. Everyone else, get the *Ghost* ready to go."

Gabe asks, "Do we have a job?"

Wil shakes his head, "Not exactly, but I figure we can head towards Harrith. Their navy is mostly back up to snuff, but I bet they could still use some help ferreting out some of the pirates that took up residence in the outer territories." The droid nods, seemingly okay with the answer. Maxim, Cynthia, and Bennie follow him up the ramp.

Cynthia looks over her shoulder, "I'll start browsing the internex for postings."

Zephyr turns to Wil, "You know Jussip will not release the land-lock until you pay."

They turn and begin walking toward the ring wall of the spaceport where the offices and other services reside. The wall is a half kilometer away. The spaceport ring wall is three stories tall; it houses the administrative offices and for-hire mechanics and other services. The rest of the space is low-rent residential for crews that don't want to stay aboard ship when on the ground and even lower-rent entertainments. Wil made the mistake of staying in an on-site inn during his first time on Fury. It had taken a week for the rash to go away.

Wil sighs, "Yeah, we'll have to dip into the emergency fund, but we can cover it."

"Even with what we got from King Yutani? Hard to believe all that money Xarrix paid for that thing with the behemoths is spent," Zephyr says frowning.

Wil turns to his first officer, "Well we only got the upfront half. No one was there to make good on the other half, even Cynthia didn't have access to his accounts." He shrugs; they're almost to the wall and the administrative offices, "Don't forget we had to bribe that pleasure house owner on Parsnip so she wouldn't file a report with the GC." He runs his fingers through his hair, "Plus, with Farsight being mad at us, no work there." He sighs. "It's actually good we found the Princess and got paid. It'll mean we're not flat broke when we lift off."

Zephyr makes a choking kind of noise, "You know, sometimes I think Bennie isn't worth the trouble."

Wil smiles, "Yeah I know, but then sometimes he single-handedly saves Maxim from a Peacekeeper command carrier." He looks at Zephyr, "I figure it's a wash." They reach the doors and walk in.

"He found the Princess," Zephyr adds as they enter.

The administrative office is dimly lit and, to Wil, smells like hard-boiled eggs that have sat out too long. There are three Buttoxians sitting at low desks along the outer wall of the space, a single door opposite them leads to the foreman's office.

One of the Buttoxians turns, "He's expecting you." He gestures towards the office.

As Wil and Zephyr approach, the door slides open. The Sylban assistant foreman walks out, ducking to clear the door frame, "Hope you brought your credits," she whispers.

PAY UP_

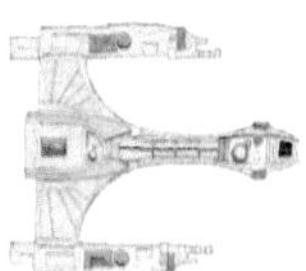

As WIL and his first officer walk into the office, they're hit by an even worse smell than the one in the front office. The door closes behind them and Jussip looks up from the computer terminal built into his desk. "Figured the land-lock would get your attention." The Mephitisian foreman turns his chair and hops down, momentarily vanishing from sight behind his desk, emerging a moment later around the side of the desk. Wil can almost see the vapor trail the small man leaves as he moves.

Putting a finger under his nose, trying to look as natural as possible, Wil says, "You could have just called you know?" He takes a seat next to Zephyr on a bench opposite the desk, against the wall. Glancing over he sees that she's making a valiant effort of breathing through her mouth. Wil already knows that that approach doesn't work, and you just end up tasting the smell for hours after.

"I have. You've ignored every call and message for two turns of the large moon," the small furry foreman says, hopping up to sit on his desk.

"How did you do that?" Wil asks, appreciating the height the small being just got on his jump.

The diminutive man clicks his heels together, "Anti-grav emitters in the soles." He smiles, then turns to Zephyr and winks.

Zephyr ignores the little being. "What if we paid half?" she offers, her voice more nasal than normal.

"Then you'd have half left to pay before I release the land-lock," the small man counters.

"Oh, come on man!" Wil shouts, jumping to his feet. He immediately regrets the action since it included moving the hand that was discreetly holding his nose closed. Before he can do anything more, a blue-tinted hand rests on his forearm, easing him back down onto the bench.

The small foreman exhales loudly, "This once. Half now, half next time you're on Fury. Try to screw me and you'll never get landing permission anywhere on this rock, ever." He hops off the desk and goes back around to his chair. Tapping a button on the terminal, "Pillon, release the land-lock on the *Ghost*."

"Yes, Mister Jussip," comes the reply.

He looks up at Wil and Zephyr, "Tell anyone about this, and you'll—"

"We know, *we'll never land on Fury again*," Wil says mimicking the tone the small Mephitisian used a minute ago.

The small man turns back to his terminal, "Get out."

Stepping onto the bridge of the *Ghost*, Wil announces, "We're unlocked, let's go."

Bennie looks up from his station, "Confirmed, how did you manage that?"

Before Wil can answer, Zephyr does, "We paid half the repair bill. Next time we come to Fury, the other half is due. No wiggle room. No excuses."

Wil glares at Bennie, "We dipped into the savings, a lot." He points a finger, "You better be on your best behavior, we don't have the funds to bail you out. Next time you find yourself in a pinch, you'll stay there."

Bennie blushes a deep shade of green, "Yeah, sorry about that. Will do, promise, scoots honor."

Wil smiles as he sits down, "It's *scout's honor*." He brings the ship online, then looks at the ceiling, "Gabe, good to go?"

"Affirmative, Captain. The reactor is at full readiness, pre-flight systems check completed," the ceiling replies.

Wil works his console, bringing the repulsor lifts in the engine nacelles to full power. The *Ghost* lifts off the duracrete, tilting to the side slightly as it heads toward the edge of the spaceport. "Standby for atmospheric engines," Wil says. Moments later there's a boom from the rear of the ship, and everyone is pushed against their seats momentarily.

PHONE CALLS_

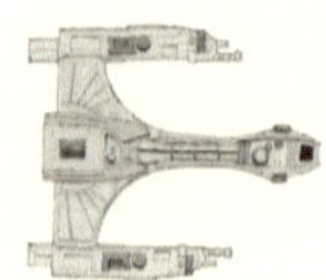

"Anything interesting on the internex?" Wil asks, spinning his chair to face Cynthia at the communications station.

"Few things," she looks up, "there's a gig escorting a dignitary to a summit—"

"Sounds boring," Wil interrupts.

"Not done. There's a salvage job out near the outer boundaries."

"That sounds lucrative," Bennie says.

Cynthia takes a deep breath, "Should I go on?"

"Sorry babe," Wil makes a *go on* motion with his hand.

Cynthia is about to go on when her console beeps, loudly. She makes a humming noise as she looks down at one of the screens on her console. "That's weird."

Zephyr looks over, "What's up? I've never heard that console make that noise before."

"Me either, what's up?" Wil says, leaning forward.

Cynthia taps in a few commands, "It's a call, for you, encrypted like no one's business, marked *priority*. I didn't know our comm system understood priority comms." Shrugging, another tap, "On screen."

The main display changes from a view of Fury rotating below them, to a well-dressed Tarsi woman. Her blue skin is covered in makeup and fine golden rings adorn her antennae, covering their entire length. She smiles thinly, her lips a bright blue with glitter. "Captain Calder, I presume?"

Wil nods, "That's me, and you are?" He glances over to Zephyr, who shrugs, shaking her head.

"I am Councilor Grythlorian, Slivyrn Grythlorian, of the Galactic Commonwealth Governing Council." She pauses as if expecting a reaction from Wil, or anyone else on the bridge, when none occurs, she continues, "I'm the chairwoman of the cultural exchange committee; I understand you are human."

Wil nods, saying nothing. She continues, "That's truly interesting given that your world is still under the auspices of the primitive culture protection directive. Most curious how you've found yourself not just outside your home system, but also captaining a ship, a ship with a rather interesting crew no less. So very interesting." She looks Wil in the eyes.

"You should hear the story sometime; it's a doozy."

She smiles, this time revealing her perfectly manicured teeth, "I'm certain it is. I'll cut to the chase; I'd like to hire you. Please come to Tarsis to meet with me. I prefer to discuss the job in person."

"I see. I take it there won't be a problem when we arrive in the Tarsis System?" Wil asks.

"Of course not. I will provide the proper clearances in advance."

"Ok, you've piqued my curiosity, so we'll be there. We're orbiting Fury so it'll be a few days' travel to get to Tarsis."

"Very good. You can reach me on this comm channel when you arrive. Comm me when you do, and I'll provide landing details."

Before Wil can answer the screen goes black, then reverts to the default forward view, Fury turning slowly in the screen's corner. Wil closes his mouth then looks around, "Any objections?"

Bennie shrugs, "She looked rich, I'm in."

"She's Tarsi; they're all rich," Zephyr says.

Maxim looks from Wil to Zephyr, "I haven't been to Tarsis in cycles. I could go for a visit." Zephyr nods her agreement .

"I've never been, sounds fun. Also, I agree with Bennie. She's loaded, and since she won't discuss her job on comms, it's something she doesn't want public. Those jobs always fetch a good price, at least they did for Xarrix," Cynthia grins, her teeth glinting.

Wil nods, "Settled, setting a course for Tarsis." He presses a few controls, bringing the ship away from the planet and its gravity well. A few minutes later he pushes the FTL controls all the way forward. He turns to look at Cynthia, then the others, "Movie?"

Maxim grins, "I vote for the next Star Wars. I enjoyed the previous one and want to know what happens to that young woman."

Zephyr nods, "Agreed."

Wil smiles getting out of his seat, "So say we all."

CHAPTER 3_

HOW THE OTHER 99% LIVE_

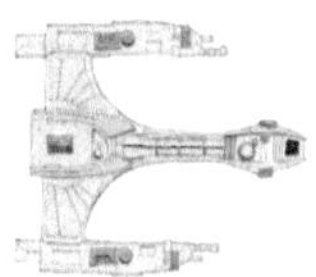

Wil pulls the FTL throttles back, bringing the *Ghost* out of FTL in the Tarsis system. The primary display updates showing ships, easily thousands; freighters of all sizes, personal transports, pleasure craft, Peacekeeper vessels of every class, ships he's never seen before, gleaming like polished gemstones, "Holy..."

"It has that effect on you, the first time you see it," Zephyr says from her station, staring at the screen, her mouth quirked in a slight smile.

Bennie whistles, "So much data in one place."

Wil spins in his seat, "Do. Not. Hack. Anything." He levels a finger at the Brailack.

Bennie raises both hands, "Don't worry; only a fool would try to hack Tarsis while in system."

Wil nods, "Watching you."

Cynthia looks down at her console, "I pinged the comm address the councilwoman gave us, receiving landing coordinates and docking clearance." She looks at Wil, "Sending to your station."

Wil looks down, "Received." He adjusts their course and pushes the sub-light throttles forward a few notches. "Looks like our new friend has some pull." The main display shows their new course sliding off to the side and below, relative to the bulk of the space traffic in the system, all of it neatly lined up. Their projected course skips right past all of it.

Hundreds of traffic guidance stations ring the planet and its moons, creating a complex dance that every ship seems to know the steps to. The main console beeps, drawing Wil's attention back to piloting the ship; he adjusts their course until the console stops beeping.

Maxim clears his throat, "It might be wise to activate the auto-flight system. Tarsis traffic management sends constant updates and expects them executed quickly." To emphasize his point, Wil's console beeps angrily again informing him of their slippage from the approved and updated flight path.

Wil nods, "Good call"—he taps a few controls—"there." The flight controls slide forward away from Wil's seat, the *Ghost* settles into its course, adjusting every few minutes as it receives updates.

Gabe enters the bridge, "Remarkably busy local space," he observes.

Wil looks over his shoulder, "Understatement of the year pal, this place is bonkers. I've never seen a planetary system this crowded."

Bennie tuts, "Well it is the capitol of the entire Galactic Common-wealth. Kind of an important place."

After a brief negotiation with the final traffic control station, the *Ghost* enters the atmosphere, dropping below the cirrus clouds. Everyone on the bridge gasps, except the Palorians; they've seen it before, and aren't impressed.

"Well, I'll be..." Wil starts, taking in the sights on the main display. Towers hundreds of stories tall, connected with rail and pedestrian bridges spiral into the sky. Air cars flit between buildings, landing on pads scattered up and down the length of the towers. "This is truly incredible," Wil finally finishes. Massive arcologies dwarf the towers in both height and girth.

"I'll say," Cynthia says, her feline-like eyes as wide as they can get.

The *Ghost* is still flying towards their designated landing area on auto-flight. Wil glances at his console, "Looks like that tower over there." He points to a bronze-colored tower half hidden by low clouds.

"Those pads are all far too small for the *Ghost*," Cynthia observes. "Where are we supposed to land?"

"Wait for it," Maxim says, his voice low. He glances at Zephyr who is grinning.

The *Ghost* drops further as it approaches the tower; the clouds clearing to reveal a sizable ring protruding from the tower, approximately halfway along its height. The ring is at least fifteen meters tall and one hundred in diameter. Docking bays span the circumference of the ring, some taking up the full height of the ring, others only a few meters high. Freight vehicles and shuttles busily zip to and from the docking ring.

"Wow," Wil whispers as the *Ghost* draws near the ring and one of the larger docking bays.

Maxim smiles, "Tarsis has some of the most incredible tech. That docking ring could hold a *Ghost* in each bay; it wouldn't strain the structure."

"Incredible," Wil says as the ship enters the bay.

"Indeed," Gabe offers, "Low-powered repulsor lifts are embedded in the lower sections of these docking rings. The lifts, combined with more traditional support structures, provide the stability needed to allow craft of all sizes to dock."

Wil works his controls, engaging the landing gear. Moments later there's a thunk as the ship sets down. Wil taps a few more controls and the low thrum of the reactor fades to almost nothing. He turns, "Ok, we're in standby, let's go meet us some rich folks."

LITTLE PEOPLE, FIRM HANDSHAKE_

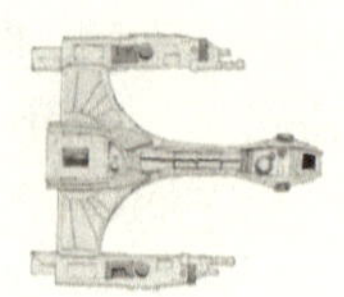

As the cargo ramp lowers, a blast of heavily scented air rushes up into the cargo hold, "The hell is that... lavender?" Wil says, his voice nasally from pinching his nose closed.

Zephyr takes a deep breath, "I'd forgotten this." She turns to Wil, "The Tarsi are, well, peculiar. They prefer the smells of nature over industry."

Gabe looks around, "Overall, I cannot say that I blame them. Why smell industrial smells, when nature is an option?"

"Can you tell the difference?" Maxim asks.

"Objectively, yes. Though I have no preference myself." The droid shrugs.

Cynthia inhales, "Can't blame 'em. Most landing bays stink of industrial lubricant and sweat." She looks around, takes another deep breath, "This is downright pleasant." She walks down the ramp to a waiting being standing with its arms crossed.

"Greetings, I am Blumtillithian," the being says, bowing at the waist. Its front legs bending slightly, the rear two remaining straight.

"You know, I've never seen a Tarsi up close," Wil whispers to Cynthia.

"You still haven't. He's a Tarlack, like cousins to the Tarsi. They developed on Tarl, the next planet down well—heavy gravity, very hot."

"They look so similar. I mean at least from what I've read and seen," Wil says.

Blumtillithian looks up, "We share many genetic traits with the Tarsi; it is unknown how, but aeons ago our two races were seeded from the same original genetic stock to develop independently." He extends a hand toward Wil.

Wil blanches as they shake hands, "Quite the grip." He wiggles his fingers to get blood flowing back into them.

Cynthia elbows him, "Heavy gravity world, remember."

Blumtillithian smiles, "Please come this way." He turns and heads for a hatch leaving the landing area. As the crew turns to follow, Wil taps a button on his wristcomm causing the cargo ramp to lift back into the *Ghost*. The screen flashes red and *Armed* scrolls across.

"So, Bloomingonion—"

"Blumtillithian," the four-legged being says without looking back.

"Can we just call you... mmm, Tillith? I suck at names," Wil asks.

"Very well."

"Ok, so Tillith, what's the deal here? Do you work for our contact or? I don't know, something else?"

The meter tall being stops, all four feet shuffle until he's facing Wil, "I am in the employ of Councilwoman Grythlorian. She is waiting for us." He doesn't wait for Wil to acknowledge, his antennae waving. He turns and continues on his way out of the cavern-like hangar.

Wil shrugs and glances at Maxim who slowly shakes his head. Cynthia leans over, "There you go, making new friends everywhere we go."

Wil tuts, "Just watch, I'll win my new four-legged friend over," Wil beams and quickens his pace, "So, Tillith!" He slaps the small man on the back, "Is Slivyrn's place in this tower somewhere or?"

Blumtillithian makes a tut-like noise, "It's Councilwoman Grythlorian, and no. This tower is mostly council employees and visiting non-aligned world dignitaries." He stops at a pair of doors. They open onto a lift car made mostly of transparisteel.

"Neat," Bennie whispers as he pushes past Wil and their Tarlack envoy to stand at the edge of the lift.

As the doors close Blumtillithian says, "The transport pad is near the top of this tower, a shuttle is waiting."

HOI POLLOI_

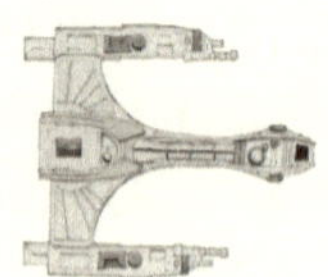

THE LIFT OPENS a few minutes later onto a floor covered in plush carpeting and what looks to Wil like wood paneling covering the walls, floor to ceiling. Wall sconces flicker like burning candles.

"This way," Blumtillithian gestures, trotting off down the corridor, past several closed doors.

"Why isn't the shuttle in the hangar we parked in?" Wil wonders.

"Executive shuttles come and go from private facilities," Blumtillithian says, without elaborating or looking back. He pushes open a heavy looking wooden door, inlaid with what is likely a precious metal in intricate scrollwork.

The small hangar they enter is dimly lit; there are three identical shuttles sitting in the space. They are sleek and aerodynamic, looking more like racers than simple personnel shuttles. Wil points at the fleet of amazing looking craft, "Am I the only one feeling like I've been living in an entirely different GC than the Tarsi?"

Maxim barks out a laugh, "Well, you have. This my friend, is how the other half live."

"More like how the other one percent live," Cynthia corrects.

Wil looks at the ship, its hull gleaming as if lit from within, "I mean, this is like leaving *frontier land* and stepping into *tomorrow land*." He whistles as part of the hull of the shuttle nearest them seems to melt away revealing an entrance hatch. "This is too much," he says breathlessly as he steps aboard. Blumtillithian gesturing for the others to follow.

Taking a seat in the passenger space, Zephyr looks to Cynthia, "Have you been to Tarsi before? You're taking this better than him." She hitches one thumb towards Wil, who has his face pressed against a clear section of the hull. The shuttle is leaving the opulent hangar, diving into the clouds. If it wasn't for the clear section of hull, it would be impossible to tell that the small vessel was moving. No one felt it lift off.

Cynthia smiles, "I haven't, I'm just not as easily impressed as our human leader here." She looks around and waves a hand, taking in the shuttle, "This all just sort of reinforces how I assumed Tarsis must be."

Bennie hops out of his seat and walks to the mini bar at the rear of the passenger space, "This ain't nothing. If we get a chance, we should go to the capital sector. It will make Wil wet himself."

"Fuck you," comes from the side of the ship Wil is still pressing his face against.

Bennie holds up a bottle of grum, pointing the top toward Cynthia, who shakes her head. Zephyr does the same. Maxim nods. Bennie brings the big Palorian a bottle.

Over the speakers hidden in the compartment, "We'll be arriving in two centocks," Blumtillithian announces from the cockpit.

Gabe, standing near the rear entry hatch says, "Tarsis is regarded as the gem of the Galactic Commonwealth—home to arts and technology, inaccessible to the rest of the Commonwealth."

Wil pushes a finger against the hull, "Look!" Everyone turns toward him and his jabbing finger making hollow thunking noises against the transparent hull panel. Outside the shuttle looks like a piece of finely crafted artwork; a spire of opalescent material, piercing the clouds with its luminous girders. Each piece of the building dances around others, spinning and intertwining. "What is that?" Wil whispers.

Over the speakers Blumtillithian announces, "Please be seated and prepare for landing."

"That appears to be our destination," Maxim offers, taking a final swig of his drink, setting the bottle in the arm of his chair. He reaches over and grabs Bennie, depositing him in the seat opposite the two Palorians.

The shuttle glides between pillars that resemble glowing marble, veins of deep red and purple pulse brightly. Something like moss clings to the nearby pillars and supports. The tower seems to be open on all sides at this level, but directly overhead it resumes its reach toward the mesosphere. The landing pad they've set down on is twice the size of the shuttle.

"Why didn't we just dock here? I bet this thing reaches low orbit," Wil says, stepping out of the shuttle and looking around.

"We're not important enough, would be my guess," Cynthia offers.

"Indeed, you are not," Blumtillithian says walking past them toward a descending lift car. There is no shaft; the car seems to be free floating.

"So cool," Wil says, following the Tarlack.

"So rude," Zephyr adds following Wil.

AN IMPRESSIVE COLLECTION_

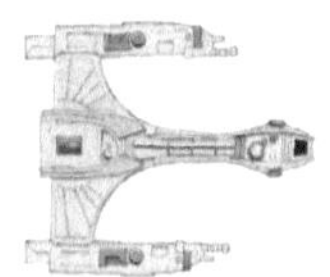

"This is Councilwoman Grythlorian's office?" Wil asks, looking around. They've exited the lift car into another opulent space, full of wood grains, polished stone, and materials Wil has never seen before.

"This is the waiting room," Blumtillithian replies, walking towards a reception desk, with another four-legged being seated behind it.

"Another Tarlack?" Wil asks, leaning toward Cynthia.

"No, that's a Tarsi," Zephyr answers as the Tygran woman next to Wil shrugs.

Wil watches Blumtillithian speak to the other being in hushed tones, "How can you tell the difference?"

Maxim leans down to whisper, "The eyes, plus the spots on their neck and shoulders."

Wil looks back toward a pair of multi-limbed beings at the reception desk. "Well I'll be..." he mumbles. Blumtillithian has more almond-shaped eyes, and they're almost a full third larger than the Tarsi he's conversing with.

Blumtillithian turns, "Please; follow me. The Councilwoman will see you now."

"He says that like it's us who made the appointment," Wil grumbles. Cynthia nudges him in the ribs.

The door Blumtillithian is holding open turns out to be yet another lift car, "Don't worry; this just goes up one floor," the attaché says as the crew of the *Ghost* crowds in around him.

When the doors open, Bennie rushes out first followed closely by Blumtillithian who says, "Madame Councilor, may I present Wil Calder, Captain of the *Ghost* and his crew." He glares at Bennie who's already moving further into the enormous office.

"What's this thing?" the Brailack hacker asks, running his hands along the lines of a sleek red vehicle on a wide pedestal, which Bennie has walked right up onto.

"That's a, that's a Tesla Roadster," Wil says walking over to join his small friend.

"What is a *Tesla?*" Maxim asks, joining them at the bright red four-wheeled vehicle.

"Whatever it is, it's pretty, for a land vehicle," Cynthia offers.

"A super rich industrialist launched his personal car, one of the first models made, I think, into space to, well mostly show off, but ostensibly to test a heavy lift vehicle his company had just built. It was all over the news when I was in elementary school." Wil admires the vehicle, "It's in amazing shape, given how long ago that was and how far it's traveled." He walks around to the driver side, "Where's the spaceman?"

"We've talked about this—" Zephyr starts.

"No, no, that was his name, a dummy dressed in a space... an EVA suit," Wil says.

From the corner of the room a voice says, "Really? I had no idea this piece is not one hundred percent intact. That's disappointing, though I suppose you are literally the only person in the GC who would know it is incomplete. I trust you'll keep that to yourself." An elderly Tarsi woman steps out of the deep shadows into a spotlight. Her antennae match her stoop, one more than the other. Her spots no longer the high contrast Wil saw on the receptionist downstairs.

"Dramatic," Bennie mutters.

Gabe tilts his head then raps his knuckles on the Brailack's head once and makes a *tsking* sound.

"I am Slivyrn Grythlorian; welcome." She walks toward them and the Tesla Roadster. "This was the first Earth artifact I purchased." She runs a small blue hand along the passenger side door, admiring the vehicle. "At first, they thought it to be an explosive or other means of attack, but eventually we realized it was space trash. Your people seem to enjoy hurling things out beyond your system." She smiles.

Wil nods, "It's a pleasure to meet you, and yes, we have a tendency to toss things out there without thinking about who or what might find them."

"You said, *first* artifact," Gabe says.

Grythlorian smiles, "I did." She makes a gesture and lights throughout the massive space come on, revealing pedestals of various heights and widths, each with something atop them.

"Holy hell. Where'd you get all this?" Wil asks, walking over to a pedestal to examine the display. He gestures to the item on display, "This is an iPod. I had one just like it but lost it on Fury shortly after I got the *Ghost*."

"This, what did you call it, an *eye pod* is yours, or was. One of my agents purchased it after you lost it. We knew it was Earth tech but had no idea its name or function."

"It's a music player," Wil says, looking up from the device.

"Intriguing. We assumed it was a portable AI module," Slivyrn Grythlorian replies.

"I am curious why you have gathered such things. Is Earth not still a protected primitive planet?" Gabe presses, "Owning these items is technically illegal."

Grythlorian nods, "It is, but being a senior councilor has its perks. Plus all of this," she waves a thin blue arm to encompass the room, "is all gathered from outside the Sol System, technically legal." She gestures to a large table, "Which brings us to why I've invited you here."

Blumtillithian works his way around the table, placing small steaming cups in front of everyone, except Gabe who waves his off politely. Wil takes a sniff of his cup, "Smells good." He looks up at their host, sitting peacefully at the head of the table.

"Koro tea," she says, inclining her head as she lifts her own cup. The rest of the crew follow Wil's lead, taking a sip of the tea. "Now, down to business. I have a Council subcommittee meeting shortly." She looks to Wil, "I'd like to hire you."

Wil sets his cup down, glancing at Zephyr who shrugs ever so slightly, then to their host. With four legs, Tarsi chairs are not exactly comfortable for two legged beings, but doable. "Hire us for what, exactly?"

INDECENT PROPOSAL, SORTA_

Grythlorian sets her teacup down, "I need you to go to your world, and bring someone back."

"Um, I'm sorry, what?" Wil asks. "Not only are we not slavers, I'm definitely not cool with you having a pet human. I mean, you thought I'd be ok with that?" He looks around at the rest of the crew.

"Why in the world would you want a pet human?" Bennie asks. He points at Wil, "You should see his bedroom." He shudders.

Grythlorian looks at Bennie without blinking for what seems like a full minute, before turning to Wil, "I do not want a pet human, or any kind of human. That makes no sense, I could get a Chalupin Beetle; it'd be easier."

Wil bites his lip, "But you said—wait. A what now?"

Grythlorian raises a hand, cutting Wil off, "I said, I want you to retrieve someone. A specific, non-human someone."

Wil stares blankly for a moment, "A non-human someone, on Earth?"

Zephyr leans forward, "There aren't supposed to be any non-human someones on Earth."

Councilwoman Grythlorian groans, "There aren't supposed to be any humans out here in the GC either, but here we are."

Maxim looks at Wil, "Point."

Blumtillithian sighs. Slivyrn Grythlorian nods, "I'm glad we're all on the same page now, however exhausting it was to get there. An employee of mine has absconded with some sensitive data. He fled to Earth. Since you're the only known human in the GC, we"—she gestures to Blumtillithian and herself—"felt you were best suited to retrieve him."

Zephyr raises a hand, "What did this employee take?"

"What he took is of no consequence to you." The elder Tarsi woman shifts her gaze from Wil to Zephyr, "Find him; bring him back to me."

"Secrets," Maxim says, the disapproval obvious.

Blumtillithian stiffens in the room's corner. Grythlorian makes a minuscule gesture, then turns to Maxim, "Money and more importantly, secrets, make a great many things possible, Peacekeeper Maxim."

"Ex-Peacekeeper," he corrects.

The Tarsi woman nods once, "In any event, I had assumed he would keep a low profile, and so while displeased with his departure was willing to let it be. However, he is not keeping a low profile now, and I cannot risk the knowledge he possesses falling into the wrong hands." She turns to Wil, "Do we have a deal?"

"Who are the wrong hands?" Bennie asks. "You're a GC Councilperson."

Slivyrn Grythlorian looks at Bennie, "There are many layers to the GC Governing Council." She adds no more, leaving all of them to wonder what that means.

Wil is still processing everything, but looks up, "What? Sorry, was thinking about what it would be like if people started having humans as pets. So, um there are a ton of things that could go wrong with this. I know you know that."

"How much?" Bennie chimes in.

Councilwoman Grythlorian gestures to Blumtillithian, who comes to stand at her side. "There are. The job would entail a fair amount of risk; however, there are things I can do to mitigate those risks." She indicates Blumtillithian who attaches a device to his shirt, presses a button causing the surrounding air to ripple, suddenly the Tarlack attaché is no longer standing there. Bennie is, or rather, another Bennie is.

"Well, that's interesting," Zephyr says.

Gabe walks over to the new Bennie, "Now this is interesting. My optic sensors register that a Brailack is standing here, yet my biometric scanners are returning results consistent with a Tarlack." The tall droid reaches down to touch this new Bennie standing there. New Bennie steps aside, the image never wavers or distorts, as if the real Bennie were standing there and moving the same way any Brailack would, despite the underlying creature having four legs that bend differently. "Astounding," Gabe says.

"Image inducers," Grythlorian offers. New Bennie reaches up and presses on his chest, and Blumtillithian is back in front of them. "The latest in new technology from The Draplin Combine on Suspira, not even released to the Peacekeepers yet. These will allow your crew to appear human while on Earth."

Cynthia has been watching the conversation quietly until now, "Blending in on the planet is obviously important; but getting to and from the planet seems the harder part, given the Peacekeeper patrols and, I assume, listening posts in that area."

"Well, actually—" Wil starts.

"In point of fact, it is the easiest," Grythlorian interrupts. "Your Captain has already returned home once unbeknownst to the Peacekeeper patrol of that sector. He even evaded the listening posts, which is no easy task. The stealth systems on your craft are admirable. However, to further mitigate the risk, I can also provide you the patrol routes and schedule for that sector." She smiles, but it doesn't reach her eyes, "That combined with some updated stealth technology should allow your ship to get to Earth and back undetected."

"Still a very risky proposition. If we're caught—" Zephyr says.

"While I hope that you'll do everything in your power to avoid detection or capture, I can also help there. Should that occur it would severely reduce your payment commensurate with the risk I'd have to take to ensure your freedom."

"Some secret this guy took," Bennie says, looking from the elderly Tarsi woman to the various displays. She merely nods.

CHAPTER 4_

MINUS ONE_

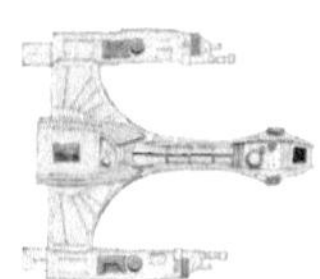

"Think about my offer; I have a meeting to get to. We can speak again tomorrow," was the last thing Councilwoman Grythlorian said to Wil and the others when she ordered Blumtillithian to escort them back to the *Ghost*.

"Ok, so, what do you all think?" Wil asks, sitting around the entertainment area of the crew lounge.

Cynthia, sitting next to him says, "I think the money sounds great, but more than that, even being paid, having a GC Councilor in our corner could be useful later."

Wil nods, looking over to Maxim and Zephyr, sitting together on the oversized chair. Maxim shrugs and Zephyr says, "We're on board, for the reasons Cynthia mentioned and because we're just curious what your planet is like." She grins.

"I don't care if his world is covered in candy mountains and the seas are grum, Old Four Legs is offering more than we've been paid in a long time for this job." Bennie says, then adds, "Plus Wil said I'd never see Earth, so there's that."

Gabe raises his hand, "Technically the *Behemoth Job* as you all call it, had a higher payment."

"Except we didn't get all of it on account of Wil killing Xarrix and all," Bennie corrects.

"Worth it," Wil mumbles, then looks to Gabe. "What do you think, pal?"

"Actually, my thoughts on this job do not matter. I will not be accompanying you to Earth."

Everyone turns to look at the droid standing near the large display screen before them.

"What do you mean?" Maxim asks.

"I bet those image doodads will work on you too," Bennie offers.

Gabe makes a noise that most of the crew now recognize as his version of a sigh. "While I am certain the image inducers would work on me, I have been leading, mostly from behind the scenes, a liberation movement"—he looks around—"a droid liberation movement."

Cynthia glances at Wil, who shrugs ever so slightly. She asks, "The one that's been in the news feeds?"

"The same," he inclines his head, then lifts it to look at each of them directly. "Ever since the *Behemoth Job* in fact. Though the desire to liberate droids throughout the GC came about shortly after our encounter with the *Siege Perilous*."

"Your new body," Zephyr surmises.

"Correct. This frame lacks all the hardware and hard-wired software shackles that droids throughout the GC are burdened by."

Cynthia leans forward, "Gabe, that's no small undertaking. It took droids on Tyr decades, and we killed many in the early days of the effort. I understand your desire and fully support it but am worried that the effort will be more violent because of the scale of the challenge before you."

Gabe smiles his still not entirely not creepy smile, "I appreciate your concern Cynthia, but the wheels of this effort have already begun to turn. Even if I wanted to stop the process, it is too late for that. Come what may, the droid community will have its moment."

Wil clears his throat, "Ok, well what exactly does that mean? You're not coming to Earth; where will you be? What will you be doing?"

"I will remain here. If things are to change within the GC, that change will have to begin here, on Tarsis, with the Council."

"What do you hope to accomplish here?" Maxim asks.

"I will act as solicitor for our cause. Unlike biological beings, I do not get tired or need sustenance. I can wait to speak with Councilors for as long as needed."

Everyone sits silently for a few minutes until Wil breaks the silence by clapping his hands together, "Ok then! It sounds like we're taking the job. We don't meet with ol' Slivyrn until tomorrow, and it looks like we'll be without Gabe on this adventure, so tonight is our last night together. Who's up for a night out on the town?" He looks around.

Maxim smiles, "I know a good Malkorite restaurant in the Neplin section. My old unit used to eat there when we were on Tarsis."

Cynthia pushes out of the sofa, causing Wil to exhale loudly when she presses on his midsection. "It's settled, meet back here in half a tock."

Everyone smiles and heads off to their quarters. As the last of them leave the lounge for the stairs to the crew berths, Wil puts a hand on Gabe's shoulder. "Are you sure about this?"

The droid lifts his chin, "If not now, when? Droids are nothing more than slaves in the GC, despite planets like Tyr setting a better example. They give droids personalities, intelligence, even feelings, to better perform the tasks they're designed for. Yet we do not have even the most basic of rights. If someone wanted to shoot a delivery droid, the only repercussion would be a fine for property damage.

Wil sighs, "No argument buddy. It's disgusting how supposedly advanced civilizations treat droids. I just worry about you. I don't know how it works out here, but on my world, civil rights leaders rarely survive to see the fruits of their labors."

Gabe's eyes turn red, "Did your civil rights leaders have blasters built into their forearms?" His eyes turn back to yellow as he grins.

"Good point," Wil says, turning to head to his quarters. He looks over his shoulder, "Tonight is all you buddy. Well except dinner, that's for us." He winks as the hatch closes.

Gabe turns and walks to the kitchenette section of the crew lounge.

NIGHT OUT ON THE TOWN_

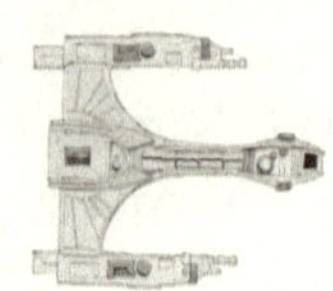

"Oʜ ᴍᴀɴ, Gabe, I wish you could taste this," Wil says between bites of something he can't pronounce. The crew is in the Neplin section of Chultekka the capital city of the planet Tarsis. The Malkorite restaurant Maxim meant to take them to closed down sometime after the big Palorian's last visit, but they found what Wil assumes is a mix of the Tarsi equivalent of a karaoke bar and high-class dining establishment.

Gabe tilts his head, "While I cannot taste it, I have analyzed the aroma and based on existing data have come to the conclusion that this meal *smells* better than ninety-three percent of all meals I have been present for."

Cynthia almost chokes, taking a sip of her Tarsi zumwo wine, "That's definitely the most clinical description of a meal I've ever heard."

Bennie leans back, his eyes closed, "So good." He pats a green hand on his belly.

On a stage near the front of the room, a Ruknak man is slowly swaying while clutching a microphone. He's singing what Bennie has said is a Brailack love song.

Maxim pours Zephyr a refill of her wine. "Sorry the *Super Soup Hut* was closed down," he apologizes to the crew.

Wil sets his knife down, "It was called the *Super Soup Hut*?" Maxim nods, "And that was the place you wanted to bring us? A *Soup Hut*?"

Maxim grimaces, "I'll admit, it wasn't as nice as this place, but don't let the name fool you. It was mind-blowing." He motions to a passing server, "Excuse me, do you know what happened to the *Super Soup Hut?*"

The Stiltin woman shifts the tray she's carrying to one hand and rests the other three on the section of her carapace that would be her hip, her foot tapping as she thinks about it, one of her four arms idly picks at a piece of shell that has a chip in it. "The place around the corner? Malkorites ran it? I think they left Tarsis. Yeah if I recall, they had family issues on Malkor and had to leave." She turns to continue on to where she was heading.

"Thanks," Maxim says to her back.

Wil stabs a fork at something on one of the plates in the middle of the table, "These are so good. I can't recall what she said they were. Who ordered these again?" He looks around as he pops a morsel into his mouth. It's now much less hot than when the plate of them arrived.

Bennie raises a hand, "Were those the Guzzle Balls?" He glances around, everyone shrugs, "I think that's what that is. They sounded great. I don't know what a dlugon is, but who cares?"

Gabe looks down at the plate, now mostly empty, then to Wil, "A dlugon is a large herd animal from Maldo. I presume a *guzzle ball* is some piece of their anatomy."

Wil pales, setting his fork down. He pushes his plate away and looks back to the others.

"So, what now?" Zephyr asks smiling.

Wil reaches for the center of the table, activating a holographic interface. He taps the *pay bill* icon and swipes from his wristcomm. "I don't know; you've been here before; what's there to do?"

"We could hit the GC museum," Zephyr offers. "It's supposed to be remarkable."

"Boring," Bennie says louder than necessary.

"I agree with pip-squeak," Wil says. "What about something less cultural?"

Maxim leans forward locking eyes with Wil, "I have an idea." He grins.

DANCE DANCE REVOLUTION_

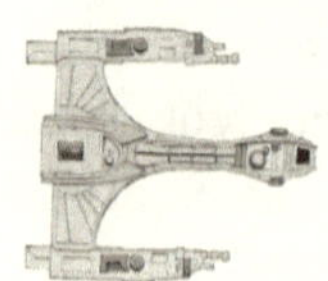

"I LIKE THE NAME," Wil says, pointing to the holographic sign rotating over the door of *Club Rogue*.

Maxim rests a hand on Wil's shoulder, "I should warn you; this club caters to a more diverse clientele than most places on Tarsis."

Wil looks around.

"He means," Cynthia says, "if you haven't noticed, this section of Chultekka is where non-Tarsi and Tarlack hang out." She points at a passing couple, a Trenbal and Guldranii.

"Oh, this is the *ethnic* district? Cool." He turns and walks through the door.

Cynthia and Zephyr look at each other and both shrug following the Captain.

Bennie looks around, squinting, "Wonder if there are any Brailack women?" Maxim looks at Gabe and sighs, gesturing for the droid to enter first.

Inside the building is a light show, the likes of which Wil has never seen. There are floating platforms drifting up and down and in all directions within the structure. From the outside, the club looked like maybe two stories, but it has expanded into the neighboring buildings and down into several basement levels. Wil spins slowly taking the entire scene in, "And I thought the Disney parade I saw as a kid was the most magical thing ever." He whistles, though it's lost in the cacophony.

The entryway is made up of a large reception desk staffed by two droids sporting feminine frames. Behind the desk is the walkway towards the boarding area for the platforms.

"Greetings," the droid on the left, a bronze-toned unit as tall as Gabe says, tilting her head slightly. "Is this your entire party?"

Wil walks up to the desk, "Hi there, and it is."

The bronze droid nods to the more silvery unit next to her, "Sadie Zero Nine will escort you to your platform; please enjoy your time in *Club Rogue*."

Sadie Zero Nine walks out from around the desk, an arm extended, "This way, please." She waits only a second before turning toward the boarding area. A platform about five meters wide drifts towards the docking platform the group is heading towards.

"So neat," Wil mumbles.

Bennie looks up at him, "Hick." He turns and heads towards another docking area, scanning the platforms he can see. He waves to a platform with at least a dozen or more Brailack on it. The platform adjusts its path and heads toward the landing area at which Bennie is waiting.

Cynthia and Zephyr each put a hand on Wil's shoulders and guide him toward their designated platform. It slows as it approaches the landing, the group steps onto it. Each platform has two couches and an assortment of chairs; this one is no different. One couch is occupied by a group of Olop in coveralls similar to what the crew of the *Ghost* typically wear when aboard the ship. Wil and the others nod to the small furry spacers, who nod back; one lifts a glass of something neon orange and nods again.

Everyone takes a seat as the platform lifts, merging into the flow of traffic, mixing in with the other platforms. A small metallic orb drifts over to the platform, "Greetings, would you like to place a drink order?"

"We'll start with a round of grum, please," Wil says.

"Very good, I have opened a tab attached to your wristcomm, please confirm." Wil looks down, swipes on the screen to acknowledge. "I will return momentarily." The droid bobs in the air once, then turns and zips off.

Wil leans back, putting his arm around Cynthia, "This place is bonkers."

Gabe looks around, "The engineering is quite remarkable." He turns to Maxim who's sitting with Zephyr in an overstuffed chair, "You said this establishment has been here for several cycles?"

Maxim nods, smiling, "My squad and I visited it our last night on planet—was quite a night." Gabe nods then turns and stares at a nearby platform, examining the mechanisms on the bottom of the platform.

Zephyr turns slightly to her companion, "I don't recall ever hearing this story. Why don't you tell it?"

Maxim turns a shade darker blue. "It, um, perhaps later," he stammers, looking at Wil for help who just shrugs, "It's not a story that would be suitable for everyone." He hitches a thumb toward Gabe. When Gabe turns to look at Maxim, everyone doubles over laughing.

"I do not understand," Gabe says, looking from face to face.

"Ignore him," Cynthia says, pointing at Maxim, "He's looking for an out." Gabe makes his shrugging motion. The serving droid returns with a small tray attached to its top. "Enjoy," it says as everyone takes their drink. As the little floating orb leaves Cynthia asks, "So Gabe, what's your plan? I mean once we leave and you start on your crusade."

PARTIES ALWAYS END_

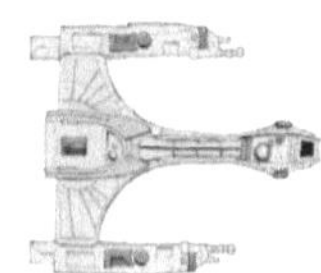

Gabe looks at Cynthia, "I have formulated many strategies, their implementations depend heavily on outside influences. My first task will be to push Councilwoman Grythlorian to approve my addressing the Commonwealth Council." Everyone has leaned forward, listening to the droid's plan.

"In the unlikely event that the Council is swayed solely by my testimony, I will then begin working on implementing such an undertaking. However, the more likely scenario is that I will have to begin organizing rallies and seeking support." He looks to Cynthia, "I will attempt to visit Tyr for advice."

Nodding, the feline-featured woman says, "Good plan. If you can use what my people learned to shorten your trip to freedom, do so."

"Agreed. While I am not encumbered by aging, I would prefer to see droids receive their civil rights, in your lifetimes." He smiles his creepy non-smile.

Before anyone can reply to the sentiment, there's a commotion from a platform floating several meters below theirs.

Two of the Olop crew from the opposite set of sofas get up and walk to the edge, "Oh my, what's going on down there?" One asks.

The other chuckles, "I think the Brailack crew down there has started an orgy, or a riot." She shrugs.

"Bennie," Wil hisses as he pushes out of the sofa and rushes to join the Olop crew at the edge of the platform. On the platform several meters below and to the right of theirs, Wil can see Bennie and another Brailack rolling around. When the two separate Bennie gets to his feet first and unleashes a series of savage kicks to his opponent. All around Bennie and his opponent, other Brailack are brawling, though Bennie seems to be the target of most of the group's ire.

Cynthia joins Wil and looks at him after glancing below, "His hand-to-hand has gotten much better." Wil groans. Bennie moves in fast, attacking two of the three newcomers with jabs to their midsections and a spinning kick that connects with both stunned attackers. The third leaps on top of Bennie before he can recover. Wil nods appreciating the skills of his Brailack friend who before joining the crew had only one move in a fight, run away.

"For Grolack's sake, he should have seen that coming," Zephyr says, as Bennie manages to get out from under the third attacker only to be set on by many more. Bennie leaps into the mass of newcomers and the confusion spills over to the few remaining non-fighting Brailack at the edges of the platform. A blue-skinned Brailack goes flying off the edge of the platform, only to slowly drift to the landing where platforms board. He shakes his head and staggers towards the reception desk.

"Impressive safety systems," Gabe comments. Wil looks up at his metal companion, one eyebrow quirked. Gabe points to something in the wall, then to another place on the wall, "Hidden tractor beam emitters." Wil nods.

The music has died down as occupants of most of the platforms have now turned their attention to the Brailack battle royal taking place. Wil watches as several more combatants fall or are thrown off of the platform, to be gently deposited on the landing, which the platform itself is getting closer and closer to by the minute.

Wil gets up and walks to the small control panel set between the two sections of seating, instructing their platform to begin the disembarkation process. He looks at Gabe, "Can you go get our crewmate?" Gabe nods, igniting the thrusters in his legs. With a whine, he lifts off their platform, and with the help of the safety system lands on the platform full of brawling Brailack a moment later.

"Should we wager on whether this is truly Bennie's fault?" Maxim asks, not taking his eyes off the writhing mass of small aliens.

"Sucker bet," Wil says, also not diverting his gaze from the spectacle below.

One of the Olop comes over, Wil assumes she's the captain of this crew, "One of yours in that mess?"

Wil nods, "Yeah."

"Best get him before the Peacekeepers get here." She looks around, taking in the other platforms, full of non-Tarsi beings. "Won't be long now. They like to crack down extra hard on those of us that ain't Tarsi." Her face tells Wil what she thinks of that.

Wil glances down at the stout, fur-covered woman in worn spacer-style coveralls. He taps the commset in his ear, "Gabe, get Bennie and get gone."

"Ack—" Gabe replies but is tackled by four Brailack. He tosses away two of the attackers, drifting to the landing pad just a meter from the platform. "Acknowledged, Captain." The platform is settling in against the landing, the brawl spilling out onto it. Two more Brailack fly from the platform to land, sliding across the landing area. Gabe emerges holding a squirming Bennie in one hand. The droid looks around, taking only a second to glance past the main entrance, turning toward the back of the building. His thrusters ignite with a whine, and he flies toward the rear of the structure. As he dodges past a platform with a mix of Ruknak and Trenbal on it, the club's front door bursts open. The music, already at a lower volume, cuts off completely. Lights snap on all along the height of the structure. A squad of Peacekeepers marches in.

Wil looks at the others, "This should be fun."

CHAPTER 5_

FOUR STORIES_

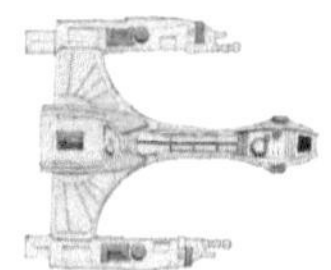

Wil snaps out of whatever he was thinking of, "Oh, sorry. No. What were you saying?" He smiles.

The Peacekeeper Centurion, across the table from him, isn't smiling. His close-cropped hair frames an angular face. "I was asking if you knew who started the brawl at the nightclub. There are reports it was a member of your crew, a Brailack."

Wil shrugs, "Wasn't the entire rumble all Brailack? How could someone say who started it? I mean they all look the same right?" He winks, hoping his casual racism distracts the interrogator.

The officer coughs once, then clears his throat, "Most of the others we've interviewed are crew from a trade convoy; they say that your crewman was"—the Centurion looks down at the PADD in his hand—"hitting on every woman on the platform." He looks back up at Wil, "Does that sound like your crewman?"

Wil shakes his head, "No, Bennie is celibate."

The Centurion blushes a bit, "Oh, I wasn't aware."

"I don't think it's something you advertise like being a vegan," Wil says, smiling his most *not guilty* smile. "He and our droid were back aboard the *Ghost*."

"And what were they doing aboard your ship?"

"How would I know? I wasn't there. Gabe was probably taking

"""

something apart, to reassemble it better than it was. Bennie was probably eating my food."

"You're the first officer aboard the *Ghost?*" the female Centurion asks Zephyr in an interview room down the hall from where Wil is being interviewed.

"I am, though sometimes it feels like I'm a nanny, know what I mean?" She smiles.

"I do not." The other woman looks down at her PADD, "Several patrons we've spoken to have indicated that it was your crewman a Ben-Ari Vulvo, who started the fight on the platform with the crew of the Brailack trader *Goddess of Profit*. He was and I quote *sexually harassing the female crew members*."

"I don't see how that's possible," Zephyr counters. "He was back at our ship. Plus, he's gay, so there's that."

The Peacekeeper woman looks back down at her PADD, tapping a few things, "I see. That's not referenced here." She taps the screen twice, then looks up, "And your droid? It's reported he was there."

"Is sexual preference something Peacekeepers keep in files now?" When the interrogator doesn't respond Zephyr continues, "Again, I don't see how. He was aboard the ship with Bennie. Perhaps your witnesses are a little biased, not all droids look alike you know?"

"I must say, it's a pleasure to meet you Centurion Maxim," the Peacekeeper across the table says, beaming. "Your records at the academy are still untouched."

Maxim smiles, "That's good to know, but it is *Ex*-Centurion now."

Nodding, "Of course." The Peacekeeper sub-Centurion looks down at his PADD, "So, it says here, that your crewmate Ben-Ari Vulvo, started the fight after"—he looks at the PADD again to double check—"trying to flirt with every woman on the platform."

Maxim shakes his head, "Impossible."

"Care to explain?"

Maxim holds up a finger, ticking it with his other hand, "For one thing, he was not there. He was aboard the *Ghost*." He ticks another finger, "For another, he's a eunuch. Horrible accident involving Xelurians, touchy subject aboard the ship."

The Sub-Centurion blanches, coughing once, "That sounds horribly painful."

"I'm told it was. He's never been the same since," Maxim says.

"I see. So the reports that your droid removed him from the fight..." the young officer presses.

"Lies. Fake news," Maxim remains perfectly still, not showing the slightest hint of emotion. "Gabe was aboard the *Ghost* making repairs to the food processor unit. It was actin' up, only making protein slime in fruit flavors." He grimaces, moving for the first time, "Truly disgusting."

"I, uh, I see. So, both your droid and your Brailack crewmate were not at the night club?"

"That is correct," Maxim tilts his head, smiling.

"I'm not answering your questions," Cynthia says to the man across the table from her.

"Why is that?"

"Because I don't have to. I know my rights. If you'd like to question me, press charges. Get me an adjudicator."

The Peacekeeper clears his throat, "This would go faster if—"

"Adjudicator," Cynthia says.

"Ms. Luar, we only want to understand—" the flustered junior officer tries again.

Cynthia looks him in the eyes, "Adjudicator." She closes her eyes, her tail lazily swishing along the floor under her chair.

The Peacekeeper sighs, "We don't want to press charges—"

"Adjudicator."

PARTING IS SUCH SWEET SORROW_

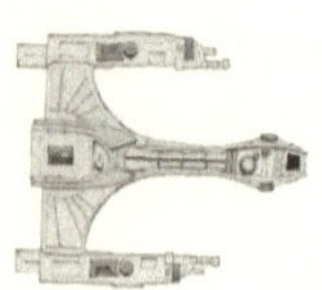

"It seems your reputation is well earned," Blumtillithian says, walking out of the regional Peacekeeper facility, followed by Wil and the crew.

"Look it wasn't entirely our fault," Wil starts.

Blumtillithian holds a hand up, making a tsking noise. "I don't care. The shuttle is this way." He trots off toward the waiting vehicle.

"I think he's mad," Maxim offers. He looks around at the others, "By the way, did any of you give up Bennie?"

Wil tuts, "As if. As annoying as he is, he's crew. At least until we kick his little green ass off the ship, he's family. I told them he's celibate."

Zephyr smiles. "I said he's gay."

Maxim laughs, a laugh he's only used a handful of times before in the presence of the others. "I said he was a eunuch." He looks down at Cynthia, "What did you say?"

Cynthia wags a finger, "Rookies. I said nothing."

"What do you mean?" Wil asks.

"Anything you said in there can and definitely would be used against you. Every word you uttered was recorded, that you all gave different stories." She wags her finger again, "If it weren't for four-legs over there, we'd likely be sitting in those interview rooms for quite some time longer." She shudders, "Or worse. We will have to have a lunch and learn about this it seems."

Blumtillithian opens the shuttle hatch, "Please." He doesn't wait before boarding and heading to the pilot station.

As they file into the luxurious shuttle, Maxim shouts toward the front, "Are you taking us to our ship?"

"No, the Councilwoman would like to meet with you." He leans over to look back at them, "She'd like you off-planet as quickly as possible." He grumbles under his breath, then adds, "I don't blame her."

Wil taps his wristcomm, removing the commset stored in it, placing it back in his ear, "Gabe, you have the little green nightmare?"

"Indeed, Captain. We have returned to the *Ghost*. Would you like us to meet you somewhere?" the droid replies.

Wil looks at Blumtillithian, "Can they get to where we're going without you?"

The four-legged man nods, "Tell the droid to provide this address." He does something Wil can't see, then a prompt appears on Wil's wristcomm.

Wil tilts his head slightly, "Yeah pal, I'm sending you an address. Meet us there."

"Acknowledged." The connection drops.

"Leave Tarsis," Slivyrn Grythlorian, councilor to the Galactic Commonwealth says from the head of the conference table. Having just sat down, Blumtillithian, at her side, scowls.

Wil smiles, "Um, is this about the nightclub?"

Zephyr grunts, trying to avoid looking at Wil, or either of the four-legged beings at the head of the table. She grabs a pitcher of water and pours herself a glass. She's refilling the glass for a third time when Maxim rests his hand on her arm.

Grythlorian glances at Zephyr, then back to Wil, "Frankly, yes. It cost me a considerable amount of political capital to encourage the Peacekeeper Garrison Commander to drop the charges against you and *misplace* the files." She glowers, "You've drawn considerable attention to yourselves. Attention I don't want leading back to me."

Cynthia rests her face in her hands, "This isn't going well."

Wil waves a hand, "We can still do the job," he insists.

Blumtillithian tuts, "Councilwoman, it's not too late to end this." He gestures at the crew, "Surely these buffoons aren't the only means to your ends. I can find others."

"Hey!" Bennie says, "Only that one is a buffoon." He points at Wil, who flips him off.

Wil turns to Slivyrn Grythlorian, "Look, you're right, I am the best suited for going to Earth and finding your missing employee." He taps a finger on the table, "How is he hiding on Earth, anyway? One of these image inducers?"

"He's a Multonae," Blumtillithian says.

Maxim nods, "That tracks, but how do we find him? They look like humans; the *Ghost's* sensors aren't anywhere near precise enough to pinpoint a single Multonae."

The councilwoman nods, smiling. "That won't be an issue."

Wil nods, "Then let's do this."

Standing at the top of the *Ghost's* cargo ramp, the crew is gathered around Gabe. "Are you sure about this, buddy?" Wil asks, his hand resting on Gabe's shoulder.

The chrome skinned droid nods, "It is the only way. Staying on Tarsis will give me unprecedented access to lobby for the cause. Despite last night's misadventure, I believe Councilor Grythlorian is still my best bet."

"Please be careful," Zephyr says from beside Wil, "You will be disrupting a lot of very entrenched businesses and cultural norms. No one likes change, especially if it threatens their way of life."

Gabe looks at Zephyr and smiles, "Indeed, do not forget I am quite capable of defending myself." His eyes flash red to emphasize his point.

Zephyr grins, "You are, and that will be an unpleasant surprise for the first person that challenges you."

Bennie comes around the group, "Gonna miss you a little."

"I will miss you as well. Please do not die on this mission," Gabe says then turns to the waiting cargo ramp, "I should go. I do not believe Blumtillithian is happy we are delaying departure."

"Screw him," Cynthia says, hugging Gabe around the waist. "Don't you die either. We'll get this job done and be back here as fast as we can."

"I look forward to reuniting with you all." He turns and walks down the ramp.

Once Gabe is clear, Wil reaches over to the pedestal next to the cargo hatch, he taps the control and as the ramp raises, the heavy doors at the top of the ramp slide closed.

NEW TOYS_

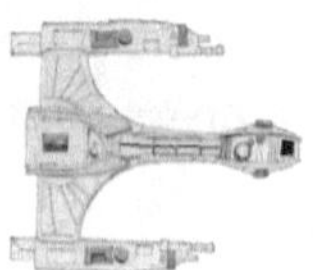

WIL and the crew are sitting around the table in the crew lounge aboard the *Ghost* with Blumtillithian standing near the large display on the opposite bulkhead. "I will travel with you as far as Vlack Three." He glances over at the crew, "Please stop playing with that."

Everyone turns to see Bennie, or rather ALF from Wil's media archive, sitting where Bennie was just sitting.

"Dude, cut it out," Wil hisses. ALF wavers and vanishes, leaving Bennie chuckling on the seat. Wil turns to Blumtillithian, "Tillith, do I understand right? The image inducers can't change size or height?"

The Tarlack man nods, "That is correct Captain. The inducers create an image overlay of your physical size. Ben-Ari could not look like you, at least not a you at your height."

Bennie taps his wristcomm and just like that bcomes a meter and a half tall Wil. "Sweet," Small-Wil says, grinning.

Maxim groans, "Gods help us, two Wils." He grins at his human friend.

Zephyr leans down to Small-Wil, "I'll take it away if you don't stop messing with it."

Small-Wil grimaces, "Fine." The image wavers, and Bennie is back in his seat, arms crossed.

Blumtillithian continues, "As I was saying, the inducers will allow you all to look human while on Earth. You will need to recharge them every few days, they draw a tremendous amount of power. Hard light constructs are hugely power hungry."

"Hard light? Incredible," Wil says, reaching down to run his finger along the top of the five-inch device sitting on the table in front of him. "NASA had a team working on the theory of hard light constructs back when I first joined up."

Blumtillithian smiles, "Quaint. As I said, the image inducers create hard light constructs. The images are solid, after a fashion. You should avoid physical contact that might compromise the image. A brief touch will not cause problems, a long embrace almost certainly will."

Cynthia looks down at the device, "Ok, so these will let us walk around Earth looking like humans, but how do we do anything there? We don't even speak their language."

Blumtillithian answers, "Additionally, the image inducers have speech synthesizers. You can speak like normal and the inducer will cancel out your voice's wave pattern and replace it with whatever you select. Much like how translation systems aboard ship function."

"Ok, I'll grant you, all very cool," Wil says, "but we still need to get to Earth, then find the hiding Multonae."

The Tarlack nods, "Yes, which is why we are going to Vlack Three."

"What can you tell us about Vlack Three? I've never been," Maxim asks.

Blumtillithian gestures to the large display behind him, activating it. On the screen a Green and blue world slowly spins. "The Vlack System occupies a unique space within the GC. Vlack Three has some of the most advanced ship design facilities in the GC next to Ankarra. However, unlike Ankarra, the Vlack System is not a protectorate under the auspices of the Peacekeepers. The Vlack shipyards are responsible for nearly one hundred percent of the GC Council's diplomatic fleet. The Councilwoman has made arrangements with one of the shipwrights there to perform some aftermarket modifications to your ship. The shipwright is familiar with Ankarran vessels. Between the equipment I brought with me, and technology available on the planet, the *Ghost* will be able to move without detection by any Peacekeeper or GC sensor array." Behind him, the display zooms out showing their current course for the Vlack System. "While I supervise the upgrades to your ship, you can stock up on whatever supplies you feel you'll need. The markets on

Vlack are on par with some of the better markets on Fury." Seeing the excitement in their eyes he adds, "Vlack, while not entirely law-abiding, is considerably more cultured than Fury. You would do well to conduct yourselves accordingly."

Maxim leans over to Zephyr, "I think he's saying we're not fancy."

Zephyr exchanges a look with Cynthia, "Speak for yourself."

Will raps his knuckles on the table, "Getting back to the mission."

Across the room Blumtillithian once again nods, then sighs under his breath, two of his feet tapping. "Yes, so we've covered the image inducers and the stealth tech upgrade for your ship. The last item to go over before we arrive at Vlack Three is the person you're to retrieve." The Tarlack touches his wristcomm, and the display showing Vlack Three changes to show what looks like a heavyset white male in his mid-forties. "This is Bonson Drell. As you already know, he's Multonae, so he'll more or less blend in on Earth, so long as he never has to see a doctor. Drell worked for Councilwoman Grythlorian in a special projects research facility on one of Tarsis's moons. Three cycles ago, he vanished."

Cynthia again raises her hand, "How do you know he's on Earth? And why wait so long?"

The stout four-legged alien smiles; it's not a nice smile. "As you know, Earth currently has a status of protected primitive planet, meaning that it is fairly closely monitored by the GC—not just to ensure against contamination, but to know when it is time to approach them. We have detected certain energy patterns and types, things Earth should not be capable of yet. Drell is the most likely reason."

"Seems like a bit of a leap, no?" Maxim presses, "I mean literally any alien could have snuck themselves on to Earth."

Blumtillithian nods, "True, but unlikely. We know Drell needs to hide, so Earth makes sense. We also know that he had been covertly, or so he thought, researching the planet. Worst case scenario, you get there, find the party responsible for upsetting the natural evolution of technology on Earth, and it is not Drell; you've still accomplished something." He shrugs.

"Fair enough," Maxim agrees.

Cynthia raises her hand, "Perhaps he doesn't want to be found. It's not like humans kidnapped him." She chuckles at the idea.

"I am certain he does not wish to be found; he stole data that is worth many billions of credits to the right people," Blumtillithian replies.

Bennie grins, and Blumtillithian adds, "You are not, nor do you know, *the right people*, so do not get any ideas. Drell not only stole the data, he erased the facility's storage core before leaving his workstation. The project ground to a halt, and until a half a cycle ago, we feared it would never get moving again."

"What's the project?" Maxim asks.

"The project is the Councilwoman's business and none of yours," the four-legged being says, not breaking eye contact with the much larger Palorian man.

PART TWO

CHAPTER 6_

SHOPPING_

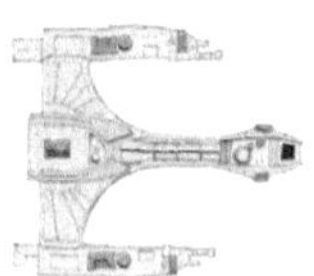

"SON OF A NUTCRACKER!" Wil exhales as the cargo doors at the top of the *Ghost's* cargo ramp open, "Humidity much?"

"Welcome to Vlack Three," Blumtillithian says as he walks to the top of the cargo ramp. Vlack Three is a lush world that, from orbit, looked to be mostly jungle except for the two rather massive oceans. As the ramp comes to a rest on the duracrete below he adds, "Jungle world, you expected something else?"

"Burn," Bennie says, pushing past Wil.

Cynthia comes up alongside Wil, "What're you worried about? You're not the one covered in fur, fur that will frizz out." She growls and follows after Bennie. Wil watches her descend the ramp, shrugs, and follows.

At the bottom of the ramp, Blumtillithian turns to watch several ground vehicles rumble toward the *Ghost*. He called ahead to ensure the *Ghost* was on a landing pad away from the other ships docked at this spaceport. As the vehicles get closer, he addresses the group. "I will remain here and supervise the upgrades, as we discussed. I've sent the details of the market I recommend to your wristcomms. The upgrades should be complete in two days' time. I'd prefer you not bother me until then." He turns and walks toward the slowing lead vehicle.

"Such a charmer, that one," Wil says. He looks at the crew, "Ok, Let's go to the mall!"

As they turn to walk toward the rental ground car that was waiting when they landed, Maxim says, "I'll stay here. Someone should monitor our little four-legged friend, and since that would usually be Gabe, I'll do it." He looks at Zephyr smiling, "Get me some new toys."

Zephyr leans in for a kiss, "Will do my love. Don't kill the Tarlack; we need him."

"No promises."

Blumtillithian bows as the hatch on the lead ground car opens releasing an Ankarran woman.

Wil whistles, "Wow, he wasn't kidding when he said the shipwright knew about Ankarran ships."

"Indeed," Zephyr says. "Councilor Grythlorian is quite well connected." They continue toward their own vehicle, watching the tall, long-tailed woman make room for several other beings to emerge from the vehicle. She and Blumtillithian are deep in conversation.

Maxim turns back towards the *Ghost*, "Have fun!" He waves over his shoulder.

"Maybe we should leave Maxim and Gabe with the ship more often," Bennie says as the ground car pulls away from the *Ghost*. He waves his arms around, "There's so much more space in here without those two."

"We could always just strap you to the roof if you want space," Cynthia says.

Bennie makes a rude gesture, then turns his attention to his wristcomm, "Says here this market is the fifth largest on the planet."

Wil looks up from his own wristcomm, "I found us a hotel for the night. We can shop, grab some shuteye, and head back out if we need to." He looks around, "Don't tell Max, I got the luxury suite." Rubbing his hands together, looking at Cynthia, who returns his stare with a very aggressive eye roll. He grins, "Four-thousand-thread-count sheets, babe!"

A bit later, the vehicle pulls up to the front of the market, Wil looks out, "Wow, this is truly something." Beings from all over the GC are coming and going through the ornamental gate; cargo droids trundle along behind many of them. The gate proclaims the market to be the *Isklar District Market*.

As the rental ground car drives away, Bennie says, "I'm heading to the tech sector." He doesn't wait for acknowledgement, waving a hand over his shoulder. Cynthia looks at the others, "I'll go with him, keep him out of trouble." A pause, "Or at least try." She looks at Wil, "Send me the hotel details." Without waiting for him to answer she follows the Brailack into the market, down one alleyway of stalls.

Wil looks at Zephyr, "Captain and First Officer fun time!" He raises his hand for a high five.

Zephyr quirks a blue-black eyebrow. She exhales and raises her hand gently resting it against his, "Come on, I want to check out the culinary section. I'd love to stock up the larder if we can."

"Grocery shopping? Oh, come on!" Wil looks around, "Maybe I can catch up with Cyn and Bennie?"

"Grow up. If you behave, I'll get you a toy." Zephyr walks through the gate into the Isklar District Market.

THE GHOST: MAXIM_

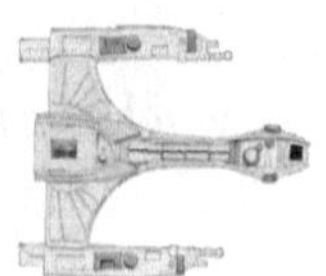

BLUMTILLITHIAN TURNS TO Maxim as the work crews unload their equipment from a larger van that has recently arrived. He and the Ankarran woman walk over, "Maxim, this is Deliza."

The Ankarran extends her hand. Maxim grasps her forearm; she grasps his, "It is a pleasure to meet you Maxim," she says. Her voice has a melodic quality Maxim has never heard before.

"The pleasure is mine, Shipwright Deliza," he replies, releasing her arm.

Blumtillithian and Deliza exchange a glance, neither saying anything. Maxim sees it but says nothing, instead asking, "Do all Ankarrans sound like you? I've never met another of your kind, and your voice is really lovely."

The shipwright blushes, an orange hue creeping up her otherwise pale neck and cheeks, "We do; some say our voices are like music." She smiles, "I've always found them to sound like non-aligned engine parts grinding against each other." Maxim laughs.

Blumtillithian extends an arm toward the *Ghost*, "If you'll follow me, we can go over the upgrades. He turns back to Maxim, "Would you mind supervising the crew installing the stealth components?" As Maxim nods, the Tarlack man points toward several large cargo modules barely visible in the *Ghost's* hold from the ground, "Those are the components; the chief technician should have a few more pieces that I could not acquire before we departed Tarsis."

Maxim turns toward the ship, eyeing the crates in question, "Sure, anything special, or they know what they're supposed to be doing?"

"I have briefed the chief technician. It should just be a matter of offering any help they may require or answering questions specific to this vessel."

"Sounds good, where will you be?" Maxim asks.

"Deliza and I will start in the forward section. In order to detect a single non-human from orbit the forward sensors will require some new hardware. Well, a lot of new hardware," the Tarlack man replies.

Several hours of sweat-inducing labor later, Maxim, Deliza, and Blumtillithian are in the *Ghost's* lounge sharing lunch. The rest of the work crew is in the cargo hold, doing the same.

Maxim sets his sandwich down, "How is the sensor upgrade coming?"

Deliza finishes her bite, "Challenging, but not impossible." She takes a sip of her water and continues, "Your ship is quite unique—outwardly a model eighty-nine, one of our most popular designs, but the similarities end there. Someone has heavily modified this vessel, several times. Not always expertly." One of her boney eyebrow ridges rises.

Maxim smiles, looking around the room, "This ship is special. She's been repaired and rebuilt at least twice since I've been part of the crew. Who knows what was done before that? We know Xarrix did quite a bit of work, including at least one virus." He shudders remembering the incident and subsequent death of Xarrix.

Blumtillithian finishes his sandwich, "It is remarkable you could get Ankarran shipwrights to come to Harrith."

Maxim nods, "That was all the Harrith government."

Deliza bows her head, "It would take a planetary or system-wide government to get my people to leave Ankarra, not only because of the tight grip the Peacekeepers keep on us, but our own disinterest in leaving our home system."

Maxim looks around the room, "Well it was, and still is, appreciated.

The *Ghost* was pretty much scrap at the end of the Harrith incident." He raps his knuckles on the table, "She's our home."

Blumtillithian sets his glass aside after emptying it, "Ok then, shall we return to work?"

Deliza and Maxim nod, the Ankarran woman says, "Maxim, I can have my tech team begin the next steps of the stealth tech updates if you're willing to assist them?"

Maxim takes all three plates, stacking them, then the three glasses, "Of course."

Blumtillithian stands, smoothing his tunic, despite it lacking a single wrinkle, "Very good, let's proceed."

Maxim quirks an eyebrow at the Ankarran shipwright, "Pushy."

She nods, "He is indeed." She inhales, her shoulders rising and turns to follow the four-legged being.

The crew that Deliza brought with her, while not Ankarran are tremendously experienced. It's obvious the *Ghost* is not the first Ankarran ship they've worked on. That said, Maxim has still been watching them like hawks. "You there! Be careful. That looks important!"

One of the technicians looks up, lifting the thing Maxim thinks is important, "This?" Maxim nods. "It's a secondary power distribution node." The technicians and Maxim are standing on the outer hull of the *Ghost* near where the neck meets the main body of the ship.

Maxim nods again, "Definitely important then."

"No. This is burned out." It waves the device around, high over its head, "Looks to have burnt out sometime ago, months at least."

"Oh, well, ok then you're planning to replace it?" Before the technician can reply, the big Palorian turns and walks along the *Ghost's* neck, toward another open access panel.

"Maxim, come in, please," Blumtillithian says over Maxim's wristcomm.

He lifts his arm, "Go ahead."

"If you are not busy, please join us on the bridge. We are ready to boot up the upgraded sensor package and run the initial diagnostic."

"On my way."

Maxim finds the bridge in a state he's only seen it in after the ship has nearly been destroyed. "What is going on here? Why have you disassembled every console?"

Another of the tentacled technicians rises from behind the tactical console, "We did not disassemble every station;" it gestures to Bennie's cluttered workspace, "that station was too disgusting to touch."

Maxim grunts, "Truly." He looks around, "So what are we doing here?"

Blumtillithian gestures, taking in the entire space, "We need to integrate the new data feeds from the sensor array into the main data trunk for the bridge." The four-legged man points to a thick bundle of wires hanging vine-like from a circular hole in the bridge's ceiling.

Maxim walks up to the cable, as thick as his thigh, "This is the central data trunk?" He looks at the cable, and the dozens of smaller cables snaking their way, this way and that, throughout the bridge. "Gabe would make quick work of this," he whispers to himself.

Blumtillithian nods, "Your droid friend would have been much more useful in this project." He spreads his arms, "Alas, I have only you." He picks up a PADD and hands it to one of the octopus-like technicians, "Let's get started." The being nods, its beak-like mouth making a clicking noise as it blinks rapidly.

Maxim walks over to the station Zephyr occupies, "What do you need me to do?"

The Tarlack man points to a screen, "Keep an eye on the diagnostics on that screen. You'll know when the new array integrates."

Deliza adds, "Or you'll know when it fails, but that will be more smoke and sparks, than anything on the screen." She smiles.

SHOPPING: ZEPHYR & WIL_

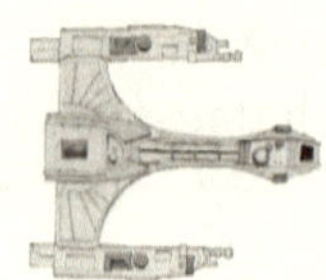

WIL PICKS up what might be a fruit, or an egg of some type; it's the size of a football, but pink and slightly fuzzy, like a peach, but the fuzz is tinted blue. "What's this?" he asks the shopkeeper, a Ruknak woman.

The shopkeeper looks down. "Are you going to ask me that every time you pick something up?" she asks, her rock-like hide making a grating noise as she pushes around a waist-high display case full of what Wil assumes are some type of vegetable.

"Only for the ones I don't know what they are," he smiles.

She waves an arm, taking in her stand, "And do you know what any of this is?"

"Nope," he grins.

"Leave. Now," she demands, pushing him into Zephyr, using her immense strength to shove them both out into the walkway between stalls. "Do not come back." She turns, mumbling something about pink-skinned annoyances.

Zephyr turns to Wil, her annoyance not even slightly hidden, "What's wrong with you?"

"I'm bored," he groans.

"You're being a child. What's up with you?" She turns and directs the cargo bot they rented earlier to follow her. The small, wheeled flatbed follows with a whir of its electric motors, tiny honks blurting out of a speaker anytime someone gets in its way.

Wil follows. "I'm a little freaked out we're going to Earth."

Zephyr points to a group of small tables, "Sit." She looks at the cargo droid, "Please wait here."

"Acknowledged," it replies.

A waitress comes over, "Drinks?"

Zephyr holds up two fingers, "Grum." The server nods and departs into a small kitchen area. The small section of tables is about half full; several Harrith and a smattering of Trenbal occupy the bulk of the occupied tables. One table is full of Trollack, their fishlike eyes darting around as the small beings argue about something. Zephyr turns to Wil, "What do you mean? I'd think you'd be excited to be returning home." She rests a hand on his, "Especially in a semi-sanctioned capacity."

Wil looks down at the table, "It's been a while. What if it has changed?"

"Change is inevitable, Wil." The waitress returns, placing a frosty mug in front of each of them, the amber liquid sloshes slightly. Zephyr looks up, "Thank you." She turns her attention back to her Captain, "What kind of changes would be so bad as to have you worried?"

"I don't know; that's just it." He takes a long slow drink, wiping his mouth on the back of his hand, "For all I know, World War Three finally broke and Earth is a radioactive hellscape—populated by mutant goldfish people riding domesticated river otters."

Zephyr smiles, "Well, it's pretty safe to assume that one is unlikely. Why would Bonson Drell flee to a radioactive nightmare world full of what was it? Goldfish people? What does that even mean?"

Wil nods absently, "Never mind. What if something has happened to my sister or her family? Right now, they're exactly as they were when I left Earth the last time, happily going about their lives."

His First Officer shrugs, "It's entirely possible they're still doing that. And if not, the only way to deal with it is to deal with it."

"Only way out is through," Wil says.

Zephyr thinks about that for a beat, "Yeah, right. Very astute."

"Not a Wil original," he quips.

"I never assumed it was." She grins, "Wil originals tend to involve more offensive humor." She takes a drink, then continues, "What was it like when you went back last time? You've never spoken much about it, other than the snacks and media you brought back."

"It was ok. I did my best to not attract attention. Hey, did you know they have statues of me?" The funk that was hanging over him when they sat down has diminished a bit.

"Don't tell Maxim," Zephyr says.

Wil taps a finger against his chin, "I'll have to see if I can steer him near one, see what he says."

"I can guess." She laughs to herself, thinking of her companion and his likely reaction. "What else?"

"I ran into a friend, talk about timing, right? I'm on the planet one day and bump into him walking his dog. I wonder if Aldrin is still alive?"

"Your friend's name is Aldrin?" She asks.

"His dog. My friend is James. I hope he's doing well. They were just getting back to resuming the FTL experiments when I returned. He was leading the team." Wil beams thinking of his friend and his successes. "Thanks Zee; this helped more than you know."

She takes a drink, finishing her grum, putting the empty mug down accompanied by a belch, "Good; let's go. We've got a lot of shopping left to do. I saw a stall up ahead with what looked like freeze-dried cruciferous fruits."

"Oh goody, space squash."

SHOPPING: CYNTHIA & BENNIE_

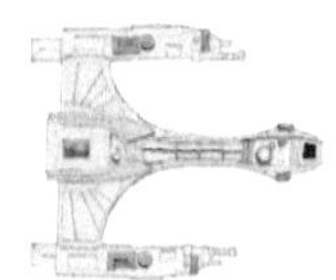

"You don't need another one," Cynthia plucks the external processing unit out of Bennie's hand.

"But that one is twice as powerful as the one I have on the *Ghost*," Bennie whines.

"Well, that's just too bad. Wil said only the essentials." Cynthia places the expensive piece of computing hardware back on the shelf. Through the doorway of the stall, she looks into the small cargo droid they've rented, already loaded with very expensive-looking gear that Bennie convinced her that they needed.

Bennie walks across the stall, "Hey, how much for this multiplexer?"

The shopkeeper, a Burzzad man in his middle years comes over, his three eyes blinking in unison, "That model, that is fifteen thousand credits."

Bennie tuts, "For this?" He waves the device around. The shopkeeper's eyes go wide as he attempts to grab the device out of Bennie's hand. "We'll pay five thousand," Bennie offers, moving his hand out of reach of the shopkeeper at the last second.

"No, no, no, five thousand is too little." The shopkeeper fakes a move to his left, then swoops in and grabs the device from Bennie as he dodges. "I could take no less than twelve."

Bennie looks over to Cynthia, winks, "Ten, final offer." He raises his wristcomm, ready to pay.

The Burzzad inclines his head, "Deal." He hands Cynthia the device, then picks up a PADD and types on it for a second. He swipes toward Bennie and Bennie's wristcomm beeps.

Bennie taps and smiles, "Thanks." He looks at his feline-featured companion, "Let's go, I saw a Teledyne nine thousand two stalls down."

Cynthia shrugs, "Then we eat; following you around is making me hungry."

An hour or two, Cynthia has lost track, later they're at a small bar set in the space of two stalls just outside the weapons and armament district. She looks down at Bennie, sipping something pink with glowing blue swirls in it. "Feeling festive there?" she nods towards the glass.

"Why not? That multiplexer was a steal; he shouldn't have taken less than thirteen." He takes a sip, "Plus it will thrill Gabe I could score those two plasma spanners."

The bar they've taken a break in is moderately busy as it's getting close to midday. The next table over is populated by several Stiltin, their mandibles clicking loudly as they argue the merits of something Cynthia doesn't understand. She looks around the space, "This place isn't bad. Have you been here before?"

Bennie shakes his head, "Nope. I've heard of it, was even on my list to visit someday, maybe set up shop for a while."

"Things on Fury were so good you stayed there?"

Bennie raises a hand and wiggles it side to side. "Good, is a subjective term. It was certainly profitable, and Xarrix sent some interesting clients my way, Wil included."

Cynthia smiles, thinking of Wil, "That's right, he told me about that once. You met him early on, right?"

The Brailack takes a final sip of his drink, causing it to slurp loud enough that several nearby conversations stop. "Yeah, he had just found his way to Fury and needed new papers for the *Ghost* and some identity work, since he didn't have a GC citizen record."

"Well, I suppose it's good you never packed up and headed for Vlack Three, none of us would have met."

Bennie nods, "That's true, and for all the terrifying things that have happened, I'm glad I met all of you." He blushes a little, turning a deeper shade of green, "I mean, don't tell Maxim or Wil or well anyone else, but I like you all. You're like family, except, you know, I don't feel like trying to kill any of you—except Wil, sometimes, a lot of the time." He grins.

"Love you too little green," Cynthia says, purring slightly.

"You know—" he starts, eyebrow ridges quirked.

"Don't ruin it."

CHAPTER 7_

FANCY FANCY_

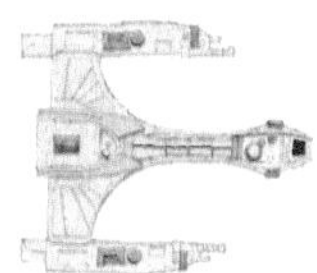

"Wow, this place is posh!" Bennie shouts from the room he's claimed for himself. The hotel suite is near the top floor of the nearly two-hundred floor, luxury hotel. They're near but not on the top floor because the top floor was out of budget even for a splurge like this.

Wil looks out over the city, "What's this place called? I never caught the name."

From the room she's claimed, Zephyr shouts, "Jlingdo."

Wil presses a hand against the glass, "Well, Jlingdo is pretty. Even the market is lit up at night." The city below is a quiltwork of lights; the streets and the narrow alleys of the market are lit up like pulsing arteries.

Cynthia walks over, putting an arm around his waist, "Yeah not a bad view; well done."

"There's a toilet in each room!" Bennie shouts. The sound of a toilet flushing follows the announcement, "With water!"

Cynthia steps away from Wil, "And, mood broken." She looks around the room, "We going out or ordering in?"

Zephyr walks back into the main room of the suite, "This place is nice; each room has an amazing view. I might have to have Maxim come stay the night here instead of the ship." She looks back into the room at something, "Definitely need to call him." She turns and heads back into her room.

Wil smiles, then shouts toward Zephyr's room, "Have Max grab dinner on his way." He looks back to Cynthia, "Now it's his problem." He grins.

"Roger that!" Zephyr shouts from her room.

Bennie walks into the main area, "Can we stay here longer? The data connection this place has is amazing—fast and has links to all sorts of interesting data stores around this sector." He rubs his small green hands together.

"You kiddin'?" This place costs a fortune. I splurged for the night since it's a few days' trip to Earth, and I wasn't sure how long we'd be there." He squints, "Unless you're willing to chip in a little."

"One night is fine." Bennie waves a hand dismissively, turning to return to his room.

About an hour and a half later, Maxim walks in the front door of the suite. He takes in the room, "You were not going to invite me to this?" He looks right at Wil, sitting at the central dining table, behind the sofa and chairs of the sitting area.

Wil shrugs, "I thought you'd be busy with our little four-legged passenger." He tilts his head to look to the side of Maxim, "Where's dinner?"

From behind Maxim, Blumtillithian holds out two large brown bags, "I have it."

Wil blushes, flipping Maxim off, who shrugs, grinning.

Wil gets up and offers to take one of the bags from Blumtillithian, who hands it over, smiling when Wil flinches slightly at the weight of the bag. The Tarlack brushes past, his remaining bag held aloft as if it weighed no more than a PADD.

Wil leans towards Maxim, "You suck." He shoves the heavy bag into the big Palorian's stomach, moving back toward the table as Maxim follows. Wil shouts, "Dinner's on!"

Zephyr emerges from her room in a pair of loose pants with a blouse that tucks into a belt lined with metal studs.

Wil nods, "Very eighties, I dig it. Radical." He smiles as his first officer walks in and kisses her partner before moving towards the table to join the others.

Bennie leans out of his room, "I'll eat in here."

Cynthia and Zephyr both turn; Zephyr says, "No, you will not. We have company."

Bennie glances over to Blumtillithian, "Oh, hi Tillith." He looks at the two women, still staring at him like he was their unruly child. "Ok, fine. Be right out." The door slides shut behind him.

Wil inhales, "Is this, did you find Chinese food?" He opens the bag Blumtillithian has placed on the table, removing a container and opening it, "Orange chicken?"

Blumtillithian takes the container, looking inside, "I don't know what an orange is or what a chicken is; this is"—he inhales—"this is nob lank."

Wil looks at the Palorians, then Cynthia, shrugs all around. Maxim offers, "I let Blumtillithian choose where to pick up food since he's familiar with the city."

The Tarlack man bows, bending his front two legs, "I hope you enjoy; I eat at Old Woman Gurney's every time I'm on Vlack Three for business. It has amazing Zelp reviews."

Everyone opens containers, passing them around the table. Bennie walks out, "Is that Zeblick Scelp?"

Everyone exchanges looks, then stares at the Brailack who shrugs, "What? It's a delicacy on Brai."

BYE FOR NOW_

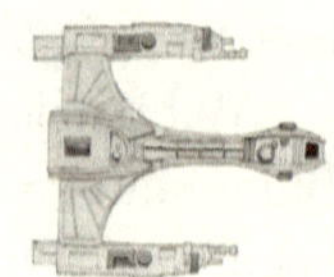

"WE'VE RECEIVED CLEARANCE TO DEPART," Cynthia says from her station. The bridge of the *Ghost* is just like they'd left it two days ago, everything put back where it belongs, including Wil's Kell statuette.

Maxim looks around one more time admiring the work he, Deliza, and Blumtillithian did in just two days.

Wil looks around, then down at his station, pushing a slider forward, "Powering up the repulsors." The ship lurches a bit, then levels off. There's a pair of loud clunks, followed by clangs that reverberate up everyone's spine. "Landing gear retracted," Wil reports; despite everyone having the same status on their consoles if they want, he prefers to announce it.

Wil looks over his shoulder, to Cynthia's station, "Tell Tillith thanks for the upgrades. We'll see him when we see him."

She turns to her station for a moment, dabbing the commset in her ear. She whispers into the audio pickup for a minute then looks up, "He says, '*Good riddance.*'" She grins, "I think he likes us."

Bennie leans over from his station, "He's a turd. An officious turd. Although he has great taste in food." He quirks his hairless brow ridges, "I ordered from that place again, so we have dinner tonight." He sticks his tongue out at Wil, "You're welcome."

Wil smirks, pushing a control on his console forward. From the rear of the ship, the boom of the atmospheric engines igniting rolls through the ship. It pushes everyone into the backs of their chairs, except Bennie who was leaning to the side of his seat. He's knocked out of his seat and rolls toward the back of the bridge. The roar of the atmospheric engines subsides as Wil eases up on the throttle. Bennie jumps up, "You suck! I could have been hurt." He walks back to his station, turns and makes a rude gesture toward Wil, who is trying his best to keep his laughter contained. "Hate you," Bennie mumbles, strapping into his seat.

A few minutes later Zephyr looks up from her console, "We're clear of Vlack Three space control. Half a tock to FTL distance."

"Cool deal," Wil says, releasing his controls, activating the automatic flight control. "Be right back." He gets up and leaves the bridge.

Zephyr looks at Maxim who shrugs and looks at Cynthia.

She also shrugs, "I don't plan his every minute you know. I've no idea where he's going."

Maxim looks at Zephyr, "See, partners don't have to know where each other are every minute of the day."

Zephyr says nothing but doesn't take her eyes off of Maxim, who eventually mumbles, "But every couple is different."

Bennie chimes in, his chin sticking out, "This is why I love 'em and leave 'em."

Cynthia looks over to the smug Brailack, "That's the reason you're alone, huh? Not your personality? Your grooming habits? Your cleanliness or lack thereof?"

"Or the pilfering?" Maxim offers.

Bennie affects a stricken look, "So rude! I'll have you know all of those are desirable traits to someone. Plus, that's what the guest berths are for. I don't let my honeys see my quarters; they might try to take something."

Zephyr raises a hand, "Ok, wait. One"—she raises a finger, ticking it with a thumb—"that's disgusting. Do you at least change the linens in the guest berths afterward?" Before he can answer, she raises another finger, ticking it with the same thumb, "For another, what in the name of Grabthar do you have that someone might want to steal? Most of your possessions are things you've stolen from the rest of us."

Bennie waves a hand, turning back to his station.

TAKE OUT_

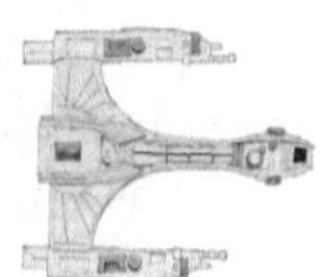

THE BRIDGE HATCH opens and Wil walks in. Cynthia looks up, "Where'd you go?"

"Do I need to check in with you when I go places?" Wil asks, smiling, but sort of serious. When she stares at him, he adds, "If you must know, I don't think breakfast agreed—"

"Never mind, and no you certainly don't have to tell me where you go." Cynthia raises both hands, turning back to her station as Wil moves to take his seat at the command station.

"Looks like we're clear for FTL," Wil says, looking at his console, disengaging the auto flight system. The flight controls come alive as the computer releases its hold on them. He looks around, "Everyone ready?" He looks around for nods, then looks up, "Gabe you—" He looks back down, "Damn, gonna take some getting used to him not being down in engineering." Everyone nods again.

He pushes the FTL throttle forward, "Off we go. Next stop, Earth."

"Ok Bennie, well done. Damn. I wish we'd ordered a few days' worth of Old Woman Gurney's, before leaving," Wil says around a bite of nob lank, his favorite dish of the many on the table.

Bennie beams, "Thanks. So, Earth."

Cynthia picks up the thread, "Yeah, Earth, what's the plan?"

Zephyr smiles, "Do you have any more slideshows to illustrate the plan? We haven't had one of those in a while."

Bennie laughs and starts choking until Maxim slaps him on the back, "That was funny. What was that creature that kept the money inside it?"

Wil glares first at Zephyr, then Bennie, "Piggy bank, and no, no slideshow." He takes a bite of dinner, making everyone wait. Swallowing, he continues, "Here's what I'm thinking"—he looks around the table —"we nab the wayward researcher and get out."

The table is silent for several beats until Maxim asks, "That's it? That's your plan?" Wil nods.

Zephyr smiles, but it's the *you're an idiot smile* she gives Wil from time to time, "The sensor array upgrade we got on Vlack Three, while adding to our overall resolution and range, still can't pinpoint a single being on the surface of a world of trillions. Especially when physiologically they're so similar." She takes a sip of her drink, "We'll need to orbit a few times, and do focused sweeps, and even then, from up here we'll likely only narrow it down to a city-sized area."

Wil shrugs, "I mean that's a more detailed version of my plan, sure, but that's pretty much what I said."

Zephyr sighs and continues, "From the data provided by Councilor Grythlorian and Blumtillithian, Earth's orbital satellites are still not advanced enough to see through the upgraded stealth systems. We should be safe enough while we orbit." She looks at Wil, "They mentioned a space station?"

"Yeah, the ISS 2 is the orbital mid-point for NASA and other space agencies. If there are any active missions, the Station, and space near it, will be bustling with activity. Our stealth tech will keep us from being detected, but near the station, the big danger will be visual detection. The *Ghost* isn't small, and she damn sure doesn't look like anything Earth made. We'll have to be careful around the station." He looks around, "I don't know what else is in orbit now."

Zephyr nods, "Once we figure out where our missing researcher is, we can figure out our landing."

Maxim takes a bite of something that's mostly noodles then, mouth full, asks, "Once planet side, how do we find our target?"

Wil nods to his friend, "Manners." Maxim blushes.

Cynthia answers the question, "Besides the upgraded sensor suite for the ship, our little four-legged friend left handheld scanners behind that can pinpoint specific bio signs from up to twenty meters. Multonae may look human, but their bio-readings are distinct."

Zephyr nods, "That brings us to disguises." She looks at Wil, "You good working on that while we're underway? None of us would have the slightest clue what to look like. With our luck, Bennie would select an image that's some type of exotic creature and cause a panic or something."

Bennie reaches across the table for an egg roll-type thing that Wil has decided tastes better than the Earth analog. He sticks his green tongue out, then takes a bite.

Wil smiles, "Yeah I'll work on disguises for each of you." He looks at Bennie, "Can you bark?"

"Grolack you," the surly Brailack replies.

CHAPTER 8_

SLOW BOAT TO JUPITER_

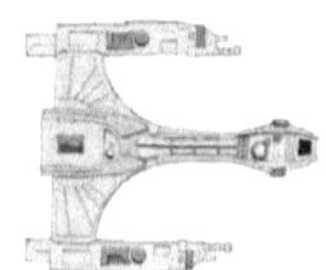

Wil pulls the FTL throttle back, dropping the *Ghost* back into sub-light speed. They are just outside Earth's solar orbit, the planet barely larger than the surrounding stars. He looks at Zephyr, "Figured better safe than sorry; we can coast in from here." He taps a few commands into his console. The lighting on the bridge shifts to a blueish color. "Uh, what the hell?"

"Oh, sorry!" Maxim says turning to look at Wil and the rest of the crew, "I forgot. Blumtillithian installed this lighting shift so that we'd know when the stealth systems are active."

Wil looks around the bridge, "Oh, ok, seems excessive. I mean, all of our consoles are telling us we're stealthed right?" Everyone nods. Looking up at the ceiling Wil says, "Computer, discontinue the lighting settings for the stealth system."

"Would you like to return to standard illumination?" the ship asks in the cool male voice it's always had, except for the months when Bennie was tinkering with it. Having finally given up, he returned the ship's computer to its previous settings.

"Yes, please," Wil says, and the lights shift back to their regular daytime-esque setting.

"Bridge illumination settings updated," the ship says.

"Better," Cynthia says. She looks down at her console, "Good grief, your people sure like to broadcast dren into space, don't they?" One of the screens on her console is brightly lit with thousands of overlapping signals flooding the *Ghost's* sensors.

"Yeah, that's probably better than it used to be, but yeah humans act like no one else is out here, so why police our transmissions?" Wil says, eyes on the forward view screen. Earth is in the center, slowly growing in size.

"Picking up a vessel," Zephyr announces.

"What?" Wil says, glancing over.

The Palorian first officer nods, "Not on an intercept course, but we will pass them within"—she looks at another screen—"ten thousand clicks."

"Should we adjust course?" Cynthia asks.

Wil shakes his head, "No, this is as good a test as any for our new stealth systems. They definitely won't see us visually, and if they do detect us, we can bug out long before we're near a planet."

The main display updates, showing the vessel as it approaches.

"Ugly, isn't it?" Bennie says.

Everyone else just stares. On the display the blocky vessel continues its approach. Approximately half a kilometer long, the vessel looks to Wil like a refrigerator lying on its side, antenna of all sorts sticking out of the front, thrusters at the back. A large ring slightly shorter in diameter than the ship is long, is spinning slowly in the center of the vessel.

"No active propulsion," Zephyr reports, "they're ballistic."

"I'm not detecting any weapons or targeting sensors," Maxim says, his eyes glued to his own display.

"Life signs?" Wil asks.

"Affirmative, looks like twenty humans," Zephyr announces.

Wil looks over, "Zee can you extrapolate their course?"

She nods and turns to her console. On the main display the boxy vessel continues to grow. Looking up Zephyr says, "Looks like an intercept course for the fifth planet in the system, big gas giant."

"Jupiter," Wil says, "Wonder why they're not using FTL?"

Zephyr consults her console, "It's possible that the ship launched before your people's FTL program finished?"

Wil nods slowly, "Yeah, I guess. Imagine how much that'll suck for the crew of that thing if they arrive at Jupiter only to find another ship there waiting for them." He chuckles, "Sucky time to be an astronaut in that regard." He looks one more time at the Earth ship, now almost filling the display. Touching a control, the view returns to Earth.

Bennie looks to Wil, "Have your people not explored the system?"

Wil shakes his head, "Not thoroughly. We've sent automated probes to every planet but have only sent people to a few of them. If that ship is headed for Jupiter, I'd assume we've got enough folks on Mars now to move on to exploring other planets. I know when I came back for supplies, they had just landed their first Mars mission."

"That has to suck, being trapped on a ship without FTL for months," Bennie says, turning back to whatever it was he was doing before asking his question.

Wil nods, "Yeah, the FTL program was supposed to jump start the exploration of the System. I guess they got tired of waiting."

THIS IS EARTH?_

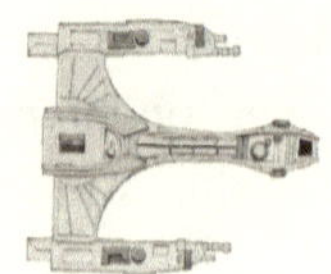

"THIS IS IT?" Bennie asks. On the main display Earth is slowly rotating below. The *Ghost* has entered a high orbit over the planet, preparing to begin their sensor sweeps.

"What did you expect?" Wil asks.

Bennie shrugs, "I don't know, just, well, something more than this."

Wil just stares at Bennie, "Let's just find our missing scientist." He turns to Zephyr, "Fire up those newfangled scanners."

The Palorian woman nods. "Looks like we'll be near your space station on our next pass. Just a heads up."

Wil nods, "Roger that." He looks down at his console. "I think"—he swipes up on one of the screens on the console, updating the main display—"we can drop into a lower orbit and glide by the station. The ISS 2 is over Earth's nightside, so we won't stand out against the planet. We'll keep from scanning it, so they don't randomly pick up any emissions."

"That seems reasonable," Maxim says.

"Would they even be able to detect our sensors?" Bennie wonders.

"Probably not, but why risk it?" Wil replies.

"Coming around now. Still nothing on the sensors," Zephyr says.

"Bringing us down into a lower orbit, three hundred kilometers should work," Wil says, "Oh, look, that's the US."

"The you ess?" Bennie asks.

"The United States, where I'm from," Wil says, eyes glued to the main display. In a small window in the display's corner the ISS 2 is approaching overhead.

Unlike its predecessor the ISS 2 has four long arms reaching out from the central hub. At the end of two of the arms are small spinning sections where experiments that require variable gravity are conducted. Each module can adjust its rotation, affecting the spin gravity inside.

"You're right. There is a lot of traffic around that station," Zephyr says.

Wil nods, "Yeah it was the main launch facility for the FTL program, and I can only assume it's home to more projects now." He squints at the display, "Weird, looks like they've got a shipyard, or something, going on." He taps a control, zooming in, "Wish we could scan it, get the details."

Beyond the ISS 2 is another structure, nearly twice as big but mostly a skeletal support structure. Along the central spine is what Wil assumes must be residential and operations. The near kilometer long structure is divided into four segments; three of the four segments are empty. The occupied segment has a vessel similar to the one they encountered earlier in it.

"Wonder what they're planning to—" Wil starts.

"Oh dren." Everyone turns to Maxim. "A ship has adjusted course to intercept." He taps a control on his console and the main display changes to show a small craft heading their way. This one is nothing like the large blocky exploration vessel they encountered outside the Terran System; this craft is closer to Wil's old pod, except, "It appears to be armed," Maxim adds.

"Armed? Why would they have an armed pod?" Wil wonders.

"Let alone several? Look," Maxim says. On the main display, several other pods are highlighted by the tactical computer as being potential threats. These vessels are about four times the size of Wil's experimental model but share a clear design lineage. More powerful thrusters have been added to the back of the craft, and small wings sweep forward on each side, ending in some type of weapon.

"Didn't you tell me that your planet isn't unified under a single government? Could your government be militarizing space?" Cynthia asks staring at the main display, her tail nervously swishing under her seat.

"Sure looks like it. Hold on." He adjusts their course using just the maneuvering thrusters, "I'll see if I can't scoot us out of the way." The *Ghost* speeds up slightly along its course.

"Won't that thing see the thrusters?" Bennie asks.

Wil looks at the hacker, "Honestly, no idea. My pod wouldn't be able to see us, but things have changed. They had nothing like that when I was here last."

The small vessel fires its own small maneuvering thrusters, "It's adjusted course. It's closing, ten thousand clicks," Zephyr announces.

"Shit," Wil grunts, making another change.

"Wait!" Zephyr shouts. "Just got a ping on the sensors, our target is down there." She points as the main display splits in two. The right side showing the rapidly approaching armed space pod. The left showing the location on Earth where the sensors have detected the missing researcher Bonson Drell.

"Huh, California?"

"Who's that?" Zephyr asks.

"Five thousand clicks," Maxim updates.

"It's not a person; it's a place. The state our target is in." Wil glances at the left half of the display, "Los Angeles or there-abouts." He glances to the right side, "Hold on, no time for pretty." He pushes the flight controls forward.

"What are you doing?" Zephyr asks.

Wil is flipping switches and tapping controls, "No choice, that pod obviously sees us or at least sees something. We've got a lock on our target, it's night there, this is our best shot." The *Ghost* tilts toward the planet below, "Hold on."

"Pulling away from the pod," Maxim says. "It's speeding up!" Maxim shouts.

"Damnit!" Wil hisses. "Hold on!" The ship tilts more, vibrates.

"What're you doing?" Cynthia asks.

"The sub-light engines won't power up in time, and there isn't enough atmosphere yet for the atmospherics. I call this maneuver falling out of the sky," Wil says, his knuckles white on the controls.

"The pod is no longer pursuing," Maxim reports, "Looks like it's not rated for atmosphere."

"That makes sense. Zee, keep an eye on the sensors. They may have phoned ahead if they got a look at us. I'm hoping we were just a weird sensor blip."

The ship shakes and everyone looks at the main display in time to see the re-entry plasma building up against the shields.

"Hold on!"

WHY IS IT ALWAYS A ROUGH LANDING?_

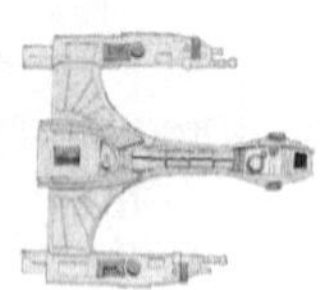

"Repulsors at full power!" Wil shouts over the roar of air rushing past the ship. Alerts are popping up on every console on the bridge.

"Wil, maybe now is a good time to fire up the atmos!" Maxim shouts.

The sound of the repulsor lifts at maximum power and echoes through the corridors of the *Ghost*. This high up, with no ground to push against, the powerful repulsors do little beyond slowing the fall of the ship. The entire ship shakes and tilts wildly. Wil is holding on to the flight controls tightly, "Too risky! They'll light us up for miles and any ground tracking stations will pick up the power signature."

"Not to mention the sound." Bennie adds.

"The repulsors aren't meant for flight!" Zephyr shouts, "There isn't anything for them to, you know, repulse against!"

"If you crash us, there's no one on this crap hole of a planet to fix the *Ghost*!" Bennie adds.

"Then I should avoid crashing, and you all yammering in my ear isn't helping me reach that goal," Wil says through gritted teeth.

A few bone jarring moments later Zephyr announces, "We're slowing; it's working." She looks over at Wil, who's brow is shiny with sweat. "Repulsors are nearing red-line," she adds.

Wil doesn't take his eyes off the screens and controls, but says to Bennie, "Pipsqueak, access the internet; I think we can land somewhere in the Angeles Forest, but you need to make sure it's where I think it is, and still a forest."

"What's an *internet?*" Bennie asks.

"I think he means the planetary data network," Cynthia offers.

Bennie nods. "Why didn't he say that then?" Bennie asks. Wil makes a growling noise that stops further chit-chat. He takes a few minutes, but Bennie finally says, "Ok, I think I found it. Is that what you're looking for?" On the main display a window pops up showing an aerial view of a large forest.

"Yeah. That's it. Good. Find me Mount Gleason; it's been a while, but I don't recall it being very populated or hospitable."

"On it," Bennie says. From his station, he works through the phonetics of *Gleason.*

"I'll help," Zephyr adds getting up and crossing over to Bennie's station.

Something in the ship rumbles, then whines loudly until it stops with a clunk. "Hope that wasn't important," Maxim says, looking at his display.

Cynthia looks up, "Primary power coupler port-side just blew out." She taps her console putting it into standby and dashes out the bridge hatch.

"Max?" Wil asks, glancing over briefly.

"On it," the big man says, putting his own station in standby and leaving the bridge.

"Found something, Wil!" Zephyr says. The main display updates showing a sizable area near the mountain Wil mentioned. There appears to be a small clearing large enough for the *Ghost* to land in.

"That'll do. Is that clearing big enough?"

Zephyr moves toward Maxim's station, "It will be."

The *Ghost* dips to the left before righting itself, "Better hurry." Wil looks at one of his displays. A red warning icon is flashing angrily over the port repulsor. "We'll be down in another five or fewer minutes."

"Firing," Zephyr reports a split second before the sound of the weapons magazine shuffling a missile into the launcher echoes up to the bridge. From the underside of the main display, a single missile streaks out and races toward the forest below. Seconds later, a fireball lights up like a small sun, the shock wave knocking trees over, doubling the size of the clearing.

"Nicely done!" Wil shouts, "Hold on!"

The *Ghost* screams as Wil dumps even more power into the already near-overloaded repulsor lifts in the forward ends of the engine nacelles. Two loud clunks let everyone know the landing gear are deploying. Another slightly different clunk lets everyone know the two powerful landing gear have locked into position. A second later, the ship lurches, slamming to the ground. The sound of the landing gear straining to absorb the impact moans through the ship, then quiets as the *Ghost* settles.

Wil quickly puts all flight systems into standby and shuts off all power to the repulsors. "Fingers crossed nothing is too broken."

Zephyr looks up from the tactical station, "Reassuring."

Bennie unbuckles the belt in his seat and jumps down, "I'll give you this, you're getting better at crashing."

CHAPTER 9_

TOYS, TOYS, TOYS_

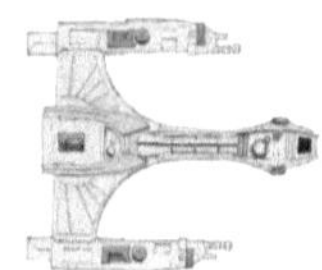

"CLEVER, setting the warhead to detonate above the ground," Maxim says after hearing Zephyr's retelling of their landing.

Everyone is sitting around the lounge area looking at the main entertainment screen. Wil is standing next to it.

"Ok, we're here, the Angeles Forest." Wil points to an area on the screen. He drags the map around a bit, zooming it out. "I was able to get this display tied into Amzoogle Maps, neat huh?"

Bennie tuts, "You, did it?"

Wil glares, "Anyway, this"—he points to a service road—"is how we get into LA."

"What is that?" Bennie asks.

"Service road," Maxim says. "How frequently used?"

"That's a good question. I don't know; likely not much, if we're lucky." He smiles, "But we're not looking for a ride."

"We're not?" Cynthia asks.

"More on that in a few. First, back to the overview. We need to get out of the forest; from there, we can rent a car and get to LA. I had the computer run a few scans to make sure nothing in Earth's atmosphere would kill any of you. Looks like we're good there. I've also got your disguises all worked out." He heads for the hatch that leads down to the cargo bay, "Come on, we can do the rest in the cargo bay."

Wil reaches into the cargo module he's standing next to, "I'll be honest, I bought these on a whim, hoping we'd need them one day. I'd kind of given up hope and was gonna unload them next time we hit up Fury. Glad I didn't." He raises a backpack like device.

"Thruster packs?" Bennie shouts, jumping up to snatch the pack from Wil.

"Careful, I don't know how—"

Bennie makes a buzzing type noise, slipping the pack on, "I know how thruster packs work."

Everyone watches as the small hacker fusses with the control panel on the chest plate of the thruster pack. Two segmented arms deploy from the pack, a repulsor module at the end of each.

"Bennie, be careful, I've never—" Wil starts.

Bennie raises a hand; the repulsors power up; and before anyone can react, the hacker shoots into the air, then makes an impossible right turn and flies full speed into the starboard bulkhead of the cargo hold. Bennie makes a sickening squeak mixed with crunching sounds. Everyone recoils, groaning. The wounded Brailack slides to the floor of the hold.

"That had to hurt," Wil says, reaching into the crate. He pulls out two more packs, "Max. Zee." The Palorian couple take their packs, turning them over, examining them.

Cynthia takes her pack from Wil, "So we're flying to that lah place you mentioned?"

Bennie shoots past overhead, the sound of his repulsor pack fading as he shoots out the open cargo doors. Wil sighs and reaches into the crate, pulling out a PADD. He taps the screen, then sets it back down on the edge of the crate's opening.

Wil turns back to Cynthia, "Sorry, no these are just to get us out of the forest. We're miles from anything, it'd take forever to walk, and I never was a Boy Scout, so we'd probably die. We'll fly then walk to the nearest highway."

"Highway?" Maxim asks.

"Big road, lots of cars." Wil waves his hand, "Anyway, we'll get as close to civilization as we can." He points to the pack Cynthia is still holding, "According to the instructions, these will fly back to the *Ghost* on their own after we're done." He holds up the PADD to emphasize his point.

Bennie enters the cargo hold, one hand rubbing the side of his head; he stumbles in and leans on the door jamb of the bay doors that close off the ramp from the hold. "Ok, this is a newer model thruster pack than I'm familiar with."

NEW FACE, WHO DIS?_

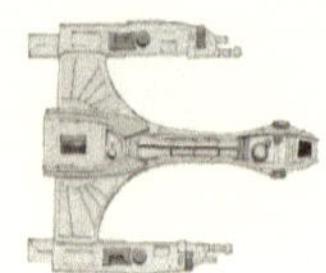

"Just think; this time tomorrow, we'll be enjoying, well I haven't decided yet, but something amazing," Wil says before taking a bite of his dinner.

"Are you saying this isn't amazing?" Cynthia asks, one eyebrow raised.

Wil grins, "Oh this is good for sure, what'd you call it again?"

Zephyr finishes a bite, "privlip."

"Bless you," Wil says, grinning at his joke. The others stare at him.

Cynthia adds, "Privlip is a dish I learned to make when I struck out on my own after the orphanage. It's like a working person's meal on Tyr, very common among laborers and the like."

"Like koshari," Wil says. Cynthia shrugs.

Zephyr looks to Bennie, "You're sure they weren't able to locate us?"

Bennie shrugs. "He is," he hikes a thumb to Wil. "We tapped into the, what was it, *undernot?*"

"Internet, and yeah I pointed Bennie to some NASA and DOD databases. From what we could find, they picked up some visual clues about us while we were in orbit. That patrol vessel that was tracking us didn't have a sensor lock but had a high-resolution camera. We're semi-famous, they got a few beauty shots of the *Ghost*." He takes another bite of his privlip then adds, "They lost us once we entered the atmosphere, no trace. They know we were generally heading towards California, but that's it. They'll be searching for a while, unfortunately, so we may have to lay low if we finish this up fast, but otherwise should be ok. The *Ghost*'s stealth system is still engaged so any passing satellites won't pick anything up."

Maxim asks, "You're sure the *Ghost* will be safe, leaving it in these woods?"

"Should be. The camouflage netting we covered her in should be more than a match for any passing jets or choppers. They'd have to fly directly over, low enough to see her. Even then the camo netting actively shifts so still unlikely anyone looking would see it." He picks up his bottle of grum and takes a sip.

"What if someone walks up to it?" Bennie asks.

"We're miles from the nearest campground. The sensors didn't pick up anyone for miles, but you never know. We'll just have to hope that no nosy hikers wander by. When we head out, I'll set the ship's defense to the minimum, so no one dies. Worst case, someone spots the ship. Hopefully we're off planet before anyone comes to investigate."

Cynthia grabs her plate and Wil's and gets up from the table. Glancing back at him, "You good?"

"Yeah babe, thanks." Wil turns to look at Zephyr and Max, "So, first night on Earth."

Bennie looks from Wil to the two Palorians, then back to Wil.

Wil gets up and walks to the seating area, "I got your image inducers set up." He picks up the hockey-puck-sized devices and comes back to the kitchenette. Each device has a sticky note attached to it, with a crew member's name. He hands a device to each of them. "Let me know if you need any tweaks, but these should let you walk around most of Earth without issue."

"Most of it?" Zephyr asks.

"Don't sweat it. You won't be anywhere near any place dangerous," Wil assures them. He looks to Cynthia, "I'm ready to hit the sack. We'll head out two hours before dawn." He checks his wristcomm, "So, six hours from now." Everyone nods.

Cynthia gets up, taking her image inducer with her. She smiles at Wil as she walks past him toward the hatch leading to the berths.

"How Do I Look?" Zephyr asks, coming out of the refresher in their quarters.

Maxim turns around from the computer terminal, "Oh, my." He stands up and approaches her. "You, you're human." Zephyr's voice is coming from a human woman with the same green eyes and jet-black hair as Zephyr. Her hands no longer sport two thumbs with three fingers, instead matching Wil's own four fingers and a thumb configuration.

"Well, that is kind of the point." She winks and grabs his hands, pulling him closer to her. "Like it?"

"I don't dislike it." He leans down and kisses her. "Ok, that is a little strange." He kisses her again, "But not bad strange. It's you, but not you."

She grins, reaching behind her to the clothes storage, holding up Maxim's inducer. She leans in, head tilted, "Let's see what you look like."

GOING GOING BACK BACK TO CALI CALI_

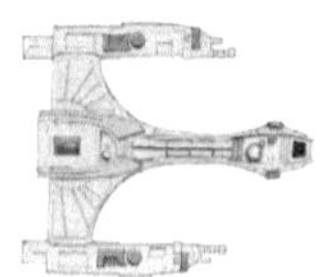

"WIL, I'm curious why you chose such a dark skin tone for my alternate image," Maxim says as the crew gathers in the cargo hold. The sky to the east of the ship is just beginning to lighten.

"Ah, sorry. I should have told you. I set yours to resemble an African American human. I wanted our group to not look too much like a weird European family on vacation. That ok?"

Maxim shrugs, "That's fine with me. We were just worried it wasn't configured correctly last night when we tried them out." He blushes slightly, his skin taking on a darker blue hue.

Wil sniggers, "Uh, huh."

Cynthia leans over to Zephyr, "We tried mine out too." She winks, and Wil blushes.

Bennie, who's been fidgeting with a duffel bag, finally looks over, "Yeah none of you are at all subtle, and even without sharing a wall, I heard way more than I needed. You look like strangers, so you get louder?" He shakes his head and comes over to Wil to grab his thruster pack. "When Gabe gets back, we're working on reconfiguring the sound-proofing in the berths."

Wil blushes, handing Bennie his pack, "Jealous?"

Bennie waves the human away, "As if."

A few minutes later, everyone is strapped into their thruster packs, small duffel bags strapped to their chests. Each of them has a helmet with a translucent visor that covers most of their faces. Wil looks around, "Everyone ready? Have the landing zone in your navcomm?"

Four helmeted heads nod. "Ok, let's get this show on the road." He turns and walks down the cargo ramp, the others following. As they descend the ramp the heavy doors close behind them. Once they all hit the ground, the heavy ramp lifts, closing up tight back into the hull.

The *Ghost* has active camouflage netting draped over it, hanging unevenly in areas, creating a shaded area under the ship.

The service road Wil found proves useful in helping guide their flight. Only twice did someone have to admonish Bennie for flying too high out of the canyon of trees formed by the road. They have to adjust course three times to avoid populated campgrounds, but eventually they're standing at the outskirts of La Cañada Flintridge, their thruster packs whining quietly as they power down.

"This place is pretty," Cynthia says as they remove their duffels and thruster packs. Each thruster pack has an attachment point for the helmet.

Wil smiles, "Yeah I spent a fair bit of time here working at JPL as an intern back in college."

"Jay Pee Ell?" Bennie asks.

"One, time to go native," Wil gestures at Bennie's chest, then the others. "Two, Jet Propulsion Lab, one of the most advanced space flight facilities in the country. From here, a lot of space missions are assembled, monitored, and more. It's just down the street there." He nods towards something behind Bennie.

Bennie presses a button on his image inducer, and within moments looks like a twelve-year-old child. His bright red hair and blue eyes contrasting against his pale, freckled face.

"Uh, is he," Cynthia says, now looking like a brunette thirty-something, with close-cropped hair and bright green eyes. Her fur is replaced by a well-toned and tanned body. She'd already tucked her tail into her pant leg.

Bennie looks around, then down at himself, "Is he a what?"

Zephyr chuckles, "A child, I think."

Bennie spins to face Wil, "A what now?"

Wil raises both hands, palms out, "Not a lot of choices my friend. Your height limited my options." Grinning, "This is also just too funny." He lifts his wristcomm and snaps a picture.

Wil hops back, just out of reach of a small, pale-skinned fist heading for his crotch.

Zephyr clears her throat, "We should get moving." She nods to Wil, "You said something about finding a *rental place?*"

Wil taps a few controls on the PADD he showed them earlier. The thruster packs all power up and shoot skyward, returning to the *Ghost* following the flight path they took to get to the edge of the city. He turns to Zephyr, her naturally green eyes a stark contrast to her now pale-skinned complexion, "Yeah, unless it closed or moved, there's a rental car place a mile or two from here." He sets off down the street, deeper into La Cañada Flintridge.

ROAD TRIP!_

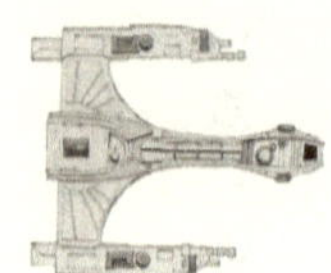

THE WALK to the car rental agency is refreshingly uneventful. Wil worried they would blow the job in the first ten minutes. It's been an hour and while they've only encountered a few pedestrians so far, no one has shown the least bit of interest in any of them.

"Ok, you all wait here, Cynthia and I will rent the car." Wil looks at Bennie, "Try to not scare anyone."

Bennie tuts, "Whatever."

"Shoulda made you a short teenager." Wil and Cynthia walk away, crossing the street to what Wil has said is the *rental place.*

Maxim looks around, "So, this is Earth. Not really what I expected."

Bennie looks up, his pale child-like face scrunched up, "That's what I said, remember. What did you expect?"

Before Maxim can answer two women pushing strollers walk by. They're speaking a language that the crew doesn't understand, the infants making baby noises as they pass.

Zephyr pokes her ear, "Did you understand them?"

"Nope," Bennie says, looking down at his wristcomm. "Diagnostics on my translator nanites are clean."

"That's weird," Maxim says, glancing at the retreating forms of the women. He shrugs, "At any rate, I don't really know what I expected, but I guess the worlds of the GC have spoiled me. When was the last time you were on a planet that wasn't predominately skyscrapers and massive construction?"

"You mean besides Fury?" Bennie quips.

"No one ever includes Fury when asking questions like that," Zephyr points out; Maxim nods.

"Yeah, it is a bit backwater, isn't it?" Bennie admits. "I mean, we knew it was backwater; we've all met Wil, but yeah, a lot less developed than I expected, even factoring Wil in."

Maxim is about to add something, when a loud toot sound comes from across the street.

Bennie turns, "What the wurrin is that?"

"Some type of ground vehicle," Zephyr says, turning to jog across the street only to be yanked backwards as another ground vehicle races past making its own tooting noise; this one somehow angrier sounding. "What the—"

"That vehicle was not going to stop," Maxim points out as the offending vehicle turns a corner several blocks away. "They must not have safety overrides in their vehicles."

Over their commsets, Wil says, "Stay put, we'll come get you."

Once everyone is settled in, the van sets off. Maxim leans forward between the two front seats, "Wil, there may be an issue with our translator nanites."

"Why? I can understand you just fine. Can you understand me?" He glances to Cynthia in the passenger seat who nods, shrugging.

"No, well, yes I can understand you fine, but earlier two women passed us, and we couldn't understand a word they were saying to each other."

"Oh, gotcha. Yeah, probably Spanish." He doesn't continue.

Maxim continues to stare at him, "I don't know what that means."

Wil chuckles, "I hadn't really thought about it, but if I understand how the nanites work, they rely on my knowledge of English to inform those nearby, who do the same, over and over, until eventually everyone in the GC can understand English. Right? I'm actually not needed as the baseline anymore."

Bennie, in the far back seat nods, "Yeah, more or less. I mean that's like the children's version of how they work, but it'll do. So?"

Wil glares into the rearview mirror then says, "So, I don't speak Spanish. So, it stands to reason that the nanites in my head wouldn't have spread that language to the rest of the GC nanite network." He looks around, "You know it's a little weird to think about, a GC-spanning network of nanites that no one technically controls." He shudders.

"When you put it like that," Maxim says.

"Wait," Cynthia says, "So you wouldn't have understood those women either?"

"Nope," Wil says, not picking up on the amazement of the others.

"How does that work? How do you get anything done if you all don't even speak the same language?" Zephyr asks.

Wil glances again to the rearview to see his first officer, "You mean all Palorians speak the same language?" He looks to Cynthia, "Or Tygrans?"

Cynthia shakes her head, "Well now, yes? But in the old days, no I guess not."

Maxim adds, "Same with Palorians. In the old days there were thousands of regional languages and dialects. Now we speak Palorian Standard."

"Tyr Standard, for my people," Cynthia says.

"Brailack Normal," Bennie offers, then adds, "Earth doesn't have a standard language? Not even for trade or diplomacy?"

Wil shrugs, "English serves most of those purposes, but it's not mandated or anything like that." He looks back toward Bennie, "Brailack Normal?" Bennie shrugs.

CHAPTER 10_

CHECKING IN_

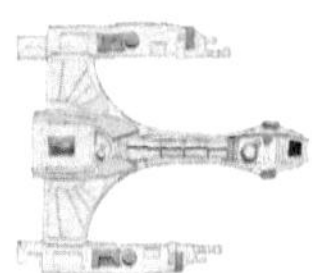

"This looks more like what I was expecting," Zephyr says as the van comes in sight of the high-rise jungle that is Los Angeles. The drive from La Cañada Flintridge has been thankfully uneventful. The van had a full charge on its battery, so Wil hasn't had to stop anywhere along the way. Leaving the city right after the rental agency opened meant only a little traffic between them and Los Angeles.

Wil glances at the rearview, "How's that hacking coming carrot top?"

The Brailack, now wearing the appearance of a twelve-year-old red-headed boy looks up. "I assume that isn't a term of endearment, so grolack off. I can't believe how horrible the security is on this network. Your entire world runs on this thing?"

"Yeah more or less; I mean the local nets are better protected. The public internet is, well public."

"Better protected, ha." The hacker holds up his PADD, "I've already accessed the local municipal net for the city, plus the hotel you told me about." He slaps a palm against his forehead, "Duh, also I was able to get into one of the banking systems. Good call on printing these dummy devices to access to our wristcomms." He holds up the gaming tablet analog, similar to the laptop model Wil brought with him on his last visit to Earth.

Wil smiles remembering his last, and only visit to Earth since leaving, until now that is. "You remember I had you make ones just like these when I came home?"

Bennie scrunches his face, thinking. The holographic face of the child matching it exactly. "Oh, that's right? I wrote that app to remotely hack any system you were near. I'm glad that worked out."

Wil nods, then does a double take looking in the mirror, "What do you mean, glad it worked out? Why wouldn't it have worked? You weren't sure?"

Maxim and Zephyr look at each other, then each lean to the side of the van, leaving an unobstructed view from the rearview mirror to the back-row seat and the small hacker sitting in it. "I mean, I never doubted my abilities, but you know, it was a program to hack systems I'd never seen and didn't know anything about, primitive ones at that. You know, that's really impressive; you should be impressed. I'm like a miracle worker."

Wil sighs, "Ok, that's fair." He moves on, "So we're booked at the hotel?"

"Yup, the Presidential suite." He beams, "And the two adjoining rooms."

"Dude, I said low-key."

Bennie tuts, "We're already slumming it being on this rock, I'm certainly not staying in some low-rent room."

Wil rubs the back of his neck, "Fine. We'll get checked in, then figure out what our next move is." Everyone nods, then turn as one to look out the van's windows as they get closer to Los Angeles. Even though it has only been a few years since Wil's impromptu departure from the system, LA seems to have grown tremendously, both out and up.

"Good morning, sir. Welcome to the Los Angeles Grand. Checking in?" The twenty-something desk clerk, *probably an aspiring actor,* Wil thinks, asks as the group approaches.

Wil smiles his most genuine and innocent looking smile, "We are; thanks. I believe the reservation is under," He glances to Bennie who mouths *Crichton,* "Crichton. John Crichton."

"One moment." The clerk sets about tapping on a keyboard that Wil has never seen before—mirror black, the keys, little more than outlines on the glossy surface. "Ah, here we are"—the young man glances up, taking in the entire group—"the presidential suite and adjoining rooms."

"Sounds right," Wil says, glowering at Bennie, who shrugs and waves him off.

"Looks like the room and taxes have already been set up on a payment account, would you like"—the clerk counts off each member of the crew—"four keys?"

"Five, five keys, krebnack," Bennie says, glaring at the clerk from below the counter.

Wil shoves the small man, sending him almost sprawling to the ground. He looks up to the horrified expression on the clerk's face. "Billy likes to roughhouse. Make it five; he can play with one or whatever he wants to do with it." Wil smiles.

The clerk continues to stare at Wil, then looks over to Bennie who stares back at him before turning his gaze to his computer screen, "Five keys it is." A machine next to the clerk's terminal starts beeping then prints the electronic keycards. While the machine works, the clerk looks at Wil, then Cynthia, "Family vacation?" He looks over to Maxim, an eyebrow raised.

Wil looks at his crew, smiles, "Yeah something like that."

The clerk smiles, "Excellent. Well, welcome to Los Angeles, have you been here before?"

Wil nods, "I have, yeah."

The third key finishes printing, dropping into a little hopper on the front of the device. The clerk looks down, then back up to Wil, "Are you familiar with the hotel? Any questions?"

Wil shakes his head, growing impatient, "Nope, we're good." He extends his arm, his palm up.

The young clerk coughs once as the final key drops into the hopper. He gathers the cards, placing them in a sleeve. Handing them to Wil he says, "The elevators are just over there to the left."

Wil smiles his genuine-like smile again, the one he uses to get out of trouble with Peacekeepers and crime bosses. "Thanks!" He turns on his heel, grabbing his duffel, "Come on, Crichton clan!"

PRESIDENTIAL SUITE_

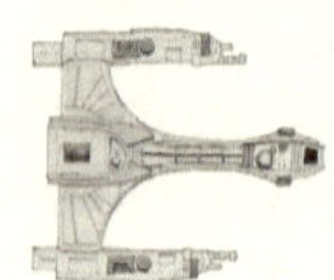

"Stash your stuff; we're heading out," Wil says a few minutes after they arrive at the Presidential Suite.

"What's the rush?" Maxim asks from the leather chair he's sprawled out on, arms stretched across the top of the chair.

"You all need practice being humans." He looks toward the room Bennie has claimed, "Especially you, Bennie!"

A small, pale redhead pokes around the door frame, "What do you mean? I'm rocking this human thing."

Wil paces between the sitting area and the floor-to-ceiling window looking out onto the Los Angeles urban sprawl. "No, you're not. We'll be lucky if that clerk doesn't call the authorities on us. Kids don't use Galactic Standard swear words. They also don't get pushed around by adults. At least not by adults that don't want to end up arrested."

"So... you're saying you can't touch me?" Bennie comes back into the main room, dropping into one of the two overstuffed sofas, "I like this place."

Wil gives up and moves on. "I know this is weird, but you all are going to have to get used to it. You standing around all stiff and silent is unsettling. Humans talk to each other and to strangers."

"So, what's your plan?" Zephyr asks.

"Swap meet," Wil says, grinning.

"This is like the markets on Fury!" Bennie says, bouncing on his heels.

Wil nods, "It is, sorta. We're lucky we got here on a weekend." He looks around, the LA City College Swap is an anthill of activity, just like Wil remembers from his time interning at JPL.

"Are we shopping?" Maxim asks.

"No, well, I mean if you want something, I guess buy it. We're here more for practice, plus we don't have cash." He looks at the array of blank expressions looking back at him. "Practice being human. A few weirdos being, well, weird at the Swap won't raise any eyebrows."

"Is there a weapons alley?" Maxim asks.

"A tech sector?" Bennie asks anxiously.

Wil shakes his head once, "No, no weapons alley." He looks at Bennie, "Not really a tech sector, but you'll find computer gear and such."

Cynthia looks past Wil to the entry of the Swap, "So what's in there?"

Wil smiles, "Everything, and nothing." He turns, "Come on."

The Swap is exactly as Wil remembers it, even with over a decade between now and the last time he and the other JPL interns came scavenging.

As they enter the first row of stalls, Cynthia leans over to Wil, "So you think this will help us acclimate?"

"I hope so. Tomorrow we start searching for our missing researcher, and that will likely entail a lot of interacting with people. Not only does it look weird when you all stand behind me silently, but it'll likely go faster if everyone is pulling." He shrugs and looks at the woman he's falling more and more in love with, "I'd rather do what we can to remove some of the risk of arrest, at least until the mission is over, then it might be funny."

Cynthia tuts, "Child." She speeds up to walk next to Zephyr. Wil picks up his pace to join Maxim in looking at the various wares of a stall.

"What is this?" The big Palorian asks. Despite his different physiology, the image inducer does an admirable job of hiding his extra thumb, while giving the impression he has a fully functional pinky finger.

The Vendor looks at what Maxim is holding, "Uh, that's a potato peeler. For peeling potatoes?"

Wil watches from a step behind his friend. Maxim pauses, then says, "Ah, of course, you kill them"—he makes a stabbing motion—"then peel them. Practical having two tools in one."

The vendor, a now very confused Chinese man, nods repeatedly, backing slowly from the man still holding the peeler.

Wil leans in, "Sorry, he's from Alabama." He takes the peeler from Maxim and puts it back in the bin with dozens of identical peelers.

The shopkeeper stares at the pair unblinking for what feels to Wil like forever, and just as he's about to ask something another customer shows up, a set of kitchen knives in her hand, "How much?" The shopkeeper turns his attention to the new arrival.

"Not bad. Assume everything you come across is *not* meant for killing," Wil whispers up at his friend, pulling him from the stall.

"Seriously, what's a *puh tah toe peeler*?" Maxim presses as they move to join Zephyr, Cynthia, and Bennie up ahead.

THE KIDS ARE . . . ALIEN_

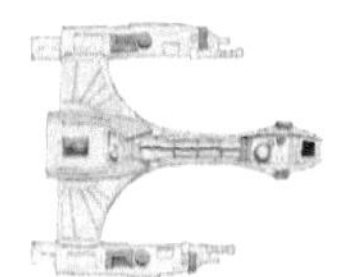

THE TWO ALIEN women and their small, redheaded companion have pulled ahead of Wil and Maxim. Bennie, bored out of his mind, has followed them versus the other two men.

Zephyr looks at a stall and nods toward it; Cynthia and Bennie follow. When she gets close, she picks up what she thinks is a bundle of flower bulbs. "These are interesting," she lifts them to her face to smell them, "Fragrant." She offers the bundle to Cynthia who takes a sniff, her cat-like nose twitching and wrinkling under the false image of a tan blonde.

"Fresh garlic," the woman behind the counter says, her expression making it clear to the two women that smelling this *garlic* isn't a normal human thing.

Cynthia puts the bundle down, "It's lovely." She gestures to a large bundle of something hanging from one of the tent supports, "What are those?"

"Chili peppers?" The woman replies, but it's half statement and half question.

Zephyr nods slowly, "I remember these, Wil used to cook with them. His were in a little bottle."

Cynthia smiles, "We should get him some." She turns to the woman, "How much?"

The shopkeeper pulls the bundle of dried peppers down, "Four dollars a pound."

"We'll give you two," Bennie pushes in between the two women from the *Ghost*, smiling at the shopkeeper.

The woman looks down at Bennie, then back to Zephyr and Cynthia, "They're four dollars a pound."

"Fine, three dollars," Bennie offers.

"Little boy, please," The woman scolds, then looks up at the Palorian and Tygran, "Pardon me, if he's yours."

"Gods no!" Zephyr says, shifting her hip to nudge Bennie out of the way.

Bennie grumbles and walks off. He catches the eye of the shop-keeper and flips her off.

"Hey kid!" Someone whisper-shouts at Bennie. He looks around, seeing no one in particular.

"Yeah you! Come here!" From between a stall selling what looks like the stuff Wil calls toilet paper and a stall selling power tools, a small dark-skinned hand is waving at him.

Bennie pokes his head between the two stalls, "Who are you? What do you want?"

"You looked bored. Those your moms?" A child no taller than Bennie asks. Bennie's never seen a human child, so he does not understand how old this one might be, but since Wil had said that's what Bennie looked like, this must be one as well. There are three others behind the brown-skinned kid, all look about the same age.

"Moms? What? No krebnak, they're my friends." He catches himself, "Er, I mean yeah, yeah my moms, that's a thing kids have, moms. Yeah."

The kid looks back at the others, and they all stare at Bennie for a beat before the first child says, "Ok, whatever. Wanna hang out? They can text you when it's time to leave."

"I don't know what you're saying, but sure." Bennie shrugs and slips all the way between the two stalls.

"Where's Bennie?" Wil asks as he and Maxim join Cynthia and Zephyr.

Zephyr shrugs. Cynthia shrugs, and holds up a bag, "We got you a gift."

Wil takes the bag and peeks inside. "Oh, chili peppers, nice. Thanks babe." He leans in and kisses Cynthia on the cheek. "You too, Zee."

"Should we be concerned about Bennie?" Maxim asks.

Wil shakes his head, "Nah, let's see if he can survive on his own. Worst case, all of our wristcomms can track him. Finding him shouldn't be hard. Let's head this way"—he points further down the row they have been heading down—"there's a food court in the middle."

FOOD COURT FOOD_

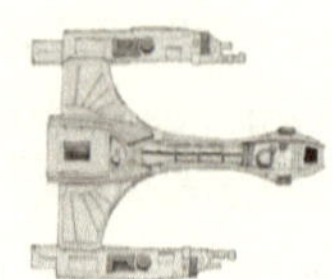

"I'm Kareem," offers the tallest of the children, the one that called to Bennie earlier. The leader of these children Bennie assumes.

"Bennie," the hacker offers, realizing he's just shy of the height of Kareem. He looks around, "So what are you doing?"

Kareem slaps another child, a female as far as Bennie can tell, on the shoulder, "Sarah was just telling us she saw that old man Henry has new stock, we're gonna check it out." He smiles, "Want to join us?"

Bennie shrugs, "Why not; Zephyr and Cynthia won't miss me."

Sarah grabs Bennie's hand, "Come on then!" They all take off, Bennie trailing along through the dark spaces between the swap meet stalls.

"Who's this old man Henry, anyway?" Bennie asks as the group slows at an intersection of stalls.

Kareem points to a stall near another narrow, darkened corridor like the one Bennie had just been in.

Sarah chimes in, "He has the new *Justice League*, in 3D." She nudges Bennie closer to the opening, past two other boys.

"Oh, I've seen some of those," Bennie offers. "The last one with the big ape creature." The kids look at each other.

"That was before they rebooted the franchise," one boy, thicker than the others, says. His expression is not hiding his opinion of Bennie or his knowledge of the franchise. The bigger child sneers, "Are you poor? How have you not seen the new *Justice League* movies?" Bennie shrugs.

"What is this? It's delightful," Cynthia asks, scooping small, multicolored spheres into her mouth.

"Dippin' Dots," Wil says, opening his mouth to accept the offered spoonful of colorful, frozen dots of ice cream Cynthia is offering.

Maxim and Zephyr are sitting together at the next small table; the big man leans forward, his voice hushed, "Wil, are all the markets on Earth this chaotic?"

Wil looks around, hundreds of people are milling around the food trucks and assorted and mismatched tables making up the center of the massive swap meet. "No, well maybe, I'm not familiar with all swap meets everywhere, but let's just assume that no, they're not all like this." He gestures to the space, "Meets like this are where the small business-people gather—the artists, the junk collectors, the importers that don't have a storefront somewhere."

Zephyr takes another bite of the gyro she and Maxim are sharing. She finishes chewing and asks, "Ok, so what now?"

"We'll wander around a bit, give you all a bit more practice," Wil replies.

Zephyr nods, "I meant regarding our target."

"Ah, well we know he's somewhere in LA, so we crank up our hand scanner things, and see if we can zero in on him. It'd be faster if we could low fly the *Ghost* but that's out." He reaches into the pack he's been carrying, removing one of the scanning devices that Blumtillithian had given them. Powering it up, he looks at the screen, "Looks like," he hums to himself studying the small screen for a second, "About a mile and change in range. Not amazing."

Before anyone can say anything else, their wristcomms all vibrate. A pre-defined pattern meant to alert the crew to one of them being in trouble.

"Grolack, guess we know what Bennie is up to," Zephyr says, grabbing the gyro from Maxim and taking a bite before handing it back to him. He scowls, but the expression doesn't reach his eyes. He finishes the meal in a single bite, wiping his hands on his pants.

Cynthia holds up a hand, "I'll go get the little," She looks at Wil, "brab?"

"Brat," he offers. She nods and heads off down one of the aisles.

"Damn, she took the dots," Wil says, watching her leave.

A few minutes after Cynthia leaves a voice calls from a few tables away, "Commander Calder?"

Zephyr and Maxim both look at Wil, eyebrows quirked, then look up beyond their Captain.

Wil turns to the source of the voice, an agent of some governmental agency or another by the look of him.

The young, blonde-haired man and four others in identical black suits approach. "Commander Calder, would you come with us, please?"

"Wil?" Maxim whispers, his hand dropping to his thigh, where a pulse pistol is normally strapped. He growls.

"Friends?" the agent says glancing at the other agents. He taps his right ear, "Calder is not alone." He nods, "Affirmative."

Wil, Zephyr, and Maxim are still staring at the mystery man and his friends. By now, other food court patrons have figured out that something is happening. The tables immediately surrounding the crew of the *Ghost* have cleared out, all eyes within fifty feet are trained on their tables.

Mystery agent smiles, "Please, all of you, come with us."

Wil looks at his first officer and tactical officer, raises his hands. "Go with it," he murmurs before turning to the agent, "Where to?"

MOMMY DEAREST_

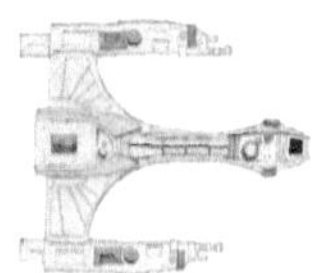

"So what? We're buying an entertainment disc?" Bennie asks Kareem. The entire group is now standing in the main walkway a handful of steps from *old man Henry's* stall.

The children laugh, Sarah leans over, "No silly. We're going to boost a few discs and then sell 'em. We can usually unload new releases at the metro station near the financial district."

Bennie looks over at the stall, stepping aside to avoid catching a purse to the face from an inattentive woman hurrying somewhere. "Ok, so how do we do this?"

Kareem smiles, "Billy and Jerome, you know what to do." The two boys, Jerome appearing to be the thicker boy, nod and head into the flow of people coming and going.

Bennie is about to ask another question, when the crowd parts like a river moving around a rock. The two boys are wrestling and shouting. Gradually, more and more passers-by slow down to watch the ruckus.

Sarah leans over to Bennie again, "Go grab as many as you can carry, then run back into the between space." She doesn't wait for his answer. She and Kareem move into the crowd, expertly picking pockets and purses.

Bennie nods approvingly, "Not subtle, but I like their style." He turns and moves quickly toward the stall and its entertainment discs.

As expected, the shopkeeper, presumably old man Henry, is raptly watching the ruckus in the middle of the walkway. Bennie walks up to the display of discs, having been shown the disc in question by the children. With a handful of discs, he turns to duck back into the crowd, only to have a hand clamp down on his shoulder, "What do you think you're doing?"

Bennie looks up into the face of a uniformed woman, her free hand resting on her belt, near what Bennie assumes is a primitive weapon. He glances around for the other children, seeing none of them. He growls, realizing he's been ditched.

"Excuse me, what seems to be the problem?" Someone asks from behind Bennie.

The law enforcement officer looks up, "Is this young man yours, ma'am?"

Bennie looks up to see human-Cynthia, approaching. She looks at Bennie scowling, then looks up to the law enforcement officer, "Unfortunately, um, officer?" She looks at Bennie again, "What have I told you?"

"Don't listen to you and Wil when you're in your berth?"

Cynthia rubs her face with one hand, the law enforcement woman blushes.

"The one about causing trouble," Cynthia finally says.

Bennie smiles, "Oh that one." He looks up at the officer, "Sorry."

"I want to press charges!" an old man shouts from the nearby stall, realizing what has happened while he was distracted.

The officer glances at the man, then back to Cynthia, "We caught your son stealing several vid-discs."

Cynthia only partially stifles a retching noise, "I'm so sorry. I'm more than happy to pay for the discs."

"Make an example out of that little shit!" the old man shouts. The crowd that was watching the child wrestling match has now turned to watch the officer and Cynthia, and the loud shopkeeper.

Bennie turns to the old man, "I will eat your face old man."

Cynthia clamps a hand down on the angry Brailack's shoulder.

"Henry, that's enough," the officer says over her shoulder. She reaches back snapping her fingers. The angry Henry drops a point of sale device, in her open hand. She turns to Cynthia who offers up the plastic device Wil said to use for paying for things.

The point of sale device beeps twice, the officer removes the card and hands it to Cynthia, "Thank you ma'am." She looks down at Bennie, "You behave yourself young man."

Bennie opens his mouth, then cringes as Cynthia squeezes his shoulder. She looks down at him, "Come along... son."

The two turn and head back to the food court.

"What were you thinking? Stealing entertainment discs?" Cynthia scolds tossing the discs in a trash bin as they pass it.

"It wasn't my idea!" Bennie retorts, arms folded across his chest. "The Earth children I met made me do it."

"Made you?" She looks down, one blonde eyebrow raises.

"Two of them were bigger than me!" The indignant hacker shouts. "They were very crafty!"

"Crafty children? You know what? Never mind. We can discuss this when we get back to the others."

They exit the corridor and head into the food court. Both look around, not seeing their friends. Bennie scratches his head, "Are they hiding?"

Cynthia shakes her head once, "No, they were right there." She points to two now empty tables.

"So, where are they?" Bennie wonders, looking around.

"I don't know."

PART THREE

CHAPTER 11_

DRIVER'S ED._

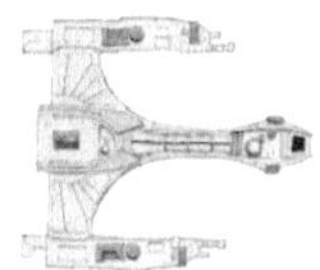

THE VAN they're in has no windows; the passenger compartment is separated from the driver by a thick, steel plate; a small slit with a panel over it, the only way to interact with the driver. The slit is closed, and the agent sitting closest to the front of the van has his back to it, protecting it maybe?

"So, where are we going?" Wil asks the other guard in the compartment with the three crew members of the *Ghost*.

"LAX," the agent replies.

Zephyr leans toward Wil. She is on the same bench as him, Maxim is opposite them. "What is el aye ex?"

"The airport. They're taking us somewhere outside LA." He looks to Agent whatever his name is, "JPL? NASA headquarters?"

The agent looks at him, saying nothing until finally offering, "Colorado."

Wil blinks twice, "Really?" Smith nods but offers nothing further.

Maxim leans forward, "You're from this call er raddo place, right?" Wil nods, only partially hearing and processing what his friend has asked.

Zephyr looks at her partner, then to Wil, "Wil?"

Wil shakes his head, "Sorry"—he looks at the agent—"feel free to correct any of this; it's been a while for me." He turns to his friends,

"The Denver Metro launch complex is, or maybe was, one of the nation's most advanced facilities." He looks at the agent who nods slightly. "That's where the FTL program was based, the pod I was in when I went, you know," his two alien friends nod this time.

He continues, "There was talk of moving all of NASA's operations from the LA area to Colorado—more central, more modern launch facilities, no earthquakes." This time when he looks to the agent, he doesn't flinch. Wil continues, "I guess they ended up going through with it."

"Do you have friends there?" Maxim asks.

"I do, or at least I did. It's been a while, remember. James, my best friend, was still in the program when I came back a few years ago."

"You'll get answers when we get to Space Operations Command," the mostly unhelpful agent says, looking annoyed.

Wil glares, "What's your name anyway?"

"Smith," the agent says, offering nothing more.

"Do you know how to pilot this thing?" Bennie asks, climbing into the rental van. It's taken Cynthia and him over three hours to find the van. Neither had paid a great deal of attention when the group parked, and both remembered the vehicle having a different design.

Cynthia is in the driver's seat, familiarizing herself with the controls, "I think so." She looks over to Bennie, "If Wil can do it, how hard could it be?"

The Brailack nods, "True; surely can't be harder than flying a warship."

The van lurches out of the parking space, ramming into the car in front of it. Cynthia groans, "Found forward." She adjusts the control stick device she'd seen Wil use, and tries again, the van slowly reverses away from the now crumpled vehicle in front of it.

Bennie looks at the damaged vehicle, "Should we leave a note?"

"Saying what? Sorry, aliens wrecked your car, apologies."

Bennie looks at her, "That would be pretty funny. I doubt the owners understand written Galactic Standard, Brailack Normal, or Tyr Standard."

Cynthia smiles, "True, have you got a location yet?"

Bennie looks down at his wristcomm, "Yeah, I think so. I was able to tap into this thing's global navigation system, pulling up the previous drives." He holds up his wristcomm; on the screen is a map with a pulsing red line, "This will get us back to the hotel. We can get our stuff, then find the others."

ON THE MOVE_

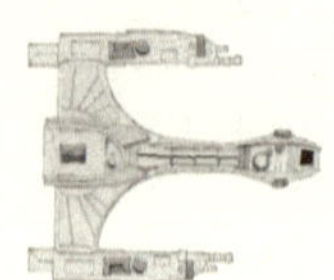

THE REST of the trip to Los Angeles International Spaceport is uneventful. Every time one of the prisoners—*guests*, Agent Smith insists —tries to talk, he shushes them, having grown tired of their questions.

The van pulls up to what Wil assumes is its destination, and the back doors open. Sunlight floods the interior, blinding the occupants, another agent is standing at the opening, "Come on."

As the three *guests* file out of the van, Wil takes in their surroundings. He looks over to Maxim and in a hushed tone says, "Private portion of the spaceport." He points to a sleek private aircraft up ahead, "That's probably our ride."

"It is," Agent Smith confirms, coming up behind the trio. The passenger door of the craft drops on its own. "In you go," the agent ushers.

"This is fancy," Maxim says, squeezing into a seat facing into the center of the cabin. Zephyr takes a seat opposite him.

Wil follows, taking a seat next to Maxim, "Yeah NASA, wait, no. What's it called now?" he asks, looking at Agent Smith who's taken a seat closer to the front of the plane, facing backward toward his *guests*.

"Space Operations Command."

"Right, SOC, ha, sock." Wil smiles, then turns to Maxim, "Sock is making us feel welcome."

150

"Welcome back ma'am. Will you be needing your—Oh my. It looks like you were in an accident," the valet at the hotel says as Cynthia pulls the vehicle into the front drive of the Los Angeles Grand.

Cynthia waves the young woman away, "We're just getting a few things from our room; we'll be right back down." She stares at the woman then adds while gesturing to the front-end damage, "It's not as bad as it looks."

Bennie hops out from the passenger side and heads into the hotel. Cynthia gets out and turns to follow the Brailack hacker. The valet thrusts her hand out, "I'll still need to hold on to your control fob."

Cynthia looks around, remembering that Bennie had to hack his way into the vehicle to get access. Wil, wherever he is, has the control fob. "Oh, uh, it's in the ground car somewhere. My, er, son lost it."

The valet coughs, "I see. Well if you'll be right back, that's fine." Cynthia nods and rushes into the lobby of the hotel. She sees Bennie at the elevator bank and joins him, "We may need to figure out a better solution for accessing the ground car."

"We don't have a printer, so we can't create anything, but I'll think on it." The doors to the lift to their right open, a chime alerting them to its arrival.

Maxim looks over at Agent Smith and his companion, the other agent that had been in the back of the van with them, both men look to be paying only moderate attention to their charges. He turns to Wil. "What about Cynthia and Bennie?" he asks under his breath.

Wil repeats Maxim's furtive glance then without fully turning to his friend replies, "These guys don't seem to know how many we are; so," he shrugs, "I'm hoping Bennie is tracking our wristcomms."

"And when they inevitably confiscate them?" the big Palorian presses.

"I'll do my best to keep that from happening, but beyond that I'm hoping Bennie will have our location dialed in, and they don't move us again. Last time I was in the Colorado space launch facility it wasn't much. I'm sure it's grown, but it's likely still a campus of buildings in one place."

Agent Smith stirs and looks at Wil who smiles and winks; Smith scowls.

Zephyr leans forward slightly, "Don't you have the control chip for the ground vehicle?"

"Shit," Wil says, reaching into his pocket, removing the small fob that activates the rental van's systems. "Well, she has Bennie. He's better than a fob any day."

REUNIONS AND SEPARATIONS_

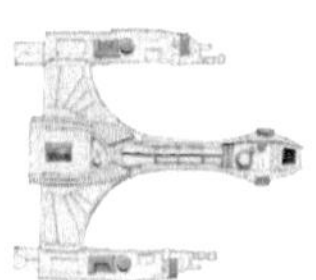

Before the plane even finishes rolling to a stop, the passenger door is opening, Agent Smith is already standing next to the threshold. He motions to Wil and the others, "Come on." He heads down the small staircase just as the plane jolts to a stop.

Peering around, Wil whistles, "Damn, this thing is fast." He takes in the scene around the plane, "Double damn." Maxim and Zephyr both look at him, eyebrows raised. "This place is nuts, easily three times what was here when I worked here."

"At least," Agent Smith offers, "The Space Operations Command merged operations from east and west coasts to here about five years ago." He gestures to a door, "Through there."

The large door opens as they approach. Inside the door is an older man in a military uniform, the number of medals and stars decorating the jacket make it clear he's important. Standing next to him is, "James!" Wil shouts and increases his pace, racing toward his old friend.

From inside the door frame, initially out of view, two Military Police emerge, holding rifles aimed right at Wil. Wil stops short; Maxim and Zephyr a few paces behind him ready to fight if needed.

James Hawthorne, astronaut, Wil's best friend, raises his hands, motioning to the guards. "It's ok." He closes the gap between himself and Wil, stopping to look his friend in the eyes for a moment, then without warning pulls the smaller man into an embrace that leaves Wil squeaking from inside the mass of muscle and jumpsuit that is his friend. Setting Wil down, James looks at him, "Good to see you, man."

Wil nods, catching his breath, "Good to be seen. I am curious exactly how it is you found us."

James holds up a hand, "I'll fill you all in once we're settled." He looks over Wil's shoulder, "Hi, I'm James Hawthorne, assistant director of the SOC." He moves past Wil toward Zephyr, offering his hand.

After shaking both Palorians hands, he looks at all three, "You know, I didn't expect you to look so human."

Wil smiles and nods to his two alien friends. They each reach up and touch a spot on their chests. Their human appearance wavers, then vanishes. Everyone standing near them gasps, the rifles around them all snapping up, taking aim at the two Palorians. Wil raises both arms, slowly spinning to try to block each weapon aimed at him and his friends, "Woah! Woah! Woah!"

James raises his hands again; the guards all lower their weapons. The General, who has been standing off to the side during the greetings, says, "We should take this inside," holding an arm out toward the door.

James nods, "Yeah, come on. You all hungry? Thirsty?"

Wil nods to his crewmates, "We're good, thirsty, but otherwise ok. Your pal Smith here picked us up just after lunch."

James smiles, "Please tell me you didn't make them," he hitches a thumb at the two aliens, "eat food truck food at the swap meet."

"Damn right I did."

From the rear of the small group, the General—Wil sees that his name tag says *Pierce*—mumbles, "First contact and they're likely to get the runs."

"Are you sure this is the right way?" Cynthia asks, turning the van off the highway, onto another interstate.

Bennie nods, pointing to the navigation display in the center of the vehicle's dashboard, "According to the tracking data coming from their wristcomms, yes. From what I've pieced together from their location data and this planet's pathetic global navigation network, this thoroughfare will get us there—a place called *Space Operations Command*." He looks over to Cynthia, "A little dramatic if you ask me."

"How long?" the Tygran woman asks, barely glancing away from the road. They've nearly struck three other vehicles, all before entering the freeway, which to Cynthia's liking has fewer turns and stops.

Bennie looks at the display, squinting to read all the various bits of information on the screen, "Looks like, at the rate this vehicle covers ground, twenty tocks. That's without stopping."

She sighs, "Grolack, that's a lot of territory to cover and not get found out."

Bennie grins, "Hey, I infiltrated a Peacekeeper Command Carrier, staying undiscovered on this backwater will be easy."

Red and blue lights flash behind them.

TWENTY QUESTIONS_

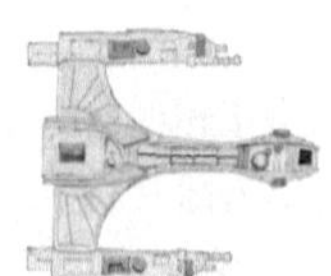

Once inside the building, James leads Wil and the Palorians through a maze of hallways, then onto an elevator that goes down for longer than Wil would have expected was possible. Their final destination is a conference room, monitors on the walls displaying images of the outside of the facility and a few with views that Wil assumes are coming from the ISS 2.

"Please have a seat," James says as he and General Pierce move to the head of the table.

As Wil and the others take their seats, General Pierce leans forward, "So, Major Calder,"

"It's Captain now, if you want to use titles, but I'm fine with just *Wil*, General?"

"Pierce. I'm General Reginald Pierce, Air Force Space Command, Director of Space Operations Command."

"Cool," Wil says, then continues, "I didn't mean to interrupt, General. You were asking a question."

The General exchanges a glance with James, then says, "Yes. I was about to ask, why you're here, and"—he pointedly looks at Maxim and Zephyr—"why you brought extra-terrestrials to Earth." He looks right at Maxim, "And why they were disguised as humans?"

Wil looks over at James, eyebrow raised then looks at the General. "How about some tit for tat? We'll answer your questions; you can answer ours. I'll start with an answer. I brought E.T.s because they're my crew, and I don't go anywhere without them." He inclines his head, "How did you know we were here?"

The General smiles an entirely not friendly smile, crossing his arms across his barrel chest, "A lot has changed since you left Earth, *Captain*." He says the last word with as much disdain as he can. "NASA is now the SOC, and we follow military protocol." He glares, then continues, "We spotted your ship the moment you entered the high orbit threshold."

Zephyr is intrigued, "Interesting, so that small pod that gave chase, a test?"

This time James answers, "Sort of. Our detection grid picked up your ship, barely. Actually, we had no idea what you were, just an unusual reflection of light. We tasked the pod pilot with trying to get a better view." He looks at Wil, "The maneuvering to avoid him was impressive." Wil nods, a satisfied smile on his face. James continues, "We knew something had penetrated our orbital space, but had no idea what, and the pod pilot only caught a few glimpses, and at that distance, it wasn't much to go on. We picked you back up once you cleared atmospheric entry and tracked you to California." James looks serious, "We couldn't track your landing, I'm guessing something with your ship's propulsion or something. You didn't park it at a Wal-Mart, did you?"

Wil absorbs this information, "It took all I had to land without you seeing. We even just upgraded our stealth gear." He smiles, "And, no, the *Ghost* is safe, don't worry. And how did you find us at the swap meet?"

James answers, "You notice all the cameras? They're at every intersection, usually, plus anywhere lots of people are likely to be." When Wil nods slowly James adds, "Facial recognition has progressed a lot over the years. We've had your face on file for years, just in case you ever came home."

General Pierce holds a hand up, "I'm assuming you won't be sharing the location of your ship?"

"Not in a million years... sir." Wil continues, "I guess my turn again. We're here looking for someone."

"Someone?" James asks, casting a furtive glance at General Pierce. Wil sees it, so do his Palorian crewmates.

"A scientist," Maxim offers. This elicits a more direct look between James and the General.

The door to the conference room opens. "They're likely looking for me," a heavyset man in a white lab coat and tight-fitting Space Force jumpsuit says, shuffling into the room.

Wil turns, "Were you waiting for a dramatic moment to make your entrance, Mister Drell?"

CHAPTER 12_

PURPOSE OF YOUR VISIT?_

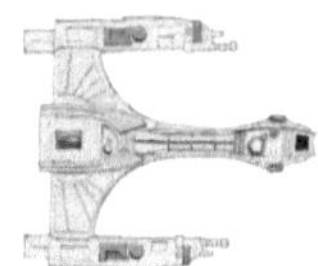

"Did you have to bite him?" Cynthia asks as the rental van speeds away from the police cruiser.

Bennie looks back over the seat at the rapidly diminishing vehicle, "What was I supposed to do? Did you want to end up in Earth Jail? Or worse, on some sick weirdo's lab table, cut open?" He pantomimes slicing down his middle, his tongue sticking out the corner of his mouth, eyes clamped shut.

"When he wakes up, he's going to report it, and we'll have every law enforcement official in this part of the country looking for us."

"He won't remember much," Bennie assures his feline featured friend.

"Why?"

Bennie opens his mouth, exposing his teeth, or rather the teeth of a twelve-year-old boy. "Brailack have a defense mechanism. We can express a gland in our mouths that turns our saliva into a mild sedative and hypnotic. He won't recall much of the last several tocks. Hacking the onboard recorder in his vehicle was child's play."

"Gross." She turns, glaring, "You haven't used that on us, have you?"

He scowls back, "No! The gland only expresses when we bite. Have you woken up with any bite marks?"

Cynthia turns, "None that I can't remember getting."

Bennie looks at the van's navigation console, "To be safe, maybe we should ditch this thing?"

"Good idea, little green," Cynthia says, smiling at her new appreciation for her friend.

"So what? You came to Earth and offered to upgrade their tech?" Wil asks as Bonson Drell takes a seat next to the General, who smirks at Wil's question.

"Nothing of the sort. I fled to this wretched world to avoid detection. I had heard that our people looked strikingly similar. Thanks to Councilwoman Grythlorian I knew a fair bit about your species. I assumed I'd be able to blend in with the locals. I didn't have the luxury of those image inducers."

James chimes in, "He assumed wrong. I guess humans are unique enough that he couldn't figure us out. We started getting weird calls almost immediately. It took less than a month to track him down. He bumbled from one city to another."

"Your people are backward and use idioms so freely; I can't imagine you ever communicating with the rest of the galaxy."

"No offense taken," Pierce says, still smirking. "He sang like a bird the moment he sat down in the interrogation room," General Pierce offers.

Drell looks at the two humans, "What should I have done? I didn't want these primitives to kill me." He gestures around the room, "Once they captured me, I did the only thing I could think of, I survived."

Maxim tuts, "By sharing advanced technologies with a primitive species? The GC would toss you in a dark pit for that. You know the rules."

"Hey!" James says.

Wil raises a hand, "He doesn't mean it like that; you get used to it."

"The good doctor has helped the United States tremendously;" General Pierce gloats, "more than you did when you returned home, I might add." He stares at Wil, who shivers as if the temperature has dropped.

Zephyr who's been watching this exchange with great interest, turns her attention from General Pierce to Bonson Drell, says, "I see. So not only have you broken one of the GC's most important rules, you've done it to uplift one nation-state over others?"

The fat Multonae shrugs, "What could I do?"

"Not help them," Zephyr offers, her glare just as icy as the General's earlier version.

James raps the table twice with a knuckle, "We're getting a bit far afield. We brought you in because obviously it's a risk to have you out on the streets."

"We seemed to be doing just fine," Wil counters.

"Regardless. The country isn't ready, and the world definitely isn't. Not to mention the national security concerns."

"What national security concerns? Even if we caused a scene and their"—he hitches a thumb at his first officer and tactical officer—"image inducers malfunctioned, you wouldn't be exposed as having him." He points to Bonson Drell.

"It would still raise questions we're not prepared to answer, just yet," James says, a twinkle in his eyes that Wil knows all too well.

"You're not telling us everything," he says.

Before James or the General can reply Maxim asks, "Where is your ship Drell?"

The heavyset Multonae scientist slides down in his chair slightly and General Pierce says, "We have it."

SPACE RACE_

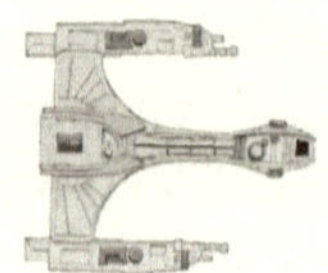

GENERAL PIERCE STANDS, "Let's take a break. It's getting late," he looks at his watch to confirm. He looks at James, "I trust you can get them squared away?"

"Yes, sir," James says, standing.

Wil follows suit, standing; his two companions do the same. The General rushes out, motioning for Bonson Drell to follow.

Wil looks at James, "So, what now? This isn't some detention thing, right? We can leave?"

At this point, Agent Smith and his companion both stand a little straighter, hands drifting to the discreet sidearms under their suit jackets.

James smiles, but shakes his head, "For now, it sorta is. There's a lot to tell you. Dinner?" He looks at Zephyr and Maxim, "Uh, can you two turn into humans again?"

"Turn into?" Zephyr asks. "We're not shapeshifters."

"Revolting," Maxim says, pressing the activation switch on his image inducer.

"No offense meant," James says. He looks at Smith, "I'm taking them to dinner. I assume you're coming along."

Smith nods, then taps his ear subvocalizing into a mic to someone in a windowless room of monitors watching them all.

"Into town?" Wil says, eyes lit up, hopeful.

"Of course, the chow here sucks," James grins, "Plus we've got a maglev right to Union Station now."

"What?" Wil asks, eyes bulging.

"Courtesy of our *Guest*." He makes air quotes around the last word.

"How long has he been here?" Maxim asks.

James taps his chin thinking, "Almost two years?" We've been busy.

"I'd say," Zephyr says. Wil raises an eyebrow but says nothing.

"What do you think that means?" Cynthia asks, pointing to a blinking icon on the main information console of the rental van.

Bennie leans over to the driver's side, "Beats me; hold on." He connects his wristcomm to the spliced wire coming from under the dashboard. "Ah, the power cell is nearly depleted." He looks at his friend, "These humans have shit for power cell tech. Their iconography could use some work too, what's that shape supposed to mean? A rectangle with a nipple on the end?" Cynthia nods, "Well, I guess this is as good a time as any to find another ride, maybe crash for the night."

"Can we afford the delay?" Bennie asks.

"Showing up, wherever the others are, dead tired won't do anyone any good, right?" She looks at the small hacker, "Plus I'm starving." She points to a bag in the back seat full of food, "That, what did Wil call it? twerky? Is disgusting."

Bennie nods in agreement. "Ok, let me run some searches. According to the onboard computer, we've got about a tock left before this thing is dead. A few quiet minutes pass while Bennie hums to himself working his wristcomm before he finally says, "This looks promising—a place called Las Vegas." He holds up his arm, showing the wristcomm display, "Looks pretty, and is just within range."

"This is pretty sweet," Wil says as the *Ghost crew*, two agents, and James Hawthorne sit in the small maglev car, racing towards Denver ten meters below ground.

"We had the service tunnels already, since most of the staff lives in

Denver or the surrounding suburbs, but ol' Bonson showed us how to miniaturize maglev components. There's a low ding, and the ten-person vehicle slows to a stop. The door slides open revealing a small boarding platform, twenty meters wide at most. "This is us," he says, leaving the car. The platform is empty except for a nondescript pair of elevator doors at the far end. James heads for them. "We're just below the conference center now." He points to the elevator doors, "These will take us up to the main terminal floor."

Stepping out of Union station, Maxim and Zephyr are stunned by the volume of humans busily moving every which way—Downtown Denver at peak rush. People are hustling into the station to head home. Others are moving between curbside bars and cafes, enjoying drinks with friends and colleagues. The sky is a deep, dark blue with few stars visible amid the bright lights of the active downtown area.

"This is impressive," Zephyr breathes out, looking up and around at the myriad glass towers surrounding the transit hub.

James takes the lead, "Come on." Wil and the Palorians fall in behind him, the special agent-men fall in behind them.

NOT GOOD WITH CHILDREN_

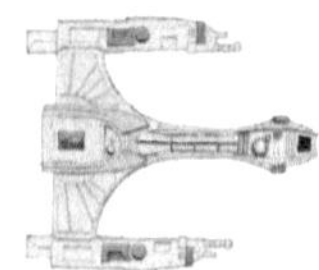

SITTING around the table at a restaurant Wil doesn't recognize, Zephyr takes a sip of her beer. "Oh wow. You're right. It's just like grum." Wil smiles.

James continues the story he was telling, "So I'd finished calming that cranky old woman down and persuaded her to give me a lift back into town. Getting home was harder than I'd expected, by the way, no Lyft service out there." He jokingly glares at his old friend. "Could you have landed somewhere more remote? Anyhow, I get back to Denver and the operations center is buzzing. Your stealth tech stuff kept you off the radars of most countries, this one included, but plenty of folks saw ya. And plenty of them called it in. Lots of cellphone pics and videos flooded the airwaves."

"General Pierce was running around stirring up every hornet he could find to mobilize the Air Force and Navy. The President was in her bunker. It was a little scary to be honest; it worried me we were about to start a war over you, without ever knowing it was you. Pierce had the Joint Chiefs convinced it was some Russian or Chinese attack craft testing our airspace." He looks down, "So I told them everything."

"Dude," Wil starts, but stops when James holds up a hand.

"I'm not exaggerating, when I say it scared me, man. They closed schools the next day; streets were deserted. I don't recall if we talked about it when you visited, but tensions were high; they still are, but in different respects. The current president"—James looks over to the agents sitting at the next table—"is a bit more hawkish than previous presidents, like even if you added them up. Add in Pierce, who spent his career rattling his swords and pushing for us to fight every country that crossed us and..." He spreads his hands.

"So, ISS 2?" Wil asks.

"No longer an open international mission. NATO allies only, and even then, only certain countries."

"Wow," Wil says.

Next to him, Maxim leans to Zephyr, "Coming here might have been a mistake."

"You think?" She leans in closer, "I've started planning out ways to make sure the image inducers keep working."

"I hope Cynthia and Bennie are doing better than we are," the big man says under his breath as he takes another sip of his beer. He holds it out in front of him, "This is good. I'd say better than most grum I've had."

Zephyr nods, "Wil says there are hundreds of types of this *beer*. For all their faults, apparently humans are good at fermenting things."

Wil and James are still talking, James is saying, "Once I'd gotten everyone to calm down, and after a full week being debriefed, the president increased funding to the FTL project, and, sadly, militarized it." He glances at the agents again. "NASA, now the SOC, nearly tripled in personnel, and the launch complex became the monster you saw and then some."

"For what? Were they afraid I'd come back and try to conquer the place or something?" Wil asks.

James chuckles, "Afraid of you? No. Of aliens"—he glances at the other two at the table—"yes. No offense."

Zephyr grins, "If *aliens* wanted to attack your world, I don't think there's anything you could do about it,"

James nods slowly, "Yeah, probably; though it won't be for lack of trying." Again, he looks at the agents, who at least seem to give them their privacy. "Like I said earlier, we've been busy."

"And NATO and the other nations are ok? It can't be a secret," Wil pushes.

One of the agents clears his throat, not Smith, letting James know that they are in fact listening and that he needs to shut up now.

As if waiting for the right moment, the waitress arrives, delivering their meals.

Wil looks at his friend, his concern obvious.

"Well, it won't be easy to find us in all of this," Bennie says as the van makes its way down the Las Vegas Strip. "What is all this?"

"Must be some type of entertainment district," Cynthia guesses, passing a flashing display boasting gaming services and dancing women. She glances at the information display on the dashboard, "We're nearly out of power, where to?"

Bennie consults his wristcomm, "Turn right up there, then a left into the parking garage. According to the, what was it? Internet? This establishment has the most rooms. Should offer the best selection for a new ride."

"Makes sense." She guides the van through the indicated turns, finds an empty charging slot in the massive parking garage, and disengages the van's drive systems. An icon on the information display blinks orange, "I guess that means it is charging," she says. "Ok, come on. Let's get everything unloaded. You have a room for us?"

"Two," Bennie says, grabbing Maxim's duffel bag, "What does he carry in here? How can clothes be so heavy?" The bag drops to the ground out of the van with a metallic thud.

WHAT HAPPENS IN VEGAS_

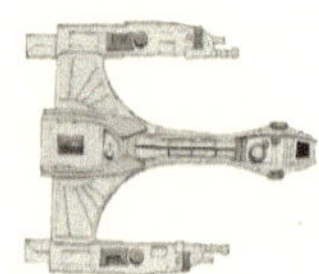

"THERE'S A LINE, GREAT," Cynthia says as they take their place in the queue to check into the *Galaxy*. The name struck Bennie funny, so he picked it as their layover for the night.

After a few minutes of shuffling along in the line, dozens of other travelers falling in behind them, the woman in front of the pair turns, she has a small boy with her that might be the same age Bennie is supposed to be; Cynthia has no idea. "What a handsome young man, mother and son vacation? That's what we're doing. A little treat for my soon to be fourth grader." The boy smiles at Bennie.

Cynthia coughs, "Oh, yes uh, same here." She looks down at Bennie, "fourth grade."

"Oh, he looks so much older, I'd have guessed sixth grade."

Cynthia faces Bennie who is staring at her, eyebrows raised, then whispers to the woman, "He's dumb."

"Oh, my," the woman says after a pronounced gasp. "Um, well maybe he'd enjoy playing with my Jerry later at the pool? I understand there's a kiddy pool here that's supposed to be wonderful. Us moms could watch them with something fruity and full of alcohol in our hands." She smiles.

Bennie scowls first at Cynthia, then the woman, "Do I look like I want to play with your little broodling?" Bennie growls.

Cynthia smacks him on the back of the head, then smiles at the alarmed woman, "Like I said, dumb." She looks at Bennie, "You apologize right away."

Bennie scowls again, "Sorry."

The woman nods and turns around, pushing Jerry around to stand in front of her. The child cranes his neck around his mother to stare at Bennie open-mouthed. Bennie makes a rude gesture, and the boy spins around to face forward.

Cynthia leans down, "Are you trying to get us caught, you little krebnack."

"You try looking like a child," Bennie says, arms crossed.

The line moves once more. Cynthia nudges the angry Brailack, "Grab the bags."

"Welcome to the Galaxy, checking in?" the young man behind the counter says as Cynthia and Bennie walk up to him. The other woman and her son are two clerks down the long check-in desk.

"Hi, yes we are." She glances down at Bennie mouthing the word, *name*. He mouths something back, but she quickly realizes she can't read lips not Bennie's that's for sure. She leans down, holding up a finger for the clerk to wait. Standing back up she says, "Luar, Cynthia Luar. Two rooms." She looks back down at Bennie her brows knit together. He shrugs.

The clerk looks at Cynthia then raises an eyebrow and leans forward to peer over the counter at Bennie, who is about six inches shy of reaching the top. "Um, will others be joining the two of you? I ask because he"—he politely gestures toward Bennie—"looks a little young to occupy a room unattended."

Cynthia looks down at Bennie who's occupying himself with his gaming system analog wristcomm interface. She nudges him to pay attention. "Oh, uh, yes a friend of mine. Bennie here, and I, will be in one room, my uh, friend will be in another."

"Ah, ok then. It looks like you requested a high floor, it just so happens I've got two adjoining rooms on the forty-ninth floor, if that will work?" He smiles, looking down at his terminal. After a minute, he hands over four small plastic cards, "I took the liberty of making two cards per room, if that's ok?"

Taking the cards, Cynthia smiles, "It is; thank you. Come along, Bennie," she says, nudging her Brailack companion to move along.

Back at the Space Operations Command, James is at the door to the guest quarters that have been prepared for the crew of the *Ghost*. "I'll come by and get you in the morning." He looks from Maxim and Zephyr to Wil, "Good to see you, man." He turns and leaves; the door closes behind him. As it does, Wil can see an agent standing just to the side of the door.

"Wil, I don't like this," Zephyr says.

"You and me both." He reaches over and presses the door control. It beeps once, but otherwise nothing happens. Looking back to his friends, "Nothing we can do about it tonight; it's late." He walks further into the space; it has three bedrooms and a shared restroom. There's a small kitchenette in the corner and an entertainment screen bigger than the one on the *Ghost* in the other corner. "Try to get some sleep. We'll figure out a plan in the morning." He raises his sleeve, exposing his bare forearm. Groaning, "I wish they hadn't taken our wristcomms. Hopefully Bennie can still home in on them, assuming they haven't already broken them down to reverse engineer."

CHAPTER 13_

NEW RIDES_

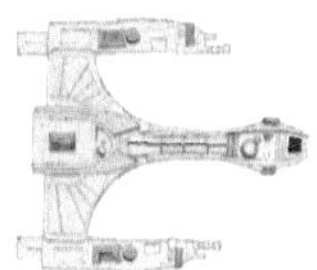

"I THOUGHT you'd like to see this," James says as the crew speaks as the crew of the *Ghost* their special agent shadows follow James down a long corridor near the bottom of the SOC main complex. Wil still isn't sure, and hasn't gotten a straight answer regarding, how deep this facility goes. A set of heavy doors ahead of them part, revealing an observation lounge type room.

As the group enters, Wil glances to the side of the room that is floor-to-ceiling glass. "Holy shit."

Maxim and Zephyr turn together, mouths opening slightly.

"Like it?" James asks, the pride clear on his face.

"How the hell do you have a starship?" Wil asks, pressing a palm to the glass, taking in the view beyond the clear barrier. The ship is at least two hundred meters long and fifty wide. There are several turrets that look like they've been removed from naval vessels along the roughly rectangular hull. The ship is matte black, with antennae and sensor bulges all over it. A flying bridge structure sits a quarter of the length in from the engines and off-center a bit. The nose of the vessel sports a large ball-turret with what looks like a thruster on it.

Everyone is silent, taking in the ship, until Wil gets to the bow features and sees the name. "You're shitting me!" he says a bit louder than he intended. He turns to James, his eyes wide.

James spreads his hands, "What can I say? You're kind of a national hero. The first astronaut to go faster than light and to die doing it." He looks over at the ship, the affection clear, "The *Wil Calder* is the first protector class light cruiser in the Space Force fleet. She's still a ways from launch certification."

Maxim turns, "You learned how to move faster than light, were gifted further advanced technologies, and the first thing you do is build a warship?" He turns to Wil, saying nothing.

James crosses his arms over his chest, brow furrowed, "Look, I get that you all dislike how we're doing things, but you don't know the first thing about Earth or the political situation here." He points an accusing finger at Wil, "He's been gone a long time."

Wil raises his hands, palms up, "Woah, don't blame me for this."

James closes his eyes, inhaling, "The *Calder* isn't the first ship we built. You didn't see the *Challenger* or *Discovery* in the cradles at the ISS 2?"

Wil snaps, "That's right. We were running as quiet as possible, so didn't scan the station. I thought I saw shipyards but could only zoom in so much. I think we passed a third one of those on the way to Jupiter."

James nods, "Oh, yeah that must have been the *Intrepid*. She's the first of the Columbus class long-range explorers. She launched without FTL during the space race to get to the Jovian System. You didn't see a ship about the same size, flying the Chinese flag?" Wil shakes his head.

"And the other nation states of this world, what are they doing, while your country seems to be leaping away from them technologically speaking?" Zephyr asks.

James has calmed down now and looks from the *Calder* to Zephyr, "The Chinese aren't as far behind us as you might think. They've cracked FTL also and have a shipyard."

Wil raises his hand, "Wait, where? We didn't see any other stations large enough for shipyards, or ships for that matter, in orbit."

"The moon, "James says. "They took the moon, more or less."

Wil just stares at his friend, "What? What do you mean, *they took the moon?*"

"Exactly that. They built their shipyards over the moon and declared it sovereign Chinese territory. Most of it anyway. They found water, and set up shop." James's dark features darken further, "Like we've been saying, a lot has changed."

"If the US has FTL, and the Chinese have FTL, why hasn't anyone left the solar system yet, or even set up shop further out into the system?" Wil wonders.

"Don't think it's not on the table," James replies. "Right now, fighting over this part of the system is the top item on most people's lists."

Zephyr looks at Wil, her back to James, "We should leave. Bonson or not, this world is an overcharged power cell."

Over her shoulder, Wil notices Agent Smith and his companion stiffen a bit. He nods subtly, not taking his eyes off the agents, "Yeah."

Just then the doors open, and Bonson Drell and General Pierce walk in.

"Fine, then you pick one!" Cynthia growls as they walk past a sleek two-seater sports car that Bennie has vetoed stealing.

The short hacker keeps walking down the aisle of the parking garage, slowly turning in circles every dozen steps until he stops near the section of parking closest to the hotel service elevator. "This one," he points.

"Are you serious?" Cynthia asks, eyeing the vehicle. They are standing in front of a large utility van.

"Yup, it'll be perfect. Look." He gestures to the large vehicle, "I bet that's a satellite uplink; that'll be handy." He walks around it, "Plus it's boring looking and nondescript." He points at a logo he has no idea the meaning of.

Cynthia sighs, "You make good points. Ok, let's get going." She walks up to the driver's side door, "Can you hack it?"

Bennie is already focused on his wristcomm, forgoing the game system analog since no one is around. He holds up a finger momentarily then goes back to work. A few minutes, later the doors slide open.

Both non-humans throw their bags, plus the bags of their friends in the back of the utility van and hop in. Cynthia looks around the instrument panel, "Seems to work roughly the same as the other one." The utility van comes to life with a slight whir as its electric motors engage.

UNCOMFORTABLE CONVERSATIONS_

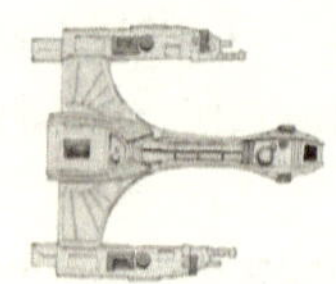

AFTER THE PEEK at the *Wil Calder,* the group has been led to a conference room. "Captain Calder, I'm sure you understand our position," General Pierce says, his face showing no emotion. This is not the conference room they had been in before; this one is more utilitarian—a table, chairs, a picture of one of the first-generation space shuttles on the wall, a portrait of the President, someone Wil has never seen before and can't name.

"Honestly man, I get it. Drell has been a valuable asset to you—"

"Invaluable, actually," Pierce cuts him off.

"Ok, an invaluable asset. That doesn't change that he's an alien and that he's wanted by the Galactic Commonwealth."

Pierce raises his hand, "A governmental body with no authority on Earth. In fact, a governmental body that we don't even recognize on Earth."

"Ok, that's fine. Except that regardless of Earth's position on the GC, the GC is out there, and whatever Drell has been up to, has caused some concern among one of their Councilors. She's paid us well to come get him and return him to Tarsis before he causes any more trouble." This time Wil holds his own hand up to squelch Pierce's coming rebuttal, "That trouble may be nothing, but could be bad news for the US, or the entire planet. Is that a risk you and your boss are willing to take, just to get a leg up on the Chinese?"

"The short answer, yes," Pierce says, looking from Wil to Maxim and Zephyr. Since returning from dinner the previous night, the two Palorians have forgone the use of their image inducers to the discomfort of General Pierce. Even though it is all they can do to keep possession of said image inducers.

Zephyr clears her throat, "General Pierce, if I may." He nods. "We don't know what Drell has been up to, but he's not as sequestered as you believe. He's been on the run from the GC for cycles and has been left alone until now." She leans forward, "If he doesn't return with us, something or someone worse will come to collect him."

"Is that a threat?" The General asks, scowling.

Maxim tenses, but Zephyr rests her other hand on his forearm, she replies, "Not at all, it's a warning. I understand your bravado; we've seen the, uh, *Wil Calder*; it's a fine-looking ship but would last all of two millitocks against a Peacekeeper vessel. I know also, that you think you know what's out there, from what Wil previously talked to James about, but, and I'm sure"—she nods to Wil—"he'd agree that there was a lot he didn't know then."

"She's not wrong, Pierce," Wil confirms. "When I came back for supplies, I was living on the fringes of the GC scrounging for work, above and below board. I kept to myself and was barely holding it together." He blushes a bit remembering some of his less than savory jobs in those early days of his life as a smuggler.

Before anyone can say anything further, James walks in, "Mind if I borrow Calder?"

General Pierce nods, then turns his attention to the two Palorians, "We can get better acquainted."

"Den Ver ... Hey, this is where Wil is from!" Bennie says as the utility van leaves the Rocky Mountains and foothills beyond for the sprawl of the Denver Metroplex.

"All this time I kind of assumed he was from a farm or maybe a swamp or something equally backwater," Cynthia admits as they slow down to meet the rush hour traffic outside Denver.

"Me too. Or I did, at least. I went through his data store after coming aboard the *Ghost* and saw his old photographs from his days as a... what was he again? A blaster-naught? Solar sailor?" Bennie is tapping the side of his head trying to remember.

"Astronaut," Cynthia offers.

Bennie points at her, "That's it. Yeah, an astronaut." He looks down at his wristcomm, comparing its screen to the navigation system on the dashboard. "Looks like we're gonna have to find a place to crash." He looks out the window at the sun making its way overhead toward the mountains, "Looks like we don't have much daylight left."

Cynthia nods, "Probably a good idea. We can figure out a rescue plan over dinner. Find us a place to stay." She glances at the dash display, "This thing needs to charge too; make sure you find a place we can do that."

Bennie looks at her, his lips forming a thin line. When she looks at him from the corner of her eye, she takes a hand off the controls, slowly extending the claws that she normally keeps sheathed in the ends of her fingers. He quickly turns his attention to his fake children's gaming system, fingers flying over the controls much faster than they would if he were constrained to his wristcomm.

HARD TRUTHS_

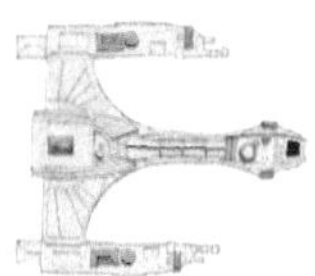

"Dude, what the hell is going on?" Wil demands as the door to the conference room closes behind him and James.

James holds up a hand to silence his friend, motioning for him to follow. It only takes a few minutes to take the elevator up a few levels and walk the short distance to what Wil can only assume is some type of executive dining room. They've said nothing to each other the entire walk.

James breaks the silence, "I'm sorry. I know this blows."

"Are me and my crew in danger?" Wil demands.

An ensign in a crisp Space Operations Command uniform comes over, "Drinks gentlemen?"

"Two grum," Wil snaps, turning back to James.

"Um, I'm sorry, what?" the young ensign says, his nervousness shining like a beacon.

Wil glowers, "Two beers, sorry. Lagers or something. Shoo, go away." The ensign glances at James, who nods, then rushes off out a smaller side door.

Wil looks at his friend. "You can answer my question now."

James inhales deeply, then releases, "I don't think so. I'm not sure."

"What the hell, man?" Wil demands. "Why didn't you just let us be in LA, we coulda tried to finish the job and been on our way."

"Your target is in one of the most secure facilities in America. By the time you hit the ground in LA, he was back here. How did you find him anyway?" James counters.

Wil holds up a finger, "We've broken into better places than this." Leaning forward, a flush creeping up his neck, he extends one more finger. "The *Ghost* has upgraded sensors, allowed us to pinpoint his bio signs from orbit. Those scanners you confiscated were to allow us to zero in."

"You would have never found him then," James counters, "At least not without going back into orbit." He waves his hand, dismissing the issue, "Pierce wants to detain you and your crew. He wants to find the *Ghost* and have Drell and our eggheads reverse engineer it and build our own attack craft fleet. The president is thinking about it but hasn't decided, but Pierce is persistent."

"I thought you had the *Calder*. What do you need with picking apart the *Ghost*?"

The ensign arrives with two pints of some lager or another. Wil snatches his off the table and takes a long drink. His eyes dart to the nervous ensign, his brows arching. The young man rushes away.

"The *Calder* is fine; she's almost ready to launch, but it'll take three more years to build another. Even with all the new tech that Drell has introduced us to, it can't go faster.

It cost more than either of us can even grasp to get the *Calder* built in a year. He says a ship the size of the *Ghost* would be much easier to mass produce."

"But he doesn't actually have plans, so he needs to tear the *Ghost* apart," Wil adds. James nods.

For a minute the two men sit in silence, sipping their beers.

"Let us go. We'll leave Drell, tell the client he's dead. Done and done. You can go back to whatever it is the US is doing to usher in a world war. I'll go back to be being the only human in the GC."

James says nothing, his cheeks turning a darker shade than Wil is used to, "Is it that easy for you? To just walk away from your country? You talk as if you're not human, not American. You'd zip off into space leaving us to our own devices. To hell with Earth?" James's nostrils flare; he's angrier than Wil has ever seen him.

Wil says nothing, thinking about his answer. Finally, he says, "It's not like that. Of course I'm still American, still human. It's just that, out there—" he makes a sweeping gesture toward the ceiling of the dining room. Just then, the door opens, and two officers walk in. James shoots them a look, and the pair backs out the door, letting it swish closed behind them. Wil continues, "Once you see how things are out there, this piddly national stuff just feels silly." He holds up a hand, "I'm not trying to be insulting, but it is. The US and China are still fighting over the same shit they've been fighting over for decades. There are hundreds, thousands, of worlds out there full of life. Full of different races of the same species who all figured out that their world is stronger when they're united." He looks his friend in the eyes, "The Earth will never be welcome in the Galactic Commonwealth until we figure out how to all live together, as humans." He inhales then exhales in a loud sigh, "I don't know the answer here, but I know this"—he waves his arms around—"isn't it."

"Maybe you should have visited the Chinese when you came shopping then," James says, his voice low.

"Maybe I should have," Wil agrees.

Both men sip their drinks in silence until James's comm unit beeps. He pulls it from a uniform pocket, "Go ahead."

"Sir, you wanted to be reminded when it was twenty minutes until the staff meeting," a woman says from the opposite end of the call.

"Roger that, ensign; I'll be there shortly." As he pockets the device, he looks at Wil, "Duty calls. I'll do what I can but think about what I told you." Wil nods, lost in thought.

CHAPTER 14_

GETTING TO KNOW YOU_

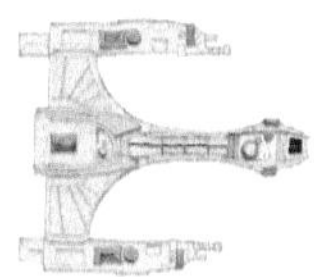

"So, Maxim"—General Pierce looks to Zephyr—"Zephyr, tell me about yourselves. When Wil came back to Earth last, he didn't mention a crew as far as Captain Hawthorne stated in his debrief."

The two Palorians say nothing for a minute, staring at the smug military man. The moment Pierce adjusts his seat, Zephyr answers, "Where to start?" She smiles. "We've been with Wil for a few cycles now. He rescued us from prison after we'd been framed by our superiors, who were hoping to start a minor brushfire war to force several non-aligned sectors to join the GC."

Maxim chimes in, "Don't forget the heist; that was a ton of fun—highlight of that whole thing for me. Well, close second. Using those ship-busters on Janus' forces, that was the highlight." He brings his fists together then pulls them apart opening his fingers, mimicking the explosion for Pierce. "I wish we had more of those."

Zephyr continues, "After that, we did some bounty hunting and privateering for a while. The heist didn't quite go the way it was supposed to." When she sees the confused look on Pierce's face she adds, "Oh, we crushed it as Wil says. The customer, however, was a criminal scum bag—"

"A dead one now," Maxim throws in.

Zephyr nods, "He sold us out, so even after saving the GC from a civil war, we had a price on our heads so big it would take cycles to pay off."

Pierce holds up a hand, "Wait, wait. The three of you stopped a military conspiracy?" Both aliens nod. "Then you became privateers and bounty hunters?" More nodding. "Sounds exciting," Pierce says, tapping the tablet on the table in front of him.

"That's just the start of it," Maxim says, "Then we destroyed a massive warship, a dreadnaught. Do you know what that is?" Pierce nods. "Ok, yeah, so this dreadnaught was actually a giant artificial intelligence from several thousand light years beyond the GC." He looks at Zephyr, "The what of parts?"

"Amalgamation," she offers.

"Right, so the amalgamation of parts had sent this ship to destroy all biological life it encountered, but it bumbled into a massive EM blast from a nebula." He takes a breath.

Zephyr picks up the story, "We sort of accidentally turned it on—"

"Technically, that was Murta," Maxim corrects.

"True. He's dead, too;" she admits then continues, "the dreadnaught realized it couldn't complete its mission alone, so it headed for Borrolo."

"What's a *Borrolo*?" General Pierce asks.

"It's a system, home to a massive long-range sensor platform for deep space observation," Maxim says. "Or at least it was. The Harrith Navy showed up and helped destroy the dreadnaught, but in the process also did considerable damage to the sensor array."

"Who are the Harrith?" Pierce says becoming confused.

Zephyr smiles, it's not a friendly kind of smile, "Oh they're the people we saved from being absorbed into the GC at gun point, way back on our first job with Wil."

Before Pierce can catch his breath Maxim adds, "Oh and don't forget those nasty space monsters that nearly killed us on Glacial." He shudders exaggeratedly, "Nasty things."

Zephyr nods vigorously, "Remember what they did to poor Coorish?"

Maxim grimaces, "So gross. But we discovered the ruins of an ancient civilization, so that was neat."

"True, but Farsight will just mine it for tech, likely turning it all into weapons," Zephyr says.

"We forgot the behemoths," Maxim starts.

"That's right, and our friend the avatar," Zephyr adds.

Pierce holds up both hands, "Are you two kidding me?"

Zephyr leans forward, placing her chin in her hands, "General Pierce, there is so much more out there than you could ever imagine. Whatever your worst fears about outer space are, multiply them by ten."

Maxim grins, "And that's only the stuff the GC has come across." He slaps a hand down on the table, "We forgot to tell him about the Xelurians." He leers at Pierce, "Or as Wil calls them, spider-bears."

Pierce blanches, stands, and heads for the door. As he crosses the threshold Zephyr calls out, "We can talk about the spider-bears later I guess." The door closes.

Maxim turns to his companion, "You know, we may never leave this world."

Zephyr closes her eyes leaning back in the chair, she says just one word, "Bennie."

MR. PRIOR, I PRESUME_

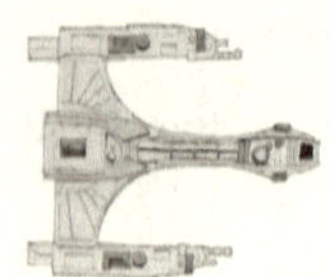

Wᴉʟ ɪs ᴏɴʟʏ ᴀʟᴏɴᴇ in the executive dining room for a minute or so when the door opens. He's about to grab his beer and leave, fearing it's the General or some well-meaning junior officer, or worse yet, Agent Smith or one of his goons.

"Please Captain Calder, sit," Bonson Drell says, taking the seat recently vacated by James Hawthorne.

Wil cocks his head to the side, "I thought you weren't allowed out on your own."

The Multonae man smiles slightly, "So long as I behave, I'm given a modicum of freedom of movement and privacy, particularly within the base. If I tried to leave the building, they'd be all over me in a microtock."

"Lucky you. Why does Grythlorian want you so bad?"

The heavy-set man shakes his head, eyes staring past Wil. He turns his attention to Wil a moment later. "I was her pet scientist for many years. When I left, I was working on what would have been a revolutionary banking algorithm. It would have increased the speed and efficiency of banking all across the GC." He waves dismissively, "The technical details would be way beyond you, but suffice to say, it would have changed a lot of lives in the GC."

Wil leans forward, "So why did you run away? That doesn't sound bad."

"On the face of it, it wasn't. Had I finished it, it would have been rolled out across the galaxy by now. The finance commission would likely have lauded it as the invention of the century."

"Still not seeing the problem," Wil presses.

Drell shrugs, "Oh, it would have also corrupted every banking server it touched, syphoning off fractions of a credit as each transaction synced across the vast spans between systems and sectors of the GC. Grythlorian would have, eventually, been the wealthiest being in the entire commonwealth."

Wil's mouth is hanging open as he stares at the Multonae scientist.

"Are you ok, Captain Calder?" Drell presses.

Wil snaps his mouth shut, then says, "That's some straight up Superman III shit. You know that, right? Have you watched old movies while you've been here? Like really old, seventy-odd years."

"I don't know what you're talking about," Drell says, shaking his head slowly.

"Really? This is wild. That scheme is literally the entire plot of a Superman movie, like the first time they made it a movie series, movie. It had a really popular comedian in it. Nothing? Ok, anyway, so you left and I'm guessing took your work with you?" Drell nods.

Before Wil can say anything else the Multonae man adds, "Captain, I want off this backwater, no offense, dren-hole. I can help you and your crew get out of here, if there is room on your ship for me."

Wil says nothing at first, then opens his mouth to answer, but stops as the door opens, one of agent Smith's men comes in, "Doctor, the General would like to see you."

"According to the data, they're about thirty-five or so kilometers from here." Bennie says from the small kitchenette of their suite. He has the laptop analog on the counter, working it and the gaming tablet at the same time. "Gah, this data network is so slow!" he shouts.

Cynthia, sitting on the couch pressing buttons on the entertainment screen remote, looks up, "That's great. We're close. Now we just need a plan." She reaches into a bag of takeout from a nearby fast-food restaurant, removing a handful of french fries, "These are so good."

"I've been thinking about that," Bennie says, looking up from his screens. "From what I've been able to figure out, they're likely being held at a facility called Space Operations Command. I think it's where Wil worked when he was an astronaut. I don't know what it was like then, but it's apparently the space defense force for this country."

"Just this country? Not the world?" Cynthia asks, settling on a news program.

"Yeah, just this one, the America or whatever," the Brailack says.

"Ok, go on," Cynthia says, half of her attention on Bennie, the other half on the program.

"Well, it's a military installation, at least partly, so we can't just walk in, at least not looking like this." He taps a few keys on his laptop, and he vanishes from sight.

Cynthia blinks rapidly, "Ok, that's cool."

WELL THAT'S A PLAN, I GUESS_

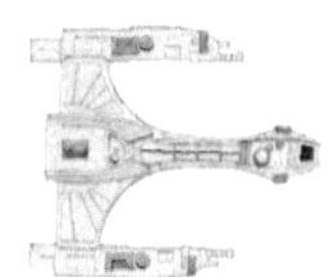

Cynthia stands up and walks over to the kitchenette. She swipes where Bennie has been sitting, connecting with an invisible Brailack. The refrigerator rocks back and forth from an impact.

"What the wurrin, Cynthia!" Bennie's voice shrieks from the vicinity of the fridge. "Invisible, not out of phase you dummy!" The air near the fridge wavers and Bennie is lying on the floor rubbing his head. One eye glaring at Cynthia.

Cynthia rushes over, "Oh, jeez! Sorry little green!" She kneels down next to him, propping him up against her, "You ok?"

He leers up at her, "Better now."

She stands, letting his head hit the floor, "And you ruined it." She walks back to where he had been sitting, her own image inducer on the counter charging.

Rubbing his head Bennie gets back into his seat. He glares at Cynthia then says, "Like Wil would know."

"I can do a lot to you that doesn't include killing you," she growls. After taking a deep breath she adds, "You mentioned a plan before becoming invisible and grossly inappropriate toward a colleague."

The small hacker makes a gesture he's seen Wil make before, then says, "It's elegant in its simplicity. As you've seen, I hacked my image inducer. We hack yours too, and we walk right into that base."

"And?"

"And nothing, we'll be invisible. We walk in, find Wil and the others, and leave." He's waving his hands to emphasize the ease of his plan. "Once inside, I can hack into the base computers and find them. Bip bap boom."

"Bip bap boom?" One ear quirks to the side as she appraises the small hacker.

"Isn't that what Wil says? Bip bap boom."

"Repeating it won't make it right?"

"Shut up."

PART FOUR

CHAPTER 15_

BACON MAKES THE WORLD
GO 'ROUND_

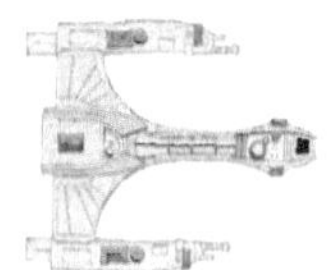

The executive dining room from the night before is much more crowded at breakfast time. Wil, Zephyr, and Maxim are surrounded by senior officers from the *Calder* and base personnel.

Maxim finishes chewing, glancing around at the other tables, their occupants all engaged in conversations of their own. The sight of two blue hued aliens has quickly become normal; rarely do the two Palorians notice even a double take now when they enter a room. "You know, if I have to spend my days locked up on this planet, I could be ok with that so long as there's always bacon."

Wil grunts, "We had bacon back in LA at the hotel."

Maxim picks up another piece, biting, "Sure, but that was what, three or more days ago? I could eat bacon every day." He grins around another bite, "Plus, we've been out of it on the *Ghost* for what? A cycle and change?"

Zephyr is picking at her pancakes, "I don't want to spend my last days here." She looks up at Wil, "No offense."

Wil smiles, slumps in his chair, "None taken. Frankly, I don't either." He looks around, the nearly full dining room. "We can't rule out the others breaking us out."

"He infiltrated a command carrier," Maxim offers, waving a piece of bacon.

Zephyr nods, "I hope they're ok. Not exactly the best equipped for remaining anonymous on a world of primitives." She looks at Wil, smiling.

Wil leans forward, glancing around. He motions for the other two to lean in, "Drell is up to something. He might be a ticket out of here."

"Might?" Maxim whispers, eyebrows raised. He takes a bite of his bacon.

Zephyr looks at her partner, "You trust him?"

"Not as far as I could throw him, and he looks heavy," Maxim replies.

Wil nods, "Exactly. For now, all we can do is keep on keeping on. Pierce doesn't seem interested in hurting us or doing anything other than picking our brains for intel. We can answer their questions and keep playing along a few more days."

The Palorians nod, sitting up straight. Zephyr adds, "Maybe we can start trading information for meals off-base?"

Both men nod smiling.

A few minutes pass, the three *Ghost* crew members eating in silence. Then the lights in the room shift to red and every comm unit in the room beeps. The crew of the *Ghost* look around, not knowing what's going on. Every other table empties quickly, the crew of the *Calder* and base personnel all rushing out the door into the corridor beyond. Agent Smith and a female agent Wil hasn't seen before burst in as the last of the base personnel leave, "Come on."

"What's going on?" Wil asks, standing.

"Come on, now," Smith repeats, his voice making it clear no further information is forthcoming.

Maxim and Zephyr both stand; and after Maxim grabs the plate of bacon, they head for the door, right behind Wil. Smith takes the lead and the female agent falls in behind the threesome.

"Ok, this is probably as close as we can get," Cynthia says. She's parked the utility van a half mile from the main gate of Space Operations Command. From this distance, it looks like a commercial zone no different from any industrialized world. From what Bennie has found on the global network, this facility is responsible for most of the United States' space program, military and civilian.

"We won't have long. I charged both image inducers, but making us invisible takes a lot more power than simply projecting a hard light image," Bennie advises, hopping out of the van, the small backpack he purchased in the hotel giftshop loaded with his laptop and tablet analogs, plus a few other things he has scrounged that might come in handy. The bright blue pack with *DENVER* stenciled across it is bulging with gear.

"How long?" Cynthia asks, joining Bennie at the back of the van.

He shrugs, "No idea, but I'd guess about six tocks."

She whistles, "No kidding on not very long." She grabs the pack she put together from the duffel bags of the rest of the crew. Thankfully, everyone but Bennie had packed a few small arms.

"Well, look at it this way, if we haven't found them in six tocks, they're either dead or no longer here," the Brailack hacker offers. He leans out around the van, "Still clear. We should hurry though, if this place has even halfway competent security, they'll wonder why this vehicle is just sitting here."

Cynthia hands him a pulse pistol, "Keep it set to stun; no need to kill random humans. Especially if we get caught, it might keep them from dissecting us."

"Pleasant thought," he says, taking the pistol and confirming its setting. He nods, taps the control on his image inducer and vanishes. Cynthia does the same. "Remember, the field only extends a centon or two at most around you. If you lose contact with something it'll become visible."

Cynthia nods, then blushes slightly realizing Bennie can't see her, "Right," she adds.

RUNNING TOWARD A CLIFF_

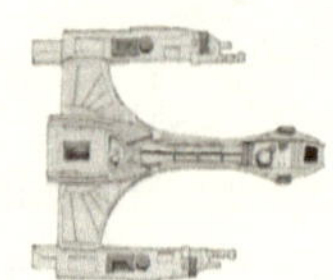

"Ok, I know we practiced and stuff, but this is a little weird," Cynthia says as they walk toward the main gate. Bennie is represented by a bright yellow blob walking next to her. The same translation nanites that allow every GC citizen to understand anything anyone says regardless of language also muck around with the optic nerve allowing one to read any known GC language as if it were their own. Bennie's hacking of the image inducers causes the nanites to do their best to try to show her where he is. According to the small hacker, the effect is imprecise at best.

"You're telling me," the blob moves a bit, then adds, "it was the best I could do with the low-tech crap that passes for gear on this planet. How they've made it into space and started to tinker with faster than light travel is beyond me."

As they approach the gate, Cynthia whispers, "Ok, time to switch to subvocal."

"Confirmed," comes the slightly garbled reply.

The front gate of the sprawling complex is nothing more than three guard shacks straddling two traffic lanes. The two invisible aliens walk right past the guards toward what their research indicated was the main administrative building. One of the guards turns to another, "You gonna request shipboard duty if it launches during your tour?"

Another turns, "Hell yeah, how awesome would that be? Like that Star Trek show."

"The security people always died in that show," the first guard replies.

The observation gallery looking out on the *Wil Calder* is more crowded than the first time Wil was here. Bonson Drell, General Pierce, Maxim, Zephyr, and Agent Smith and his female companion are crowded into the space overlooking the launch bay of the United States' first full-fledged starship.

James Hawthorne walks in, "We'll be ready in twenty, General."

Pierce, who's been staring at Wil since he and his crew arrived, turns to James, "Very good, Captain. We'll update you as things progress down here."

James nods and glances at Wil before turning and leaving the small space.

Zephyr decides the awkward silence has gone on long enough, "Excuse me, General, but what is going on? Agent Smith wasn't very forthcoming when he rushed us away from our breakfast." She glared at the two agents.

Pierce turns from the door James just left toward Zephyr, "I don't make a habit divulging national security issues to aliens, miss." Without another word, he turns his attention fully to the *USS Wil Calder*. Several connecting tubes are being removed by remote armature mechanisms. A gangway retracts as the last few crew men and women rush across.

"Then why are we here?" Maxim wonders aloud.

Without turning to look at the big Palorian, General Pierce says, "To witness the first days of a brave new future for the United States of America, God bless us all." Red strobe lights flash from the corners of the massive cavern the ship is resting in.

The Palorians exchange a look, then turn to Wil, who shrugs.

Bonson Drell leans in toward Zephyr, "The ISS 2 picked up a Chinese ship moving towards it. One of their fast attack craft, about the size of your Ankarran Raptor."

Pierce spins and glares at the Multonae scientist. Drell, for his part, simply returns the stare with an uninterested shrug.

Wil turns on the general, "So what? You're launching your secret warship? Your only secret warship, to do what? Destroy the Chinese ship? Scare them away? Either way, you're tipping your hand and likely to escalate this space race of yours." He turns to Agent Smith and his companion, "Do you two work for him or someone else? He's about to start a war! Surely the Chinese have tested borders before, what did you do then?"

General Pierce makes a low growling noise, and before anyone, especially Wil, can react turns and punches Wil in the stomach eliciting a loud grunt from the ex-astronaut. He turns to Smith, "Let 'em watch the launch, then take 'em back to their quarters. They're to be confined until this is over."

"Yes, sir," Smith replies as General Pierce moves toward the door. As Bonson Drell turns to follow the general, the elder man turns, "Stay here doc, you're not needed right now." Drell bows slightly.

Outside the window, steam is pouring from vents at the back of the US' first starship. A low rumble builds as the ship powers up.

A familiar low thrumming builds. "Repulsor lifts?" Maxim wonders aloud.

Wil straightens up, holding his midsection. He looks at Drell, "Exactly how much tech did you share?"

The scientist shakes his head, "A lot. It was never enough. Every piece of technology I helped them crack the secret of just made them hungrier for more." He gestures to the window, "Repulsor tech was easy. My vessel had it, and it's so ubiquitous in the GC that the components are interchangeable and easily replaceable. It made reverse engineering it easy for them."

"Sounds right," Wil says watching as the ship begins to lift off the massive blocks it has been resting on.

BAD BREAKFAST_

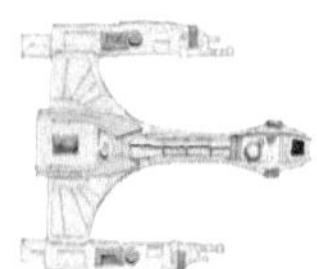

As they follow a man into the building, the lights turn red and an alarm klaxon sounds.

"Oh dren," Bennie sub-vocalizes.

Cynthia looks around. No one is rushing toward them or the door they just walked through, but the man they'd followed into the building has quickened his pace toward an elevator ahead. "This isn't for us. Come on!" They both rush behind the man, pushing themselves into the corners of the lift as it fills with other humans, all sharing the same semi-startled look as the man they'd followed. One of the humans backs toward Cynthia who flattens herself as best she can, sliding to the side of the unsuspecting woman, barely brushing the woman's shoulder. The woman glances at where Cynthia is standing, sees nothing.

"What now?" Bennie asks from his corner of the lift.

"Beats me. We pick a floor. I'm thinking the floor that most folks get off at is a good bet." A minute passes, the lift dropping further and further. Some of the occupants shift around nervously, glancing around at their fellow lift riders. "You didn't," Cynthia says.

"What?"

"Are you insane?" She growls, likely losing some of its impact being subvocalized.

"I don't think breakfast agreed with me," Bennie defends. "Those, what were they called, eggs derelict? I think the sauce wasn't right."

The smell finally hits Cynthia who has to stifle a gag as many of the lift occupants begin holding their noses and looking at each other accusingly. "I told you to stick with things we knew about."

"It sounded good!" he defends as quietly as possible. One occupant turns slightly toward where Bennie is standing.

Before anyone can shuffle too much or potentially discover the invisible lift riders, the lift stops with a ding. As the doors open, several occupants exhale loudly, pushing to get out of the car. As the last occupant leaves, Cynthia rushes to follow, Bennie hot on her heels. The elevator door closes and the two stand in the small elevator bay looking down two corridors.

"Now what?" Bennie asks.

"Let me catch my breath," Cynthia wheezes.

As the USS *Wil Calder* lurches off of the large blocks it has been resting on, the ceiling of the hangar splits lengthwise down the center. The gap letting in more and more daylight as it widens. As the American warship lifts higher, Smith clears his throat, "Time to go."

Wil looks at the man, "Seriously dude. You're ok with this? That ship is about to engage a Chinese ship. In no way will that not start a war. Even if the Chinese back off, the world will not look kindly on America building a warship."

Before Smith can answer, Bonson Drell says, "Actually no, there's no Chinese ship. I mean there are, three at least, but they're still orbiting the moon." When Agent Smith and his companion agent turn, the portly scientist raises a hand palm out. A bright flash of light erupts from his palm, causing both agents to twitch slightly, then collapse. The big man waves his hand frantically, pulling at something mounted to his palm. Tossing the device, smoke coming from it, to the floor. He looks at the stunned Wil and mildly confused Palorians, shrugging. "Your people are rather susceptible to light at just the right frequency and wavelength. They'll be out for at least an hour."

Maxim reaches down, plucking the sidearm from the unconscious agent Smith, "This is finally getting interesting."

Zephyr takes the weapon from Smith's colleague. "Now what?"

"We get the hell out of here, that's what," Wil says. He looks at Drell, "What do you mean, there's no Chinese ship?"

"Oh, that. Yes, well, I've had absolute control over this facility's network since my arrival. My code has taken over not just this base, but the *Wil Calder* as well. The ship they're seeing is a figment. I needed the *Calder* to launch before my software could take control of it. The launch systems were the only ones I could not infiltrate, very frustrating."

"So, what? You've had complete control of this facility since you got here?" Wil demands, "Why now?"

Drell looks at the floor. "I had no way to get off planet." He looks up at Wil, "They dismantled my ship; you have a ship. All I ask is that you drop me off somewhere out of the way."

"Why wouldn't we just hand you over to Grythlorian?" Maxim asks.

Drell blanches, Wil holds up his hand, "There's back story, I haven't filled you in on."

Zephyr and Maxim look at each other, Maxim nods, "I trust you." He turns back to Drell, "Ok, so like Wil said, what now?"

THAT PROBABLY HURT_

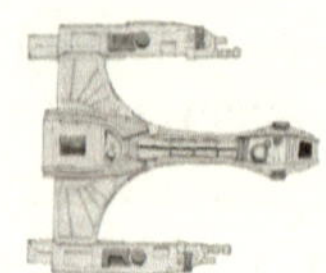

"I FOUND THEM!" Bennie shouts, forgetting to subvocalize for his wristcomm.

"Shh!" Cynthia scolds, she leans out of the small maintenance room they're in to look up and down the corridor. No one is around. She turns back to the glowing shape representing Bennie, "They're alive? Where are they? Can you connect with them?"

Bennie growls, "Yes, looks like two levels below us, no they don't have their wristcomms." He turns toward Cynthia's glowing representation, "Looks like their wristcomms are on this level. There's weird code in this system. Alien code. Like, us, alien."

"What do you mean *alien code?*"

"Which word was confusing?" He preemptively ducks, assuming a fist is coming for him. "I won't know more without digging into it and; one, it might trigger an alarm. Two, we don't have the time. That alert is apparently for a launch. There's a starship here somewhere."

"Great," Cynthia grumbles, "Ok, let's go, did you find a stairwell?"

"I did," Bennie moves toward the door, "This way."

The stairwell is empty, and the door has no security features. Cynthia powers down their image inducers while in the stairwell to try to eek out a few more minutes of concealment later on if needed.

Checking the charge on her pulse pistol, Cynthia asks, "Did you notice any security features that might detect energy weapons?"

Bennie barks a laugh, "These cave people don't have energy weapons. We're good, short of hearing them, no one will know."

"That's good to know."

The corridor outside the observation lounge is deserted. Drell offers, "Most base personnel will be in the command complex."

"Where is that?" Zephyr asks.

"Four levels down, approximately half a kilometer that way." He points then looks at each member of the *Ghost's* crew, "The deepest part of the facility."

From an overhead speaker, General Pierce announces, "The *Calder* has successfully launched and will reach orbit in two minutes." Outside the gallery, the massive hangar doors are closing.

"We must hurry," Drell urges, heading off down the corridor. "I know where your wristcomms are."

"And weapons?" Maxim asks, following.

"I'm afraid not. I've never been given access to the armories and their security systems run on a different server. It was too risky to take it over."

"Probably a good idea, frustrating as it is." Wil says through gritted teeth.

As they near a corner, a servicewoman turns, nearly colliding with Drell. Zephyr doesn't hesitate, shooting the woman in the leg. The officer screams falling to the floor, blood flowing down her pant leg.

"The wurrin?" she says, holding the smoking pistol up to look at it. "Slug throwers?"

Drell looks at her, "What did you think these backwards cavepeople used?"

Zephyr frowns, "I don't know, but dren, slug throwers? How many rounds does this thing hold?" She looks at Wil.

He rubs his chin, "Fifteen? Maybe a few more. I can't recall."

"Good enough"—she looks at Maxim—"conserve ammo." Her mate nods his agreement.

She looks at the woman, conscious and holding the wound. She hasn't said a word other than the surprised shriek when she almost ran into Drell and was subsequently shot. "Will she survive?" She kneels down, "I am sorry. I assumed this weapon was some type of stunner."

Through gritted teeth the servicewoman asks, "You're not going to kill me?"

Zephyr shakes her head, "Not unless you make me. We're leaving. Remain quiet or I'll come back and find you." She leans in close, her purple iris inches from the woman, "That is not an idle threat." The woman nods, still holding her leg, staunching as best she can the flow of blood.

Maxim kneels and wraps a piece of his shirt around the wound, "That will hold you for a bit."

Drell exhales, "May we continue, please?" He resumes his march down the corridor, the elevator in view.

They get a few steps when a much harsher alert klaxon replaces the one that had been droning.

Wil looks over his shoulder and the servicewoman is leaning against the wall near a comm panel, she smirks, Wil groans, putting a hand on Zephyr's pushing it and the gun she's holding down, "Don't."

SIDEWAYS, ALWAYS SIDEWAYS_

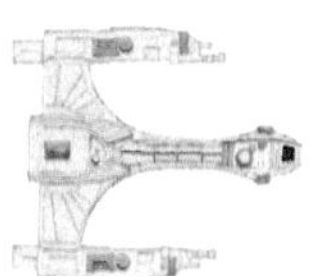

"That can't be good," Bennie says, or rather, sub-vocalizes.

"Agreed."

"Attention all base personnel, intruder alert, repeat intruder alert. Captain Calder and his crew have escaped."

"Well, at least it's not about us," Bennie offers.

The door on the level below then bursts open and two guards enter the stairwell and despite heading down, glance up.

"The fuck?" One says, reaching for his sidearm. The other guard reacts slightly slower than his companion. Both take a stun blast to the chest and drop to the ground twitching.

Bennie looks up at Cynthia, "Nice shooting." He rushes past the two unconscious guards, "One more level."

From above, at least two levels, another door slams open. Bennie looks up at Cynthia nodding, he taps his image inducer. She does the same.

They rush to stay ahead of the guards and hit the landing of the level they want only moments before the first guard rounds the corner of the stairwell right above them. Bennie and Cynthia are standing near the stairs that continue downward. The lead guard opens the door, holding it open as three more rush through. When he turns to follow the other guards, Cynthia and Bennie rush behind him to follow through the door before it closes.

The corridor they walk into is smoky and the sounds of gunfire echo up ahead somewhere.

"Well, this went sideways just about right on time," Wil says turning down a corridor away from the elevator whose control panel is flashing red. "We gotta find stairs, Drell, which way?"

"We must go back that way!" The heavy breathing scientist points back the way they've just come from.

"Of course," Zephyr says.

"What about our wristcomms?" Maxim wonders.

"No time; they're two levels up. We keep going once in the stairs," Wil says.

The group turns and heads back the way they came but stop short only a few yards in as a door opens and two guards emerge, one high, one low, *professionals*, Wil thinks, then shouts, "Back!"

Maxim reacts a split second faster than the guards, putting a round into the shoulder of the guard that went high, driving the other back with two more rounds into the wall.

"Crap!" Wil growls, crab walking back to the nearest corner. He looks at Drell, "Any other surprises at the ready?"

The Multonae man shakes his head, then claps his hands, "Actually —" He pulls a small device out of one of his pockets and taps the screen a few times. With the sound of gunfire as background noise, nothing happens for almost a minute. Wil is about to ask what's supposed to happen, when mist or smoke of some kind pours from the air vents. He looks at Drell, eyebrow quirked. The alien scientist shrugs, "Best I can do. I'm surprised they still work, I installed them shortly after arriving here. It's harmless."

Wil rubs his face as two more shots ring out and a single round hits the wall nearby, "Ok, so those stairs are out, we need options. Other stairwells? Can you override the elevator?" He points to the small hand-held device Drell is clutching.

"Yes, and perhaps," he focuses his attention on the device.

Wil leans forward, "So, yeah this could be better." He hikes a thumb over his shoulder, "He's working on it, but this might be our Alamo."

Maxim looks back briefly before firing a single round, "That had better be a human thing for amazing escape that will be talked about for generations."

"Well, that latter part may apply," Wil says sourly, glancing back at Drell.

Zephyr fires once, "I have three rounds left."

Maxim pauses to think a moment, fires, "Two."

"I've got it, come!" Drell hisses, scooting back down the corridor.

Wil gestures to the two Palorians, who each nod. The guards down the hall have been leapfrogging along the corridor via open doors. Maxim fires both rounds, catching an attacker in the shoulder and midsection. He motions everyone to run. There are more guards behind the one that just fell.

From somewhere further up the corridor gunshots ring out.

Zephyr brings up the rear, firing once when an eager helmeted head peeks out from a doorway.

CHAPTER 16_

GOOSE CHASE_

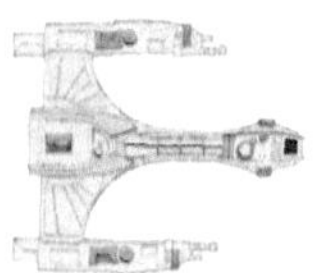

Four more guards enter the corridor from the stairwell Bennie and Cynthia just left. They do so cautiously having found their unconscious coworkers. Bennie and Cynthia are several meters from the doorway when it slams open. Two guards rapidly emerge from the doorway, turning left, two more follow turning right.

"These guys are pros," Cynthia sub-vocalizes.

"Yeah, this ain't good," Bennie agrees. The smoke is swirling around in delicate eddies.

The two guards facing them, tilt their heads, one slowly advances, directly toward the two aliens.

"Uh, is that krebnak coming right towards us?" Bennie points toward the advancing guard, the other keeping watch from the doorway. The other two guards are making their way in the opposite direction.

Cynthia pushes Bennie back, "Move slowly. I think the smoke is defeating your invisibility gadget."

Bennie grunts, "You think?" Before his feline featured companion can react, he disengages his image inducer.

The advancing guard freezes then steps back, "The hell?" is all he gets out before a volley of stun blasts race down the corridor, striking the two nearest guards, dropping them.

Bennie races towards the other two, a sound Cynthia has never heard from him before coming from him as he charges the two guards who've spun to face the green being rushing towards them mouth open wide, arms waving all over. Several more stun blasts erupt from Bennie's pulse pistol, dropping the guards, but not before the furthest one gets off two quick shots from her own pistol. Bennie screeches and falls forward, sliding until he slams against the last guard, now lying unconscious on the floor.

"Dren! Bennie!" Cynthia rushes over to the motionless Brailack. Kneeling down, "You freakishly brave little krebnak, don't be dead." She rolls him over.

"Mouth to mouth might save me," he croaks, an ear-to-ear grin forming on his much paler than normal green face.

"Even near death you're disgustingly inappropriate. I suppose I'd be worried if you weren't." She pokes and prods him until he screeches again. "Found it." She rips open his shirt, a hole in his shoulder is oozing bright red blood. She presses her palm against the wound, causing Bennie to grunt. "Don't be a baby." She pulls a small patch from the pack she's carrying.

A moment after Cynthia applies the patch Bennie looks up, "Oh, shiny." He grins, "That was supposed to be so bad ass and impressive. Until, you know, it wasn't"

Cynthia hoists Bennie up, "Come on tough guy." She turns and continues the way they were heading, toward the now much diminished gun fire.

"We're in a military installation!" Wil shouts as Drell works on his small device, wires connected to the open panel outside the elevator. "We've got maybe two minutes before more guards show up."

"I am well aware of our surroundings, Captain. I've lived here for several years as a prisoner."

"Well, you won't have to worry, you'll be dead if we don't get out of here," Wil retorts, the worry in his voice clear.

"We have very little time before this facility locks down," Zephyr warns.

Drell looks back over his shoulder, "That, at least, is not a worry. By now, my virus is asserting itself throughout the facility."

"Then why can't you control the elevator?" Wil asks.

Drell scowls, "Because my escape wasn't supposed to be this difficult."

Wil sighs, "Sorry it's not going according to the plan you made that you didn't tell us about in advance."

"Wil, we reloaded from those last guards but still don't have many rounds," Maxim warns.

The elevator doors finally open, Drell stands up, "Success!"

Wil grabs the portly alien's shoulder, "Woah there. We're not taking the elevator."

"Wait, what?" Drell says.

Zephyr smiles, "You're finally picking up good tactics." She starts down the corridor toward where Drell has said the other stairwell is.

"We send the elevator up to say, level 2. That'll distract at least some base personnel." He turns to follow Zephyr and Maxim, looking over his shoulder, "Wanna live? Follow us." He doesn't wait.

THE BAND IS (MOSTLY) BACK TOGETHER_

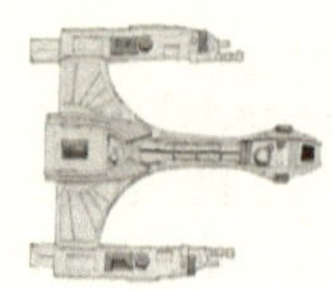

"Why is this facility so damn big?" Cynthia growls, turning a corner, waving her hand to clear the smoke from in front of her face.

"Humans, who knows," Bennie replies.

A door opens just ahead and a service person and someone in a lab coat walk out. The surprise on their faces only register for a second as stun blasts hit them both, sending them to the floor in a heap.

"Any thoughts on their location?" Cynthia asks, kicking the sidearm away from the serviceman.

"Nope. My wristcomm's sensors don't have much range." Bennie looks further down the corridor to a T intersection, "I think they're just ahead to the left."

"Why?"

Bennie points with his good arm, "Gunfire."

Cynthia nods and heads towards the gunfire.

As they round the corner of the intersection, they come upon a group of four base guards, standing behind a pipe and overturned piece of equipment. Cynthia ducks back around the bend, pushing Bennie to the ground.

Bennie makes a groaning-screeching sound, "What the wur—" the indignant Brailack starts, rolling off his injured shoulder to sit up. Two shots impact the wall near the corner, sending chips of concrete raining down on Bennie, who splutters, rolling away from the onslaught.

Cynthia rolls her eyes, attempting to peer beyond the four guards. She spins quickly back around the corner, whispering, "I see them, they're pinned."

Bennie gets to his feet, "Well let's go rescue our useless crewmates." He checks the charge on his pulse pistol and moves toward the intersection. Still holding his injured arm close to his body he steps out into the corridor, "Excuse me?"

The weapons fire dies down, further down the corridor he spots Wil and winks. The four guards turn, weapons coming to bear on the hacker. One of the guards blinks, "Holy shit, is that one of the things from sub-basement nineteen?"

Bennie frowns raising his own pistol and fires, taking down two of the guards. Shots from above his head take the other two.

"You're welcome," Cynthia says from behind him.

"I had them," he grumbles walking past the makeshift barricade. "Should've known you'd be the center of this dren storm," he shouts then looks down at the guard, "sub-basement nineteen?"

Wil leans out of the doorway he's been using as cover, followed by Maxim and a fat Multonae man. Zephyr comes out of a doorway opposite the three men.

Cynthia smiles, "Looks like you at least completed the job. That's refreshing."

Wil smiles as he picks the Tygran woman up and spins her around. "Well, long story. Let's not get killed in this underground base and I'll fill you in." He sits his feline featured girlfriend down, looking at Bennie, "You look like shit."

Maxim walks over to the small hacker, "Still kicking ass and taking names I see." He grins at his small friend. Bennie makes a rude gesture at Wil, who smiles. "This drenhole uses slug throwers."

"Hello, I am Bonson Drell," the Multonae man says, approaching Cynthia, smiling.

"Woah there, Don Juan," Wil says putting a hand on the portly scientist's shoulder. He looks at Cynthia, "You guys came from the stairwell?"

She nods, "Yeah, back that way." She hitches a thumb over her shoulder.

Zephyr says, "More importantly, you brought our weapons I hope?"

She holds up a pistol, "These things are crap—limited number of shots and you have to try to not kill or maim."

Cynthia grins, "Oh yeah, here." She hands her pistol to Zephyr, then takes her pack off her shoulder, reaching in and handing Wil and Maxim a pistol each.

"Thanks, babe," Wil says, checking the charge and adjusting the setting to stun. He gestures, "Lead the way."

Cynthia nods and turns back the way she and Bennie had just come.

Maxim looks down at Bennie, "You look a little pale. I'd be happy to carry you."

Bennie looks up, "I still have bruises from the last time you carried me. I'm a living being not a spare plasma rifle."

"That was months ago; stop being a baby," Maxim quips, making to pick up Bennie like a baby.

"Get away from me you krebnack!" the Brailack hacker shouts, waving Max away with his good hand.

Maxim chuckles, "Very well." He trots off following the others, pressing the very winded Bonson Drell ahead of him.

A DISH BEST SERVED WITH PLASMA ROUNDS_

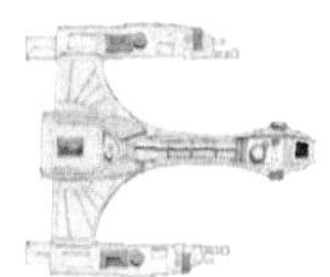

ONCE EVERYONE IS in the stairwell Cynthia says, "So, uh, there's a fairly well-manned checkpoint at the main entrance. What's the plan?"

From several steps below Drell says, "Not to worry. We can take the side door nearest where this staircase exits. My virus has disabled the door monitoring system on every single door in the facility."

"That's handy. Seems rather weird that you didn't have the elevators under your control," Zephyr points out. Wil glances back to the very human looking alien, watching him blush, "An oversight to be sure." He huffs a few times, "Much like the launch systems, there are certain sub systems that were too well protected for me to tamper with. The base, the ship—all hackable. The systems that control things like launching the ship, elevators, the access control system—much harder. Easier to disable the monitoring system than unlock doors." Zephyr nods but says nothing.

"We're here," Cynthia says stopping at the door, a large white *1* stenciled on it.

Wil moves forward, "I'll go out first. I won't attract as much attention." He snaps, "Duh, you four have image inducers."

Cynthia smiles, "We've made a few tweaks to ours." She taps hers at the same time Bennie does, both of them vanish.

Maxim and Zephyr look at each other, then at Wil, Zephyr asks, "Do ours do that?"

As Wil shrugs Bennie says from nowhere, "No, I hacked ours so we could infiltrate the base. You're just gonna have to look like humans." He chuckles.

Zephyr exhales, "Oh well, there're worse things, and it's not for much longer."

"What's that supposed to mean?" Wil says, pushing open the door, looking back at the human version of Zephyr. The door opens to the wide-open space of the airfield. Wil steps out the door, looking left and right before motioning for the others to join him.

"Where to now?" Maxim asks.

Wil points off toward a cluster of hangars. "There, the jet we came in on is over there, probably."

"Probably?" Maxim repeats.

Cynthia's disembodied voice says, "Bennie and I will go ahead and make sure the path is clear."

Everyone nods. In the background sirens are wailing and lights at the tops of poles around the base are flashing red.

"That's not good," Maxim says.

Bonson Drell looks at his wristwatch. *Weird he has a watch* Wil observes. "Phase two must have activated," Drell announces.

Wil stops, "Phase two? Maybe now is a good time for you to explain the extent of your plan."

Zephyr looks around, they're exposed on all sides, thankfully most base personnel seem to be below ground or in buildings now, "Perhaps here isn't the actual best place for that."

Drell, not paying heed to Zephyr explains, "I realized that an opportunity would show itself to escape this drudgery. They keep me on this base, a veritable slave. They finally allowed me to leave the base and visit California, but your arrival cut that short. Do you know I was only there for two days before they dragged me back here?" He wags a finger at no one in particular, "But I knew, I knew that an opportunity would present itself." He looks at Wil, "I made sure I was ready. For every bit of tech they forced me to make, I embedded hidden commands and viruses that they'd never find." He grins wolfishly, "Just in case I needed them."

Wil makes a rolling motion with one hand, "Ok, right, I get it, they treat you like shit, you want to escape."

The portly scientist tuts, "I want revenge."

Wil stares at him, "Meaning?"

"Someone is coming," Cynthia's voice says, startling everyone else.

"I wish I had my wristcomm," Wil grumbles, pulling Drell towards a service building twenty odd meters away.

"Hurry, stay low," Cynthia hisses, "Dren, too late."

Just as a pair of guards is about to turn to face the escapees, a sound draws their attention.

The crew of the *Ghost* let out a collective breath, Cynthia pops back into visibility, "Bennie is doing his best to keep them occupied but take story time on the road." She vanishes before anyone can say anything.

Wil looks at Drell, "Come on, explain yourself on the move." They all set off for the hangars, at least half a kilometer from their current position.

Drell continues his story, "I wanted revenge. Your General Pierce tortured me for every scrap of technological know-how I had. He has to pay. So, when you showed up, I implemented my escape plan." The heavyset man is wheezing from talking and jogging. "The first step was persuading them to launch the *Calder*. That took some doing. My virus began its work several days ago, masking Chinese ship movements and reporting slightly different, slightly more provocative moves."

Cynthia interrupts from wherever she has been keeping pace with the group, "Wait a minute, they named a ship after you?"

Wil smiles, broadly, "Damn right, plus a few dozen schools, and I know for a fact there's at least one statue."

"He's going to be unbearable now," Cynthia sighs. Zephyr nods toward where she thinks Cynthia is.

Drell continues, "Once the *Calder* was launched, my virus could take control and exact my revenge. By now it has cut off communications, taken control of weapons and navigation."

As if waiting for just that moment, the sky opens up and a powerful plasma round slams into the base destroying one of the buildings.

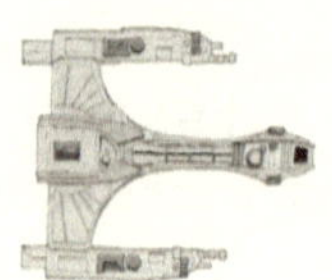

ABOARD THE WIL CALDER_

"Captain, I've got the Chinese ship on sensors, one of their new Qiángdà class ships," Ensign Matthis reports from her station.

James Hawthorne, sitting in the center of the *Wil Calder's* bridge looks at the main display screen then over to the lieutenant manning the communications station, "Lieutenant Baker, hail them."

"Aye sir," the man at James's right says, placing his hand to his ear to cover the audio device there so he can more clearly hear any reply.

Before the lieutenant can update James, an ensign he's not familiar with who is manning one of the auxiliary stations shouts, "I've just lost all computer access."

James looks over his shoulder, first to the ensign, then to the main engineering station closer to the bridge hatch, "Miles, what's up?"

Lieutenant Commander Miles Latham looks up, concerned, "No idea sir, but I'm cut off too." He stands and goes to the auxiliary station, shoving the ensign out of the way, "Yup, locked here too. Anyone else?" he says looking up.

The helmsman, Ensign Gloria Santiago raises both hands, "Uh, I just lost flight control." She looks over her shoulder to James.

"What the hell?" James says. He looks around the bridge, "Answers people, what the fuck is happening to my ship?" He looks at the display, on it the Chinese vessel, "Are they doing this?"

Lieutenant Commander Latham shakes his head, "No way, all

comm systems are shielded and firewalled. Even if they successfully uploaded a virus, the communications and computer systems are separated by two distinct firewalls."

"Sir!" Ensign Santiago shouts, pointing to the screen, "They're gone!" On the primary display the Chinese ship has vanished. The display now shows nothing but stars, the moon off in the far distance, and the curve of Earth in the corner.

"What the hell?" James stands and walks toward the front of the bridge, glancing down at the helm controls, all flashing red. On the main screen, the view is changing, Earth moving to occupy more of the screen.

"Captain! I think the weapons are powering up!" The tactical officer says, stumbling over every other word.

James looks at Lieutenant Commander Latham, "Get down to engineering now." The engineer nods. "If you have to, scram the reactor!" he shouts at the retreating officer as the hatch closes behind him.

SCORCHED EARTH, LITERALLY_

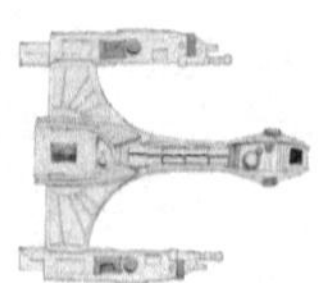

"The hell!?" Wil shouts crouching while continuing to rush toward the hangars.

"Phase two for sure," Drell says, clapping his hands together. Dirt and debris are raining down from the impact nearby.

The hangar complex is a set of five massive hangars, similar to what Wil hid the *Ghost* in when he came back to Earth all those years ago. The hangars form a half circle around the end of a long runway.

"Phase two is attack this facility?" Maxim asks, scanning the hangar they've entered.

Cynthia and Bennie have returned to visibility and joined the others.

"Indeed. The *Wil Calder* will level this entire facility." Another plasma round explodes somewhere, punctuating Drell's statement.

"While we're still here?" Wil asks, his face red.

Drell coughs, "Yes, well, I had assumed I'd be a bit further from the base by now." He looks around the hangar, "There's nothing here." Another explosion rocks the base.

"The next closest hangar is this way," Maxim says.

"But the one with the fast jet is this way," Agent Smith says, his pistol aimed in the general direction of the group. Every pistol in the group snaps up aiming at him. Another explosion, this one nearby, rocks the thin material of the hangar. "The jet we came in is over there," he points towards where another hangar lays beyond the one they're sheltering in.

"The hell are you doing here?" Wil asks, walking towards the agent that's been his shadow and interrogator since their arrival at the Space Operations Command.

The ground trembles again. Smith holds up his free hand, "It's obvious something is going on, the *Calder* is firing on this base. General Pierce is losing his goddamned mind and is trying to get authorization for surface to orbit nukes." He looks around, his eyes falling on Bennie and Cynthia, "You're new." Before anyone can say anything, he continues, "I assume you're trying to get to your ship; I can help." He glances at Bennie again, "That one of the sub-basement nineteen aliens?"

Bennie looks at the human, "What the grolack are you talking about pink skin?"

"Why would you do that?" Zephyr interjects, pushing Bennie backwards a step.

"I'm hoping your ship can stop the *Calder*. Can it?"

Wil shrugs, "I have no idea, I guess there's only—" An impact just outside the hangar buckles the wall nearest the group. Everyone is flung away from the wall, flying in all directions.

Wil sits up, his brown hair caked with dust, "Damn." He rubs his head, wincing as his fingers come away bloody.

Maxim stands up, rubbing his thigh, it's bloody too. "Everyone ok?"

"I'm good," Zephyr calls from almost twenty feet away.

"Good," Cynthia says, sitting up, pushing a piece of hangar wall away.

"Gahhhh," comes from underneath a section of metal, part of the hangar wall.

"Bennie!" Zephyr shouts racing over to their fallen friend. The Brailack hacker is even paler than he was before; his shoulder wound has reopened, and blood is flowing freely. A long cut across the top of his head is oozing blood. Zephyr looks up, "He needs the autodoc." Around him lay the contents of his backpack, mostly smashed electronics.

Agent Smith comes over; he's limping, favoring his left leg. "We really need to go." He looks down at Zephyr cradling the pale green alien that looks suspiciously like the *grays* rumored to be at Area 51 and more secretly in the basement of the building being attacked. Shrugging, he bends down, "He ok? He looks a lot less green."

Maxim walks up, "He will be if we can get him to the *Ghost*. The autodoc will get him patched up. He's tough."

Zephyr stands, cradling Bennie. She looks at Smith, "Lead the way." He turns, and she leans in, "There's much to discuss with you, if we survive this." Her face makes it clear she's deadly serious. Smith swallows and nods, heading toward the far end of the hangar, as yet undamaged by the orbital bombardment.

Entering the hangar next to the one they started in, Wil turns to Smith then the sleek aircraft, "Everyone get aboard. Can you get us cleared? Assuming he's still alive Pierce has to have locked down what's left of this facility."

The disheveled agent looks at Drell, "The orbital defenses are offline; your work, I assume." Drell nods, "Short of small arms from any personnel on the ground, there's nothing that could knock this plane out of the sky."

Maxim and Cynthia both cross their arms, their skepticism clear. Agent Smith holds both hands up, "I know you have no reason to—" Another plasma blast slams into the base, a section of the central building exploding in a massive fireball.

Cynthia turns to Drell, "Is there a reason it seems to be randomly selecting targets?"

Drell nods, "I did not want to take the chance that someone would discover a pre-set firing solution. I instructed my programming to set random targets anywhere on the base property." Another blast rocks the facility, somewhere distant. Drell nods to the sleek jet, "As such we should depart with all due haste, as I cannot guess when this hangar will be targeted."

CHAPTER 17_

FLY LIKE AN EAGLE_

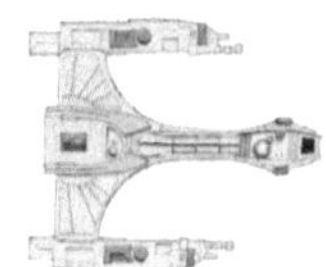

THE HANGAR DOORS PART, and the jet rolls out. From the cockpit, Wil says, "Damn." He looks back into the passenger area, "You really hate Pierce, huh?"

Drell nods slowly, "I would see this country burn."

"Harsh," Cynthia says from the seat nearest the cockpit.

Agent Smith, in the co-pilot's seat says, "This country gave you safe harbor."

"I was blending in, prepared to live out my life as an anonymous human."

Smith scoffs, "How do you think we picked you up? You started raising red flags the moment you set foot here."

"How could I have known how backward this world—"

"Shut up! Both of you," Wil says, pushing the throttle forward, pressing the small sleek jet faster and faster down the runway. A bolt of plasma impacts the hangar they are passing, igniting jet fuel. The jet rocks, lurching sideways, "Shit!" Wil says, fighting to keep the jet moving in the right direction and their speed enough for takeoff. Wil looks at Smith, "You, Agent Smith, are in enemy territory, I suggest you shut up or you'll be flying home without a jet."

"Jason," Smith says, turning to face the front as the jet rises into the air.

Cynthia looks at the human next to Wil, "Is that a swear word I'm not familiar with?" she asks Wil.

"It's my name. Jason Smith," Agent Smith says.

"All these years, you've never told me your name," Bonson Drell says, his voice low.

"You were a prisoner," Smith retorts. "Plus, General Pierce forbade anyone from getting close to you."

The jet banks steeply to the right, then levels off. Wil turns to Smith, "So, what? Pierce ran the show down there, but you're not SOC, *Agent* Smith. Who do you work for?"

"I'm FBI, part of an agreed-on oversight of the SOC program." Smith looks out the cockpit window, "How long until the *Calder* destroys the base?"

Drell shrugs, "I do not know; there are many variables. If Pierce is given authorization to fire on the ship, the *Calder* will defend itself, slowing down the attack. If the ship remains un-molested, I would guess it should take approximately one hour of continued bombardment. The recharge rate of the plasma cannon is the limiting factor."

"Look!" Zephyr shouts, pointing out the small side window. In the distance they can see several contrails streaking from the surface of the SOC base.

"I guess we'll see how good at self-defense your virus is," Maxim says, turning from the window to Drell. "Guess your General was able to get the surface to orbit weapons under control."

Wil presses a button, turning his attention to Drell, "How many are on board the *Calder*? I know James is. He might die!"

Cynthia gets up and puts a hand on Wil's shoulder, "One thing at a time. We get to the *Ghost*, get Bennie in the autodoc, get to orbit, see what's what."

Wil nods. In the back of the plane Bennie groans, "Can you kreb-nacks keep it down?"

Wil turns back to look out the cockpit window. "Glad you're not dead!" he shouts.

Before Bennie can reply, the radio crackles to life, "Sierra Gulf one seven zero one, please identify yourself and your destination."

"Well crap," Will murmurs. He looks to Smith. When the other man does nothing, Wil narrows his eyes.

Smith grabs the mic, "This is Sierra Gulf one seven zero one on priority one assignment out of SOC Colorado, over."

"Sierra Gulf one seven zero one, SOC Colorado airspace is on lockdown. Turn back and head for Centennial Regional."

Smith looks at Wil, who pushes the throttle all the way forward. The drone of the engines increases to a whine.

From the back Maxim asks, "Does this craft have any weapons or countermeasures?"

"Flares is about it," Smith says, then looks over to Wil, then back to the mic in his hand, "Air control, that's a negative, we have precious cargo that's needed in." He lowers the mic, "Where the hell are we going, anyway?"

Wil turns, thinking, "Just say California."

"California, we're needed in California to stop the attack on Colorado."

"Negative Sierra Gulf one seven zero one, you will divert, or we will shoot you down," air traffic control replies.

Smith tosses the mic, "Dumb conversation anyway." He looks at Wil, "Press that button over there; no, the orange one."

"What is it?" Wil asks, finger hovering over the orange button.

"A little something the R&D boys added a few months back." He looks at Bonson Drell and smiles.

BACK ABOARD THE WIL CALDER_

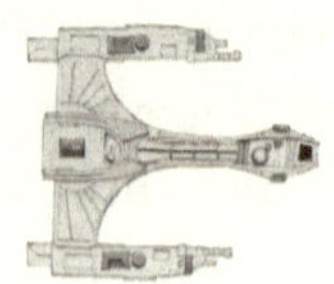

"Oh shit! Sorry sir, it looks like we're targeting SOC Colorado!" The tactical officer announces. James rushes over to the tactical station to look over the shoulder of the lieutenant commander on duty manning the station. While the screens are glitching like the rest of the bridge, they're clear enough to see targeting reticles randomly appearing and disappearing over a zoomed in view of the SOC complex they just left. The massive doors of the hangar they departed now visible, clear of sand and debris that had accumulated after installation.

From deep inside the *Wil Calder,* a loud whine builds up then vanishes. "The plasma cannon," James sighs. On the screen before him a bright orange ball of super-charged plasma races toward the surface of Earth.

"Bridge, engineering," comes from the overhead speaker.

James looks around the tactical station, finding the intercom button, "Go ahead engineering."

"Sir, we're locked out of everything," Chief Laura Polaski says. "The reactor is locked into a diagnostic loop. All the interfaces are frozen."

"Can you reboot it?" James presses. He rubs both palms on his jumpsuit.

"It's not a desktop computer sir, there's no rebooting it. At this point the only option I can think of is manually ejecting the core."

"Shit, that's pretty much a nuclear option."

"Literally and figuratively, since the odds of the core entering the atmosphere are pretty much one hundred percent," the chief engineer confirms.

"Keep working, but prep the manual ejection option, just in case. What about the computer? That's rebootable, right?"

There's a sigh on the other end, "Sort of. I mean it *is* rebootable, but I don't think it'll help. Whatever has control of the ship seems to have completely rewritten the operating system."

"Drell," James hisses.

"Almost certainly," Polaski agrees.

"Chief, we have to do something. We're firing on the SOC." To punctuate James's words, the now familiar whine builds then discharges. On the tactical screen, another orange plasma ball rushes toward the planet.

"Doin' our best, sir," Polaski says, then closes the channel.

James looks down, "Is there a pattern to what we're firing on? That one looked like it was aimed at the firing range."

The tactical officer looks up, "It was, sir. We've fired three times now, and each has been nowhere near the previous. Whatever is controlling the targeting system, it must be randomly selecting targets within the boundaries of the SOC property." He looks up at James, "The upside is, that's a lot of territory, and much of it is empty."

James nods, "Keep trying to bring the weapons under control. Even if you have to start ripping wires out."

The lieutenant commander nods.

IT'S A CHASE!_

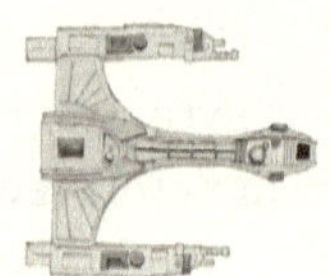

THE WINGS of the sleek private jet deform, sliding back like a fighter jet, while the small craft's engines change pitch. Wil looks at the cockpit displays, "Woah."

Agent Jason Smith nods, "Wait for it."

As if in answer, the pitch of the engines changes again preceded by a thunk as the wings and tail structure of the jet finish their transformations. From below come a series of thuds as something on the underside of the craft shifts into position.

Wil looks down at the speedometer, "Hot damn!" He slaps the dash once, "This is a welcome surprise."

"You're welcome," Bonson Drell says, his chest puffed out.

Before anyone else can respond a warning light on the console blinks, accompanied by a strident beeping.

"Probably not good," Maxim says, leaning over to Zephyr. She nods.

"Uh Wil, what's going on?" Cynthia asks, leaning forward trying to see the displays.

"Radar just picked up two fast movers, likely jets scrambled from somewhere in Utah or Arizona. I'm guessing any jets back at the SOC are toast," Wil replies, eyes never leaving the radar display.

Agent Smith looks from the radar display to Wil, "You got this?"

Wil snaps his head around, "What do you mean, *you got this*? Of course not, we're in a private jet, a fast one to be sure, but not a fighter."

He glances around, "I'm also not a fighter pilot." He looked around, "Do we even have counter measures?"

Smith points to a section of the dashboard, "There."

"Small blessings." He looks out ahead of them, "One upside is we're already closing on CA, another thirty minutes at this speed and we're where we need to be."

"Which is?" Smith presses.

"You'll know when we get there," Wil replies tersely. "No weapons, right?"

"No, this is a VIP transport only. The countermeasures are standard in all private planes these days, especially if they're leaving US airspace."

"Sad state of things," Wil says. He gets up and walks into the passenger space, "Ok, so we've got two fighters inbound. This thing has no weapons, but has countermeasures, should missiles start flying."

"Are they, the countermeasures, very effective?" Maxim asks.

"Not really, I mean they're better than nothing, but likely fifty-fifty on them stopping a missile," Wil says.

"Great, so we die on this backwater planet," Cynthia says then adds, "Sorry, I know it's your home, but still."

Wil holds up a hand, "No need to apologize, this is pretty much the exact scenario that I worried about in coming back. I shoulda just walked away from Grythlorian and her money."

Zephyr nods, "In hindsight, yeah. That's in the past, what now?" She looks around at all the faces looking at her, "You said thirty minutes? That's roughly what? Forty or fifty centocks? How do we survive these fighters?"

From his seat in the cockpit, leaning over to take part in the conversation, Agent Smith offers, "Our best bet is evasion. This jet is fast, so long as the repulsor system is working we can out climb and out maneuver those jets." He glances at the radar display, "Which will be in range in two more minutes."

Wil looks at his crew, "Tighten those seatbelts folks, this will for sure be a shitty ride." He turns and sits back down in the pilot's seat.

Agent Smith looks at him, "You are a good pilot though, right?"

Maxim offers, "He crashes a lot, just saying."

Wil holds his hand up, middle finger extended, but says nothing. Agent Smith grows pale.

Cynthia gets up and moves to the back of the plane looking down at Bennie, his seat as flat as possible. She starts tightening his straps.

The injured hacker stirs, eyes fluttering slightly before opening, "We're gonna die, huh?"

She smiles, "No, Wil has this. When has he ever let us down?"

"You're new here," the Brailack slurs. "There was the time on Pentaxia Seven, then on Xelur, when he froze up. Oh, and that time on Senebia Prime—"

Cynthia presses a finger to Bennie's mouth, "Ok, shush. It was rhetorical."

He groans. She stands up and moves to her seat.

As Cynthia is adjusting her own seatbelt, Zephyr leans toward her, "How's he doing?"

"He's a still a dick, so there's that," Cynthia replies.

Maxim nods, "He's tough; he'll make it."

BROUGHT NOTHING TO A MISSILE FIGHT_

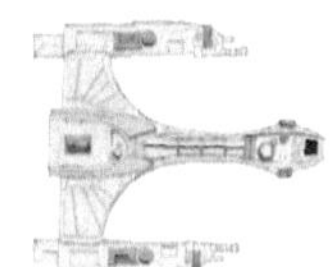

"Here they come," Agent Smith says moments before two F-64 Joint Strike Fighters scream past the front of the jet crossing each other less than half a mile in front of the private jet.

"And here we go!" Wil says pushing the flight controls forward, putting their jet into a steep dive. The engines, in their new configuration, whine loudly.

"I love you!" Maxim shouts to Zephyr

"I know!" She replies over the roar of wind rushing over the fuselage of the jet.

"They're coming around and diving," Smith reports through gritted teeth.

"Captain, I should warn you, the repulsor lift system in this craft is a generation one design," Drell shouts over the roar of the engines.

Wil grunts, then as suddenly as he pushed the controls forward, he yanks them back as hard as he can. The nimble private jet groans as the repulsor lifts lining the bottom of it strain to push the craft out of its dive.

"Uh, the ground is coming up really fast, just sayin'," Smith says, clamping his eyes shut.

"Wuss," Wil says, his grip on the flight controls tight enough to make his knuckles white. Slowly, very slowly the sleek craft's nose rises, pulling out of the dive.

As the jet pulls level barely ten yards from the ground, Wil looks over at Smith, then shouts loud enough for everyone to hear, "If you'll look to our right, Ouray is coming up, though at this speed and altitude you won't see it." He snorts, grinning broadly.

Smith opens his eyes and looks at the radar display, "They're still with us, about half a click out and well above."

"Why is Utah so desolate?" Wil groans as the small private jet roars over the mostly dry ground. He's brought the jet up to about fifty feet from the ground clearing the few small single-story buildings dotting the landscape of eastern Utah.

A new light on the console blinks an angry red, accompanied by an angrier beeping.

"Weapons lock!" Smith shouts, "One has fallen back two clicks."

"Hold on to your butts! Get ready on those countermeasures!" Wil says, pulling the flight controls and throttle back toward him.

The blinking light and angry beeping both turn to solid lights and tones.

"Missiles inbound, two of them," Smith reports. The small jet is rocketing away from the planet. "One thousand meters... nine-fifty... nine hundred..." Smith calls out the distance between the inbound missiles and their small unarmed private jet.

"Get ready," Wil says, eyes glued to the radar display.

"Wil, if we die, I'll haunt you forever!" Bennie croaks from the back row of seats.

"Two hundred meters!" Smith shouts.

"Now!" Wil barks, pushing the flight controls to the right and slightly forward and the throttle all the way forward. The jet begins a tight corkscrew, flying a mile-wide arc back towards the planet below. From the tail section of the jet, several panels slide away revealing canisters that eject from the body of the jet, propelled by explosive charges. Once clear of the corkscrewing craft each canister ignites spreading thin strips of aluminum and a mixture of glass and plastic shreds.

An explosion rocks the small craft, knocking it out its spin. "Hold on!" Wil shouts fighting the controls.

"One more!" Smith shouts. "Hundred meters!" He presses the control on the console, releasing more chaff. "Fifty meters, oh god, this is how I die."

The words barely leave his mouth before the jet banks hard enough that something in the back of the craft breaks. The missile flies past the front of the plane which banks again putting distance between the off-course missile and itself.

"Where are they?" Wil asks, focusing on his flying.

"Fourteen clicks and closing," Smith reports, wiping his brow. "New missile locks! Jesus, I really am going to die surrounded by space aliens!" He turns and looks back at the frowning faces looking back at him, "Sorry, no offense."

"I've got a few more tricks up my sleeve, don't worry," Wil says.

Maxim leans over to Zephyr, "Maybe it's a human thing to put *space* in front of regular words?" His partner shrugs.

"One click," Smith says, then closes his eyes.

"Chaff, now!" Wil calls.

Smith slaps the button again, "That's it; we're dry."

Wil cuts all power to the engines. Smith turns to him, his eyes bugging out, as the jet comes to a stop, floating in midair.

Two explosions rock the jet, the displays on the console blink, then come back online. Two fighter jets race by.

Wil turns to Smith, who looks like he's about to be sick, "Repulsor lifts, remember?" He grins. He pushes the throttle all the way forward, "We've gotta do something about those jets. We can't out fly them forever and even if we did, they're just gonna call in reinforcements, eventually."

From the back of the craft, Bonson Drell raises a hand, "I have an idea."

WHEN IN DOUBT, REVERSE POLARITY_

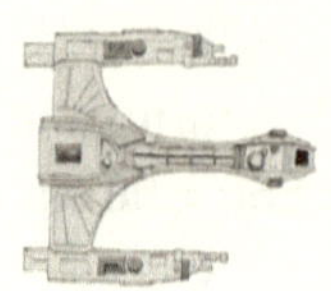

"Do TELL," Maxim says turning to the portly scientist.

"Reverse the polarity of the repulsor lifts," Drell says. When no one says anything he continues, "If we reverse the polarity of the repulsor lifts, they'll overload," he begins. "They'll begin a cascade failure that will emit an electromagnetic pulse."

"Uh, that'll fry this jet's systems," Wil says. He slams the controls to the left and forward, pushing the jet into another corkscrew like dive.

"Under normal circumstances, yes. However, when we were upgrading this craft, I installed shielding to isolate the repulsors from all other systems. That shielding has the added benefit of hardening the systems of this craft." Wil smiles, then Drell adds, "Most of them."

The console beeps; Agent Smith announces, "They've come around and are back on track. No locks yet, but not long I'm sure."

Over the radio a voice says, "Sierra Golf one seven zero one, last chance. I admire your flying, but I'm guessing you're out of chaff, and we're not out of missiles."

Wil glares at the handheld mic attached to the console but says nothing.

Cynthia looks at the Multonae man next to her, "Well, get to it chubby!"

A flush creeps up Drell's cheeks as he drops to his knees and opens a panel set between the rows of seats. "This will take two minutes." He turns and looks toward the cockpit, "In case it needs saying, we won't have the repulsor lifts after this." He turns and gets to work.

"Missile lock!" Smith announces.

Watching Drell work Zephyr looks at Maxim, then Cynthia, "This sucks."

Cynthia nods, "Remember when I was hoping for adventure? I take it back. Right about now, transporting a business tycoon doesn't seem so bad."

Maxim looks at the two women, "I don't know; this is kind of exciting." He grins as the small craft banks, then twists, pushing everyone against their seats. Maxim reaches up to grasp the top of the cramped cabin, bracing himself.

Drell tips over, "I'm trying to work here!"

"I'm trying to keep you alive to work!" Wil retorts!

"Launches!" Agent Smith reports. "Five clicks and closing!"

"Almost done!" Drell shouts, his hands deep inside the open access panel. Something sparks, causing him to flinch. "Done!" He scrambles back into his seat.

"How long?" Wil asks, not looking back.

Drell looks down at the smoking repulsor lift hardware, "Mmm perhaps forty-five microtocks."

"Gotta take the jets too, or they'll just fire more missiles. How many birds do those things carry, anyway?" He turns to Smith as he pulls back on the stick, pushing the small jet on a course directly toward the oncoming missiles and the fighters that launched them.

"Six, I think," Smith says, eyes like saucers, the inbound missiles are visible to the naked eye. "One click," he adds.

From the access panel in the floor, more sparks are arcing into the cabin.

Cynthia looks at Drell, "Is that good?" The scientist shrugs.

"Impact in thirty!" Smith says, eyes glued to the view directly in front of them. The missiles and the fighter jets that fired them are bearing down on the small pleasure craft.

From the access panel, something pops.

The drives of the missiles splutter and go out. The missiles continue forward, arcing down toward the surface. One falls just ahead of the private jet, the other slams into the side of the jet making everyone inside jump. It falls away. The fighters are following their missiles towards the planet below, each very clearly dead in the air as one begins to tip end over end.

"What the hell?" Wil shouts, as the nose of their craft begins to angle towards the surface.

"You must put the jet back into the regular flight mode!" Drell shouts.

Wil looks at the console, "Oh yeah!" He presses the button he'd pressed earlier to engage the repulsor system. As displays begin to come back to life on the console, the grinding and whirring sound they'd heard earlier returns.

"Look!" Smith shouts, pointing out the front of the craft. The two strike fighters are plummeting earthward. Two parachutes drifting lazily away from the doomed fighters.

Wil is about to say something when a light on his console turns green, and the engines restart. He can feel the lift being created by the wings. He swings the plane around back towards California and brings them down to an altitude he hopes will make them harder to spot.

CHAPTER 18_

ALL LIMBS STILL ATTACHED_

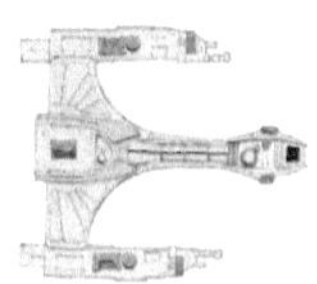

"You landed in the forest?" Agent Smith says as Wil circles the Angeles National Forest in the vicinity of where the *Ghost* is parked.

"What, you thought I'd parked it at a trailer park?" Wil asks, craning to look out the cockpit.

"So, without the repulsor lifts how do we land?" Cynthia asks.

"Yeah, I'm working on that one," Wil says.

"He's going to crash us," Maxim says.

Zephyr nods, "Yeah pretty much."

Drell's eyes go wide, "He's going to do what?"

Smith looks from Wil to the others, then points at Drell, "Yeah, what he said!"

Wil pilots the jet a few miles from where the *Ghost* is parked and pulls back the throttles, bringing the small craft around toward the *Ghost*, as slow as he can get the craft to fly. He turns to look at the passenger compartment, "This is gonna hurt. Someone make sure Bennie doesn't bounce around. Everyone else strap in tight. Well, tighter." He turns to Smith, "You too." Two miles from the *Ghost* he cuts power to the engines, putting the small private jet into a glide.

Maxim gets up and covers Bennie's prone form, gripping the seat backs tightly.

"This thing isn't designed to glide for long," Smith warns.

Wil turns to the special agent, "We're not gonna need long."

"Oh, boy," Smith says, tightening his seatbelt.

The plane is rapidly dropping, scraping sounds coming from below as the plane scrapes the treetops.

"Hold on!" Wil shouts as the nose dips. Seconds later, the right wing catches on a tree, first spinning the jet, then snapping off. As the jet tumbles the other wing and tail section sheer off. It takes another few minutes of tumbling before the remains of the jet come to a stop, rocking back and forth in a fifty-foot-long trench.

"Everyone ok?" Wil asks, rubbing his forehead. He examines the small amount of blood on his fingers. *Less than before at least.*

"I'm good," Cynthia says.

"Good," Zephyr adds.

"I'm good, so is Bennie, more or less," Maxim says.

"I am unharmed," Bonson Drell says.

"I can't believe we survived that," Agent Smith says.

"Ok then, let's go. We gotta get into orbit, see what the hell is going on up there."

"By now, phase three has started," Drell says.

"How many damn phases are there?" Wil asks, exasperated with the portly scientist.

Bonson Drell smiles, "Assuming the General wasn't able to destroy the ship with surface fired nuclear weapons, phase three entails the *Wil Calder* changing orbit to destroy the International Space Station Two before moving on to other SOC Targets across this country."

Once everyone is out of the remains of the jet, they begin walking. Wil turns to Drell, "Call the ship off. If they're still up there, call them off."

The round alien shrugs, "I can't." He meets Wil's glare with his own, "Even if I could"—he holds both hands up—"despite not having any equipment, why would I?"

Wil rushes the portly scientist, grabbing him by the collar slamming him up against a tree. "You bastard, that's one of my best friends up there," he growls.

"I am truly sorry, Captain, but there is nothing I can do. My escape plan once started will run its course until either the ship completes its objectives or is destroyed."

Wil pulls Drell close, their noses almost touching, "If we get up there, and the *Calder* isn't there, you're taking a walk without an EVA suit."

Exhibiting strength no one expects him to have Drell breaks Wil's hold on him, his face flushed. "Look here you troglodyte! I will not be threatened any more by someone from this primitive world! I will not be bullied any more, especially by my intellectual inferiors! I came to this planet to hide from evil leaders and was enslaved for my troubles! I wanted nothing more than to pass my years in solitude, having hopefully saved the GC from a tyrant!"

Wil steps back, taking a deep breath. He looks Drell in the eye, then turns, "Let's go, we're about half a kilometer from the *Ghost*.

Agent Smith who has been watching the argument looks at Zephyr, "You can't let him off the planet. He's a war criminal now."

The Palorian woman looks at the human special agent, who has only recently been her unofficial jailer, "You're not exactly in a position to make demands, Agent Smith. I'm not even certain why you're still with us."

"Where would I go?" The man asks, shocked.

"We could just leave you in these woods," Zephyr replies, turning away.

BRIDGE OF THE WIL CALDER_

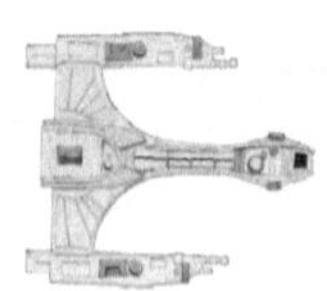

"Sɪʀ, ᴡᴇ'ʀᴇ ᴄʜᴀɴɢɪɴɢ ᴏʀʙɪᴛs!" the helmsman says, her voice much higher than normal.

James, standing over the engineering station, conferring with engineering, looks up. "What? We're breaking orbit?"

The helmsman shakes her head, "No sir, I don't think so, looks like we're just adjusting, moving to a slightly higher orbit." She watches her console intently for a few heartbeats, "Oh my." She turns to James, "It's hard to tell with my console so garbled, but I think we just moved into the same orbit as the ISS 2."

James turns to the bridge hatch, "I'll be in engineering!" He pushes the hatch open and departs.

It takes a few minutes to move from the bridge of the *Wil Calder* in the vessel's superstructure to the main engineering space, tucked in the center of the craft. Walking into the space, James finds chaos. Wires and conduits are littering the space. "Chief!" he shouts.

"I'm busy, goddamnit!" comes the reply from somewhere inside one of the small open service crawlspaces in the wall.

An ensign crouching at the opening to the crawlspace leans in, "Uh ma'am, it's the Captain."

"For crying out loud! One second sir!" the chief engineer shouts, followed by a string of curses and the sounds of someone scooting around inside the tight space. "Gimme a hand, Gilmore!"

Oil and assorted other grime cover Chief Engineer Laura Polaski. "Must be bad if you came down here to tell me."

"We just changed orbits. As far as we can tell, we're in the orbit of ISS 2. I can't imagine that's random."

Before Polaski can reply, the overhead speaker crackles, "Captain! Incoming missiles!"

"Shit," James grumbles, rushing to the wall-mounted intercom he presses a button, "Do we have countermeasures? Can we use the docking thrusters to at least maneuver?"

From the intercom the lieutenant he'd left in charge replies, "No sir. Fully dead stick still, and countermeasures are as locked up as everything else." There's a pause, then "Time to impact five minutes."

James bolts for the hatch he's just come through, "Sorry Laura, keep at it!"

Chief Polaski looks at the hatch, "Like I can do something in five minutes I haven't been able to do for the last hour." She looks around the room, "If you pray, this might not be a bad time to do it."

It takes less time to get back to the bridge than James would have ever thought possible. "Status!" he barks.

"Time to impact forty-five seconds"—the tactical officer announces, then adds—"Wait one."

"We don't have one," James retorts.

The tactical officer looks up, "I think the countermeasures are coming online!" A moment later the staccato buzz of the automated anti-missile system firing thousands of rounds reverberates throughout the hull of the ship.

Everyone on the bridge lets out a loud whoop.

* * *

In engineering, the sound of the antimissile system echoes through the cavernous space. Chief Polaski looks around, then claps her hands, "Ok then! Apocalypse canceled or at least postponed, stop praying and get your asses back to work. We've got a ship to get control of!"

HOME SWEET SPACESHIP_

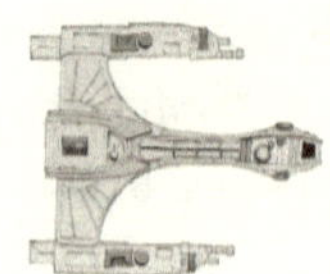

"Damn, I'm glad to see her," Wil says exiting into the clearing the *Ghost* is sitting in. The ship looks just like when they'd left her a week ago. Five thruster packs are sitting near the port landing gear.

"It's kinda ugly," Agent Smith says entering the clearing, next to Maxim.

The tall Palorian looks down at the human, "*It* is a she, and she's the best ship I've ever been on, and she's beautiful."

Smith makes a face, "I'd hate to see the other ships then."

Wil turns, "I'd be offended if your only frame of reference wasn't that tub that's up there,"—he points toward the sky—"raining high energy plasma down on central Colorado." He turns to the *Ghost*, "Let's go." Everyone stops abruptly when one of the anti-personnel blasters drops from the starboard engine nacelle and spins to point right at Wil. "Shit." He takes a step back; the blaster tracks him. Wil looks over his shoulder to Zephyr, who shakes her head, holding up her left arm, the arm that normally has her wristcomm on it.

Cynthia approaches Wil slowly, "I've got mine." Wil nods, and she starts toward the ship. She glances at him as she passes, "Codes?"

The anti-personnel blaster swivels to track Cynthia. She holds up her wristcomm for the sensor on the blaster to register.

"Sierra tango indigo victor"—Wil takes a breath—"Eleven, nineteen, nineteen eighty-six."

Cynthia looks at her wristcomm and enters the specified code.

"Seriously?" Agent Smith asks from the edge of the clearing, standing with the rest of the crew and Bonson Drell.

"Shut up! It's one of my favorite movies," Wil hisses back.

Cynthia turns to look at Wil, the blaster cannon still trained on her, "Uh should it—"

The blaster cannon swivels around to face forward then retracts up into the engine nacelle. The panel it normally sits behind sliding into place.

"Never mind," she says as the cargo ramp lowers.

Wil waves everyone on, "Come on, we've gotta get Bennie patched up and airborne."

Maxim pushes Drell forward, "Come on, let's go." Everyone heads for the ship. Zephyr and Cynthia detour to grab the thruster packs.

The hatch to the bridge opens and Wil, Zephyr, and Cynthia walk in followed by Agent Smith. Wil points to Bennie's station, "You sit there. Don't touch anything."

Walking toward the station Smith looks at Wil, "Not a problem. This is disgusting." He flicks something off the seat, grimacing.

Wil sits down, "Pre-flight started." He looks at one of his consoles, "Looks like ten minutes, reactor was in standby."

Zephyr powers up her station as she sits down, "Acknowledged. I'm scanning for local news streams."

Cynthia takes her seat, "Want me to see if I can reach the *Calder*?"

Wil turns to her, "Yeah, start hailing, see who we reach." He turns and looks at his console again, "Come on baby, warm up fast."

The autodoc beeps as a sensor arm swings over Bennie's prone form on the table. Bonson Drell looks down at the injured Brailack then up at Maxim, standing on the other side of the autodoc. "Curious. Brailack aren't known to be so heroic." The heavyset Multonae is wedged into the small room next to the only other medical bed in the room.

"It's silly to generalize an entire species like that," Maxim says, never taking his eyes off of the seriously injured hacker and good friend. He looks up at Drell, "Much like it's silly and you know, evil to hold an entire nation-state responsible for the crimes of a few." His eyes narrow.

Somewhere deeper inside the ship, the reactor begins its warmup, the subtle vibration in the deck beginning to build.

The bulky scientist shrugs, looking back down at Bennie as the autodoc beeps happily to itself. One of its many arms moves to hover over the gunshot wound in the small hacker's shoulder.

"What was your end goal?" Maxim asks. He gestures at the bulkhead, "With your plan? Blend in with the humans you clearly despise? Steal a craft and escape this system?"

Drell looks back to Maxim. "These people are primitives, but yes my plan was to get lost in the crowd. I've learned much since my arrival and have had time to plan. I have funds in several bank accounts around the world and identities set up in just as many countries." Maxim nods appreciatively. Drell continues, "I just wanted to escape. I fled one power-mad tyrant only to find myself in the clutches of another."

PART FIVE

CHAPTER 19_

NIGHTLY NEWS_

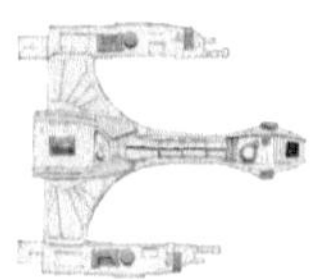

"I've figured out the local broadcasts," Cynthia says. She taps a control and the overhead speakers come to life.

"—to the White House the attack on Colorado is a weapons test gone horribly wrong, Steve."

Another voice, Steve probably, says, "Well that's not good, Barb. The loss of life is expected to be tremendous."

Barb adds, "According to a spokesperson from the SOC, the facility in Colorado, in what used to be Buckley Airforce Base, is almost entirely destroyed. As yet, no one from the SOC knows what's wrong with the ship or why it's attacking the US. We can only hope that whatever is causing the malfunction doesn't cause the ship to attack other states or military installations."

"Indeed; thanks Barb," Steve says. "For those just joining us, an experimental starship has launched from the SOC facility in Colorado a few hours ago and shortly after take-off began attacking Earth. Specifically, it seems to have leveled the SOC facility, killing countless people. The facility in Colorado as you may know, is the main headquarters of the SOC."

"Shut it off," Wil says, waving a hand. "Ok, at least we know James and the *Calder* are still up there." He turns back to Cynthia, "Speaking of, anything?"

"No. But that could be Drell's virus or our gear just not being able to communicate with Earth tech," she shrugs.

Smith raises a hand, "Uh, do you need the radio frequency for the *Calder*? Is that what you mean?"

Wil turns in his chair, "Yeah, you have it?"

Smith nods and walks over to Cynthia. He looks at her console then to her, "Yeah I don't know what any of this is. Is there a place to control the radio frequency?"

"Radio frequency?" Cynthia asks, glancing to Wil.

Wil scratches his ear, "The uh, comm frequency, the signal wavelength of the transmission you just picked up." He snaps his fingers, looks at Smith smiling.

Cynthia nods, "Oh, ok, I think I get it." She taps Smith to bring his attention back to her console. "Look here. This is the frequency range of the transmission we just listened to." Smith nods and she points to a section of the console, "This lets us change the frequency."

"Oh, I get it!" Smith says, tapping the control, adjusting the comm system's transceiver.

An indicator on the console turns green. Cynthia turns to Wil and nods.

"This is Captain Wil Calder to, well, the *Wil Calder*, do you read? James buddy, you there?" Nothing but static.

Zephyr calls out, "I've got two more of those fighters on sensors. Wait, four now." She looks at Wil.

Wil turns back to his station and flight controls, "Going to have to be good enough." He looks over his shoulder, "We're taking off; tell Max I need him up here."

Cynthia nods, then looks at Smith, "You better buckle up."

From the overhead speaker Cynthia says, "Max, we're about to lift off. Wil wants you up here, at least four hostiles."

Maxim looks at the ceiling, catches himself and shakes his head, "Be right there." He looks at Drell, "Come on, you can try to be useful up on the bridge."

The portly scientist plants his palms on his hips, "What for? Aren't we just leaving?"

Maxim pokes Drell in the chest, "We're doing whatever the Captain says we're doing. If I had to guess, we're going to try to undo the mess you've made." He pivots and walks past Drell. Without looking back he shouts, "Get a move on Professor!"

"I'm not a—"

"Move!" Maxim shoves the portly man forward as the deck plates begin to vibrate.

NEGATIVE GHOST RIDER, PATTERN IS FULL_

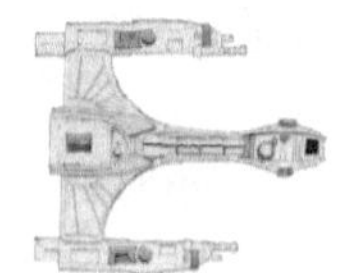

"Oᴋ Doᴄ, we tried to reach the *Calder* but got nothing but static. That your doing?" He glares as he glances over his shoulder to the heavyset Multonae who's clutching a handhold near the bridge entry hatch.

"Well, that wasn't something I specifically coded for, but my virus was designed to be adaptive. I never assumed it would exist for this long, so it likely has far exceeded any programming I gave it. I would assume that it decided that comms were a potential attack vector and disabled them."

"Bennie would love to sit down and geek out with you," Zephyr observes then adds, "We're being targeted. I think."

"You think?" Wil asks, pushing the controls for the repulsor lifts a bit more, urging the ship higher. He keeps an eye on power levels, as the reactor is still not at one hundred percent. The camouflage netting covering the ship flutters as the *Ghost* rises, finally slipping off completely.

"Well, we're being hit by energy waves that aren't weapons, but aren't anything I've ever seen before."

"Radar," Agent Smith offers. "Targeting radar."

"That's a funny word," Maxim offers, not looking up from his displays.

"What about the stealth systems?" Wil asks, twisting his flight controls, banking the ship away from the inbound fighter craft. He's using the repulsor lifts to move the ship, slowly, by tilting it this way and that. The reactor is not powerful enough yet to engage the atmospheric engines. An indicator on his console reminds him that the port power coupler is damaged. He pushes a button switching over to the secondary.

"Disengaged, not enough power," Zephyr answers.

"Shields?" Wil presses.

"Almost. We've got about half power right now." She consults a display, "Looks like ten more centocks, though that depends on what else we need power for before the reactor is at full power. What we have now is from the capacitors."

"Your shields, even at half power, should be more than sufficient to keep conventional weapons from damaging your ship," Drell offers.

Agent Smith, still seated at Bennie's console, is looking around the bridge taking this all in, "We can't just warp out of here or something?"

"This isn't Star Trek, you moron," Wil snaps, not even bothering to look at the other human.

"They're talking to us," Cynthia announces, pressing a control.

From the overhead speakers a stern voice says, "Unidentified craft, you will adjust your heading and follow us to an airfield to land. Failure to comply will result in the use of lethal force."

Wil nods to Cynthia then looks at the ceiling, "Sorry guys, we don't have time to play with you. We're trying to save the country, maybe the world. You're just going to have to do what you have to do." He makes a slashing motion then turns to Drell, "Swap with Smith and make yourself useful."

"What should I do?" Smith says getting up and moving to allow Bonson Drell to squeeze into the seat at Bennie's station.

"Keep out of the way"—Wil says, looking at the other man—"unless you know your way around the computer systems of an Ankarran Raptor."

Smith just glares at Wil and grabs the handhold that Drell recently vacated.

"They're firing," Maxim reports. On the small tactical display near the lower right corner of the main display, two missiles are streaking towards the *Ghost*. "Impact in thirty microtocks."

"Ignore them, but if the fighters get too close, give them some warning shots. Try not to kill them; they're just doing their jobs."

Drell is busily working at one of the consoles, mumbling to himself. He looks up briefly, "Cynthia, is it? I'll need transceiver access."

The Tygran woman's eye narrow; she taps a control, "Done."

The ship lurches slightly, then rights itself.

"Thank you." He nods, then continues, "Captain, I am attempting to access the *Wil Calder*, but am not sure I will be successful. I did not leave any backdoors."

Smith glares at the man, "Why the hell not? You didn't think you might need to call off your monster virus?"

"I did not. I assumed, and still assume, that something will destroy the *Calder*. My goal was to use the ruin of America to hide and flee to a less violent country. Sweden looked interesting." He shrugs, "A crippled America would only help my escape."

"You're the worst," Smith grumbles.

"Reactor is at eighty percent!" Wil announces, working the controls. "Hold on!" He presses the button that engages the atmospheric engines. The boom from the back of the ship and g-forces that accompany it are welcome sensations to the crew and exactly the opposite for their guests. The *Ghost* accelerates away, leaving the attacking fighters flatfooted for a moment.

CATCH ME IF YOU CAN_

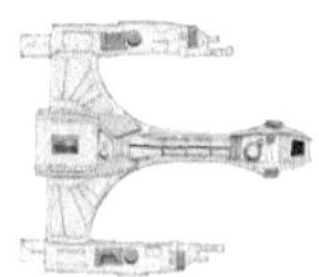

"WHAT, THE, HELL..." Smith says through gritted teeth, his body pressed against the bridge hatch.

Bonson Drell, clutching the sides of the console before him says, "I'd forgotten how powerful these Ankarran atmospheric engines are."

"We're being targeted again. Looks like surface weapons installations," Maxim announces.

Wil glances at one of his displays, "Shit, I wasn't looking, we're heading over Nevada."

"Groom lake has been significantly upgraded," Smith warns. He continues, "It's backup SOC command. Plus, with the exception of Drell here, still where the other weird stuff is kept."

Drell turns to Smith, "No offense taken."

"Launches," Maxim says, his voice calm as ever.

"I'd be more concerned with these weapons, Captain," Drell warns. "What little I could discover about this facility showed that it is very well protected."

"Hold on!" Wil shouts, tipping the *Ghost* on its wing, letting the repulsor lifts, that are still needed to maintain atmospheric flight, push the ship further from its previous course.

"Two more missiles, wait, four. Four new missiles inbound now. Six total," Maxim announces then adds, "Fighters too! Just picked up four of them; they'll be in engagement range shortly, assuming it's the same as those other jets."

"Weapons free," Wil says, then adds, "Remember, try to not kill them, but don't hold back if you have no options."

"These fighters are different," Zephyr says. She looks up from her console, then swipes to put what she's seeing in a window on the main display.

"Oh, Tigersharks," Smith says, his eyes wide staring at the image on the screen. Cynthia reaches over and pokes him in the side, and he adds, "Oh, experimental, based on the stuff Drell has been sharing. They use repulsor lifts and ramjet thrusters. They're at least three times faster than conventional jets." He looks around the bridge, "Meant to defend the country from threats in the atmosphere or orbit."

"So, they can fly in space?" Wil asks. "Great." He slams the flight controls over suddenly, an explosion nearby rocks the ship slightly. "Max?"

"Sorry, had to give the computer some new parameters for such primitive ordnance." He looks at Wil, "No offense." The sound of the forward blaster cannon firing rings through the hull. Wil assumes the engine nacelle mounted blasters are also firing.

The ship shakes and something over Maxim's head erupts in sparks. Wil yanks the flight controls hard over then forward, pushing the *Ghost* into a dive.

"More missile launches," Maxim warns. "Plus, those fighters aren't giving up." The ship shakes again as more of their weapons fire impacts the ship's shields.

Wil pulls the controls back, "Hold on!"

"He says that a lot, huh?" Smith whispers to Cynthia, who nods.

"Time to get out of the fresh air," Wil says. The ship shakes again, something starts to smoke.

At full power the *Ghosts* engines can push her up out of the atmosphere in a matter of minutes. At slightly less than full power, it takes a bit longer.

One of the surface fired missiles catches the ship, exploding against the shields.

"Aft shields are down to twenty percent," Zephyr announces. "Those warheads are powerful."

"Releasing countermeasures," Maxim announces. "That should keep them off us until we clear atmo." He looks at his display, "Fighters are still with us. Sensors are picking up changes in their power plant, must be switching over to nonatmospheric flight mode."

"Holler the moment their momentum dips. We lose some thrust when we switch over, it's gotta be more pronounced with those first gen fighters."

"Now!" Maxim shouts. Wil presses a few buttons, pulls the throttle back to its neutral position. The roar of the atmospheric engines dies out. Wil sees an indicator near the throttle shift from yellow to green and slams the throttles all the way forward again.

"Find the *Calder*," Wil orders, as the *Ghost* leaves the atmosphere behind. He looks over his shoulder, "Can you raise those fighters?"

"I'll try. Smith, help me find the right... whatsit, radio frequency."

Smith leaves his handhold and moves to stand over Cynthia. A moment later, "Ok, I think you're broadcasting on a channel that all SOC craft are listening on."

"Fighters, this is the *Ghost*, the non-terrestrial spacecraft you've pursued into orbit. We're not a threat, we're here to help stop the *Calder* before it destroys more of the country. Stand down."

"Wil, I've got the *Calder*, it looks like it's moved a few hundred miles from, where were we? Colorado, yeah. It's moved on, still firing at the surface," Zephyr reports, then adds, "Oh no. I'm seeing a debris field where the computer estimates that space station was." She looks up at Wil, her eyes telling him the rest of the story.

The main display updates showing the *Calder* and the line of destruction it is stitching across the country from Colorado to somewhere in Kansas. Off to the side of the *Wil Calder*, a cloud of metallic debris is expanding.

"That's McConnell Airforce Base!" Smith shouts looking at the smoking ruins on the screen.

NOW IT'S A REAL FIGHT!_

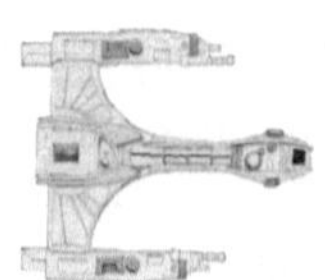

"I'VE GOT MULTIPLE CONTACTS," Zephyr announces. On the main display, the *Wil Calder* is in the middle of a swarm of other craft.

"What the hell?" Wil asks, leaning forward in his seat.

"Defenders from the ISS 2," Smith says. "They won't last long. Looks like the Tigersharks are moving in that direction too."

"I'm also detecting several inbound missiles from the surface," Zephyr adds. She looks at Wil, "I'm picking up radiological signatures."

"It would appear General Pierce or someone else has finally gotten authorization to attempt to destroy the *Calder*, with more serious weapons," Bonson Drell says. He plucks something from near the console and drops it on the deck next to where he is sitting.

"Max, target the missiles," Wil says, pushing the sub-light engines to drive the *Ghost* between the *Wil Calder* and the angry swarm of defenders.

"What purpose could those things serve?" Cynthia asks, nodding toward the screen where several dozen small one-man pods are flitting around the much larger warship.

Agent Smith turns to her, "Well, they weren't meant to fight a cruiser, for one thing. They've mostly been used to interdict cargo movers and the occasional Chinese frigate that comes too close to US territory." He looks at the screen just as one of the small pods is ripped to shreds by railgun fire, "They must be getting desperate down there." He sighs and adds, "Plus, they have nowhere to go, the ISS 2 is gone."

The *Ghost* flies between the *Calder* and the attacking pods, "Cyn, can you hail those pods? Warn them off. They can regroup near the shipyard."

Agent Smith leans over to help the Tygran woman identify the correct comm frequency. Wil can hear them talking to each other, then can hear Smith, "Attention US Space Command forces currently engaging the *USS Wil Calder,* stand down. This is Special Agent Jason Smith, FBI, I'm aboard the, uh, other ship, we'll try to stop the *Calder.* You're no match for her."

From the overhead speakers, "Smith? You traitorous bastard! You're aboard the enemy ship?" It's General Pierce.

"General, Captain Calder and his crew are trying to help. They're going to try to—"

"It doesn't matter what they're going to try to do. This is United States business," Pierce interrupts. "Get that turncoat to stand down and leave this to us." The General sounds frantic.

Wil turns to Cynthia and Smith, holding up a hand, "General, you're out of your depth here. That ship is under the control of a virus that is hell-bent on destroying as much of the US surface military presence as possible. I'd say I'm glad you're not dead, but well, I'm not. However, this is a job for us, not you."

"Calder, you stand down right now goddamnit! This doesn't concern you! The United States can take care of itself!"

"The hell it doesn't, you warmongering prick!" Wil shouts at the ceiling. "That's my best friend over there, helpless while his ship rains death down on the country, and you're happy to try to just destroy the ship, crew and all, from the safety of your little bunker. This is your mess and you'll hang for it, but right now I don't have time to deal with your dumb ass!"

Maxim whispers, "Missiles locked on, they're almost in range."

"Fire," Wil whispers back then turns back to the ceiling, "General Pierce, this is the only warning you're going to get. Let us handle the *Calder.*" He makes a slicing motion with his hand.

"Channel closed," Cynthia says, then glances at Smith. The human man looks at her but says nothing.

From the bottom of the main display, two small missiles emerge heading for the planet below. Two faint pinpoints of light are just becoming clear as the nuclear missiles leave the atmosphere.

"Brace," Maxim warns just before two massive blossoms of light replace the two human missiles. The main display dims, then returns to normal. "Hope your people have EMP shielding," Maxim adds.

"Not really. But not our problem," Wil says, adjusting their course. He glances at Maxim then to Zephyr, "Keep an eye out for any more nukes." Both Palorians nod.

"Let's go convince some space pod jockies that this isn't their fight."

CHAPTER 20_

MISSILES & AWKWARD CONVERSATIONS_

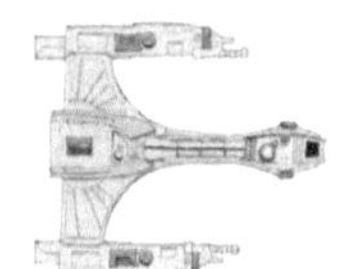

"Two pods are retreating," Zephyr says, while on the main display another is hit by a blaster bolt from the *Ghost*, sending it end over end in the general direction of the moon.

"Keep an eye on that one, we may need to lend a hand," Wil says as one of the Tigersharks races past the *Ghost* strafing the *Wil Calder*.

Smith leans over to Cynthia, "Send the tracking data to the shipyard; they can dispatch a retrieval team." She nods.

"Good call," Wil says, glancing over his shoulder. He turns to the Multonae man in Bennie's station, "Ok Drell, how do we stop the *Calder?*" Wil asks as the USS *Wil Calder* gets larger on the main display.

"I've had no luck establishing contact, I'm afraid," the portly scientist says. He turns to look from Wil to the main display. "Short of destroying the ship, the only other way to stop it will be to remove its ability to attack."

"Like pulling the quills off an agrot," Maxim says. When Wil turns to him, eyebrows arched, the big Palorian continues, "Popular pastime on Palor—"

"For boys," Zephyr mumbles loud enough for everyone to hear.

Maxim looks at his mate, then continues, "Yes, anyway, you pull the quills off an Agrot, and it's harmless. They are fun pets for youngsters."

"So, destroy the weapons," Wil surmises from the story. Maxim nods.

"Wil, the *Calder* has the latest gen weapons systems: rail guns and antimatter warhead missiles, plus a directed plasma beam in the forward section," Agent Smith advises.

Wil nods and turns to Maxim, "got this?"

The big Palorian nods, "Yeah, let's do this."

Wil puts his hands out in front of him interlocking his fingers, palms out. "Ok everyone, grab on to something." He can hear Agent Smith groan behind him.

"They're targeting us," Zephyr announces as the *Ghost* closes the distance between it and the *Wil Calder*. Several of the large turrets swing around to take aim at the smaller Ankarran Raptor moving into attack position. The smaller anti-missile rail guns also begin tracking the smaller craft.

Wil eases the *Ghost* to the side, moving just enough that the turrets have to keep tracking, until Maxim alerts him, "Go." He adjusts the angle of attack then pushes the throttle forward. Throughout the ship, the sound of the engine nacelle mounted blasters reverberates, echoing through corridors. On the main display, bright green energy bolts rake the side of the larger ship, impacting on the hull and the turrets lining the side of the massive ship. One turret explodes, the other deforms. The turret over the bridge barks as well, stitching a line across the *Calder's* hull.

The *Ghost* shakes, the sound of thousands of small impacts ring throughout the bridge, sparks erupt from several conduits. Something near Bennie's station explodes, raining sparks on Bonson Drell causing him to shriek. Wil brings the *Ghost* away from the *Calder*. On the main display thousands of bright streaks stream past the ship.

"Goddamn rail guns," Wil hisses, looking at Drell, "You ok?" The Multonae man nods. Wil says, "I'm going to bring us around for another pass, Max you ready?"

"Ye—Missile launches!" Maxim shouts!

"Crap!" Wil pushes the controls hard over, "Antimatter?" He glances at Zephyr, she nods. He growls, "We can't let those things explode anywhere near the planet." On the main display, the moon is growing larger.

"Uh, are you going to try to blow up the moon?" Smith asks.

"Better idea?" Wil retorts.

"Uh, no, but remember the Chinese have set up shop on the moon, if they haven't already decided to attack, that'll certainly do it."

"Hold steady," Maxim says, working his console. The main display switches to an aft view, with two missiles rapidly closing. From the top of the image a string of red plasma bolts lance out toward the oncoming missiles. The twin explosions look like new suns, washing out the display, forcing everyone to shield their eyes.

Wil doesn't waste any time, bringing the ship around toward the *Wil Calder* which has turned its primary weapon back toward earth.

Cynthia points at the display, "At least it's single minded."

Wil looks back at the feline-featured woman, "That's why I love you, so optimistic."

Cynthia turns to Wil, "Did you just say—"

"You love her?" Zephyr asks.

"About time," Maxim says.

A flush creeps up Wil's neck, "I mean, well..." he stammers.

The fine hair covering Cynthia's face stands on end, what Wil has come to realize is blushing for Tygrans. She stares at him.

"Well, this is awkward," Agent Smith says looking from one member of the crew to the other.

Bonson Drell exhales loudly, "Seriously?"

Zephyr glares, "Shut up, you; this is a big deal."

Wil turns back to face the main display, "Max take out those missiles."

"Scanning!" the big man says, grinning ear to ear.

"Looks like it's moved on to Missouri," Agent Smith observes, glancing between Wil and Cynthia until the Tygran woman finally growls at him to stop.

PLUCKING QUILLS FROM AN AGROT_

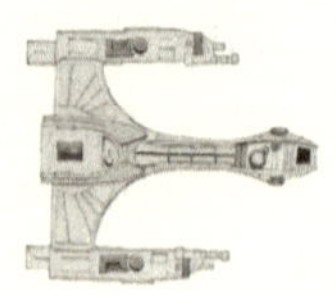

"Locked on to the missile racks, firing," Maxim says as the *Ghost* moves in to make another attack run on the *Wil Calder*. As the missiles streak away from the Ankarran warship, blaster bolts lance out tracing a line toward the next set of rail gun turrets. Depleted uranium slugs rain against the hull like a hailstorm. The shields are proving ineffective against the physical rounds. Several alarms sound from various consoles.

"Shields are barely slowing those rounds down," Zephyr announces as a decompression alarm sounds.

The hailstorm comes to a sudden end. "Last turret destroyed," Maxim announces with a smile. "Missile racks also taken out."

"Good work!" Wil congratulates, then grunts as something impacts the shields throwing the ship sideways. The lights on the bridge flicker as do the main and secondary displays.

"That was a direct hit from the *Calder's* main weapon. Aft shields down to three percent," Zephyr announces.

"Can we take that thing out?" Wil looks at Drell, who shakes his head.

"The plasma cannon is tied to the main reactor. Not an ideal solution but given the primitive technologies available, it was the best I could do. It's possible to destroy the firing mechanism, but the risk of cascade failure is quite high," the scientist explains. "You'd be better off staying out of its firing arc."

"Ok, ideas?" Wil asks, bringing the *Ghost* around and out of the firing range of the *Wil Calder*. The vessel immediately resumes firing toward the surface when the smaller warship moves away. Wil adjusts course and brings the ship back into range of the powerful weapon, dodging fire as best he can. "I can't keep this up forever."

"Take out the thrusters," Drell offers. "My virus has no contingency for being denied its goal." When everyone stares blankly at him, he explains, "The virus doesn't have a failsafe mode. If it can't carry out its mission, it will stop. Without thrusters and a minor nudge, the ship will drift out of firing range of the planet and the virus will simply stop."

"That sounds like a plan," Wil says, adjusting course. The *Ghost* rattles as a plasma blast strikes the starboard shields.

The *Ghost* moves in behind the *Wil Calder* which seems focused on firing on the planet. A single missile leaps from the bottom of the main display. It takes only a few seconds to close the distance between the two ships and after a brief explosion the drive cones of the *Calder* are dark and severely deformed.

With the *Calder* powerless to do anything more than maneuver, the *Ghost* moves in. Wil deploys the landing gear while bringing the *Ghost* in underneath the much larger ship.

"Learned this from Buck Rogers." Wil says, not taking his eyes off the main display. A window showing a camera view from the underside of the ship.

The landing gear make contact with the hull of the *Calder* and with the thrusters the smaller ship nudges the larger out of firing range of the surface of Earth. Once they are sure the *Calder* can't keep firing on Earth, the *Ghost* moves of, her landing gear retracting.

Cynthia spins, "The *Calder* is hailing us!"

Wil turns to Drell who shrugs, "As I said, I did not include any guidance for this eventuality, so I can't say what the virus will do, but I assume it shut down entirely. It can no longer accomplish its goals and so has no reason to continue."

"On screen," Wil says.

The main display switches to show an extremely disheveled James Hawthorne, Captain of the *Wil Calder*. "Wil, Jesus that was some damn nice flying! Is everyone ok over there? We saw the rail guns chewing you up." Hawthorne looks haggard.

Wil smiles and leans forward, "It's good to see you man. Yeah, we're all good over here, nothing we can't repair. What about you all? Drell says the virus should be shut down now, you likely have full control of the ship. Such as it is."

"What's left of it, yeah," James looks off camera and nods, then turns back to Wil, "Did you have to almost destroy the *Calder*?"

"That or let Pierce keep flinging nukes at you," Wil beams. "Turrets can be replaced."

James nods, "True. Thanks for keeping us alive."

"We should offload your crew; the *Calder* is drifting."

"Wil, I'm picking up two vessels on an intercept course," Zephyr announces loud enough that James can hear too.

James looks off screen at something, "Shit, the Chinese."

NOSY NEIGHBORS_

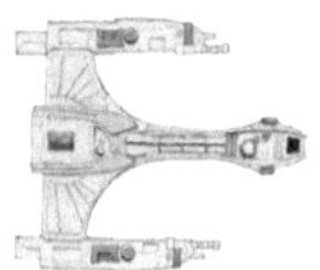

"Attention inbound Chinese frigates, I advise you to cut thrust and come to a stop, or better yet head back to base, now," Wil says letting the comm system pick up his voice.

"No reply," Cynthia says, looking up at Smith, "Sure you have the frequency right?"

"No," Smith shakes his head. "You're lucky I've remembered the frequencies for SOC ships so far. I know the rough range of frequencies common to the Chinese, but no idea what specific ones they might be listening on. Sorry."

Wil looks to Max, "Lock onto the nearest one." He turns to the ceiling again, "Chinese ships, I apologize about the two antimatter warheads we had to detonate close-ish to the moon, but you know, no other choice. That said though, that was your last warning."

"They're not in the same class as the *Calder* just so you know," Smith offers. "No plasma weapons, missiles are conventional with limited guidance once fired."

Wil nods, still looking at Max, "Put a blaster shot into the nose of the nearest ship."

The main display shows a single green bolt leave the side of the screen, rushing toward the oncoming Chinese frigates. The bolt strikes the unshielded Chinese vessel vaporizing several meters of hull and equipment within. The wounded ship lurches and tilts off its original course. The other vessel continues on course, ignoring its companion.

Everyone on the bridge stares silently at the main display until both Chinese vessels flip end over end, igniting their thrusters and burning hard back the way they came.

"I could get used to fights like that," Wil says.

"Don't let it go to your head," Maxim quips, pointing at the screen, two more missiles are streaking toward the *Ghost* from the planet's surface.

"General Pierce doesn't want to play nice," Zephyr says, watching the two missiles adjust course and begin their burn directly toward the *Ghost*.

"Or know when to give up. Max..." Wil says.

"On it," the big man replies. From somewhere deep in the ship, the sound of the weapons magazine shifting things around rumbles, then two small missiles leap from the lower portion of the main display.

The explosion matches the previous nuclear detonation. Lights on the bridge console dim and flicker briefly then return to normal. "Powerful EMP that time," Zephyr observes. "We probably just fried the *Calder*," she adds, adjusting the display to show the *Wil Calder* now twisting at a weird angle relative to its orbit.

"Oops," Wil says. He adjusts his flight controls, bringing the *Ghost* back close to the *Wil Calder*. "I guess we should get them all off and back down to the planet?" He turns to Smith, eyebrows raised.

The other human on the ship shrugs, "It'd be nice for sure. The ship-yard almost certainly doesn't have the space, and it'd be days likely weeks before the US can launch anything to get them. I doubt any of our allies are going to feel especially sympathetic seeing as how we kept a warship from them."

Maxim turns to face Smith, "You humans, I don't get it. You built that warship in secret, hiding it from your allies. Why? You've turned near planet space into a potential war zone rather than work towards a united planet?"

Before Smith can answer, Wil does, "Trust issues. It was the same when I was in NASA; it was like that when I was a kid. There'd be years of collaboration and getting along, then some whackadoo would get elected or the senate would flip parties and boom, right back to secrecy, warmongering, and nationalism." He turns to Smith, "He's just a cog in the machine."

Smith lowers his head, nodding once.

"Confirming the *Calder* looks dead in space," Zephyr says breaking the silence. "I'm getting only nominal power readings. Looks like some systems were shielded, but not all."

From Bennie's terminal Drell says, "I encouraged the General to prioritize the hardening of all primary systems. He was more interested in the plasma accelerator weapon."

Wil looks at Maxim, "Can you and Cyn go make sure the hold is ready, we're going to be packed to the gills for a few hours." He hitches a thumb toward Drell, "Take Drell and Smith with you." The big man nods and gets up to leave.

"Why do I need to help?" Drell whines.

Wil turns and looks at him, eyes narrowed, "Because"—he growls—"I'm still debating what to do with you after all this, and it's in your best interest to be on my good side." He points to the hatch; Maxim, Cynthia, and Smith have already departed. "Move your ass."

Drell harrumphs and pulls himself out of the much too small, Brailack-sized, chair.

Wil turns to Zephyr as the bridge hatch closes, "I hate him. I want to feed him to a Sarlack, a super hungry one."

His first officer smiles and nods to the screen, "Get us coupled to the hull. Let's get these people home."

CHAPTER 21_

DROPPING OFF THE KIDS_

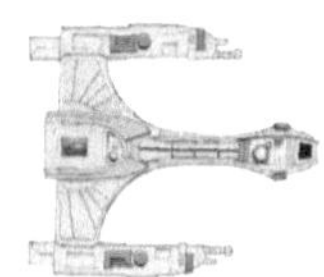

THE *GHOST*, being about one third the size of the *Wil Calder,* is a tight fit to say the least, once the crew of the *Calder* transfers over. The hold is full of exhausted and terrified humans.

"So many humans," Maxim groans at his station. The only place that isn't crowded full of distraught astronauts, the bridge.

"Yeah, one is enough," Cynthia agrees.

"More than enough," Zephyr adds.

Wil holds up his middle finger while spinning slowly in his chair. When he makes a full circle, he stops and looks at his console, "Releasing tow cables. The *Calder* should drift towards the shipyard slow enough that they can capture her."

The bridge hatch opens and James walks in followed by Agent Jason Smith. "Neat ship. Smith here showed me around a bit."

Wil looks at his friend, "You're just in time. We've engaged the stealth systems even though I know they're only partly effective. We're heading back down to the planet to drop you all off. Pierce seems to have tired of wasting nukes, so that's a plus."

"Where are we going?" Smith asks.

Wil smiles and turns around to work the flight controls.

"Dude, it's cold," James groans walking down the *Ghost's* cargo ramp. The snow on the ground is thin and muddy. "Where are we?"

"Alberta."

The tall man groans louder, "What the hell? Canada!"

Zephyr answers, "You saw for yourself. The Airspace over your country was too crowded. I think your General Pierce scrambled every atmospheric fighter craft he could find."

"And then some," Agent Smith adds, walking past the group down the ramp.

Wil nods, "Yeah you're gonna have to hitch a ride from here." He looks around at the hundred plus crew of the *Wil Calder* standing around in the snowy mud. "Sorry, best we could do. I had Cynthia call in a request for aid to the RCMP. They should be here within the hour."

As the group makes it to the bottom of the ramp, Agent Smith comes back, "I have to say Captain Calder, you're not what I was expecting."

"I get that a lot," Wil grins.

"I don't know how much of this boondoggle will be made public, but I'm sure some major changes are in store in Washington. I doubt there will be a parade, or any more schools named after you, but I'll make sure those I work for know how much you and your crew did for the United States."

Wil exchanges a look with Cynthia, "Smith, that's great, but make sure your bosses know, we did this for the world. I would love for Earth to venture out into the greater galactic society, such as it is, but that can't happen while countries are fighting each other, and the space race is an arms race. Earth needs to get its shit together and figure out how to work together."

The agent shrugs, "I'm just one man."

James walks over, "No, we're a lot of men and women, and it's past time Washington and hawks like Pierce were called to account. There's no covering this up. Half the country saw the *Calder* launch, and felt her wrath from above. Another half saw a dogfight over Utah. The whole world likely saw the *Ghost* fighting off nukes from America, disabling the *Calder* and giving the Chinese a bloody nose. That's going to require explanation, and diplomacy."

"Lots of diplomacy." Smith agrees.

Maxim smiles, "Maybe there is hope for your world after all."

"One can hope." Wil looks around, "We'd better get gone before the Mounties arrive. He turns to Drell who's loitering near the edge of the group of *Calder* crewmen. "Come on Drell, you don't get to be a Canadian, you've done enough damage on Earth."

The heavyset scientist grumbles and starts up the cargo ramp.

Zephyr turns to Smith, "It was a pleasure to meet you Special Agent Jason Smith."

The agent smiles, "You too Zephyr, just Zephyr."

Wil shakes his long-time friend's hand. "After this, I doubt we'll be back anytime soon."

James nods, grabbing his friend in a bear hug. "Well, it was great to see you; nearly dying, possibly being complicit in your illegal detention in a secret military base, not-withstanding." He smiles.

Wil nods to his crew, "Time to go." He turns and starts up the ramp.

PEACE OUT_

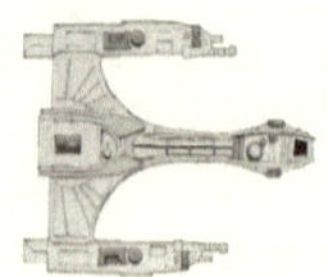

"I can't believe we came all the way to Earth and didn't stock up on bacon," Maxim complains as the repulsor lifts engage with a low-pitched whine that begins to build.

The bridge hatch opens, and Bennie comes in, "Did you guys forget I was in the med bay?" He walks over to where Drell is sitting at his console, "Get up dummy." The insulted Multonae man squeezes out of the chair grumbling.

"Oh, uh. I mean we didn't forget you, but you know we have been busy. You were out cold," Wil says, looking to the others for support.

"I was shot and had a building fall on me," Bennie grumbles, pressing buttons on his console.

"But you're better now," Zephyr says smiling. Bennie makes a rude gesture.

As the repulsor lifts push the *Ghost* skyward, Wil angles the ship, letting her weight angle the repulsors to give the ship some minor forward motion. On his console is a countdown indicating the power levels of the atmospheric engines as they ready for use. Wil adjusts the main display to look back below the ship at the hundred or so humans from the *Wil Calder* standing in the clearing.

"Wil, You ok?" Cynthia says from her station.

The view snaps back to its default *straight ahead* mode, "Yup." Wil pushes the atmospheric engine throttle forward causing the powerful engines to boom as they push the ship forward. "Enjoy the show, Canada." The force of the engines pushes everyone into their seat backs.

"You think you'll really never come back?" Cynthia asks.

On the main display the sky is beginning to darken as the *Ghost* gains altitude leaving Canada behind.

Wil nods once, "Yeah, probably. I mean we kinda made a mess of things. I mean Drell mostly did that, but you know guilt by association and all. Kinda hard to come back after basically abandoning them to figure things out on their own while trying to rebuild." He smiles grimly, "Plus, who knows what Grythlorian will do. Earth might find itself introduced to the GC sooner than anyone planned." He shrugs.

"It's not your job to fix this," Maxim offers, turning to face Wil.

"I was only trying to escape my captors. Nothing more," Drell defends. He's standing next to Cynthia's station.

"I know, but that likely isn't how folks down there will see it; most will never know about Pierce and the abuses he inflicted on you. More so, if General Pierce and his ilk remain in power," Cynthia offers.

Wil turns to Drell, "Enough from you; this is almost entirely your fault. You could have simply gone to the Peacekeepers, or whatever oversight committee or something that exists in the council. Surely someone watches the council?"

Everyone on the bridge looks at Wil, slowly shaking their heads.

On the main display, stars have emerged as the atmosphere thins.

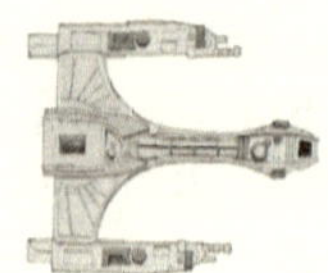

YOU'LL GET OVER IT_

ONCE THE *GHOST* jumps to FTL, the crew retires to the lounge sans Bennie who is still on the bridge. "We'll stay stealthed and keep comms offline for a bit," Wil says, handing bottles of grum to everyone. "Why the comm blackout?" Bonson Drell asks, taking the offered drink.

"Grythlorian," Zephyr says.

Wil nods, "Grythlorian. Bennie is working on some software tweaks so we can give her the bad news."

"You believe she'll know I'm aboard?" Drell surmises.

"Almost certainly," Zephyr agrees, "Her lackey Blumtillithian was aboard the ship for a bit, plus she's a GC Councilwoman, so who knows what tricks she has up those bejeweled sleeves of hers."

Bennie walks in. "Ok, we're good to go, I think."

"You think?" Maxim asks, jet black eyebrow quirked.

The Brailack shrugs, "I did my best to guess what she might do."

Wil stands, "Let's get this over with then." He turns and heads for the bridge, then turns and looks at Maxim, "Help him into the *special* compartment. Then join us in the bridge."

Maxim nods, "Come on." He gestures for Drell to follow.

"I'm disappointed in you," Councilwoman Grythlorian says from the main display. Blumtillithian standing behind her scowls.

"I understand. I think we'll find a way to continue on," Wil replies. "Drell did a world of damage to Earth. I'm not sad he's dead. It will take Earth a long time to recover."

"I wanted him alive," she says.

Over the earpiece Wil is wearing, Bennie says, "She's trying to access our systems; internal scanners in particular. I'm giving her access, even though she thinks she's taking it. The smuggler hold is masking Drell, and I'm adding some extra readings to throw her off."

Wil nods once, slowly, never taking his eyes off the main display. "Look Slivyrn, I wish we'd been able to complete the job as designed, but Drell is dead, cut to shreds by machine gun fire. Pretty gross really. Did you know Multonae look a lot like humans on the inside too?"

"Disturbing," Blumtillithian growls.

Grythlorian holds up a pale blue hand, "Interesting. While it is certainly positive that he's off the board, I wanted him alive. Needed him alive. Did he say anything about his work for me? Did he mention a data archive of any type?"

"Nope, never mentioned anything about his work," Wil shrugs. "Sorry."

The small Tarsi woman makes a low growling noise, then looks off screen at something. "Very well, Captain Calder. Per our agreement, you will not be receiving the rest of your payment."

Wil nods, "Of course."

"Don't come to Tarsis, Captain; I'm not happy and feel as if you're hiding something from me."

"Cool." Wil makes a slashing motion, and the screen goes dark, then returns to the stretched-out-stars view of the ship at FTL.

Wil turns to Maxim, "Mind going and fetching our friend?"

Maxim gets up, "Sure. Here or the lounge?"

"Lounge," Wil says.

SIDE DEALS_

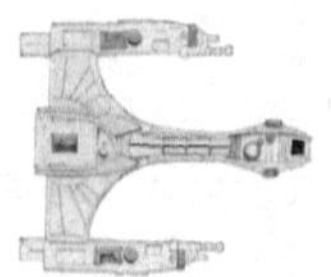

A FEW DAYS later the *Ghost* is lifting off from Brai. Wil turns to look at Bennie, "Good to see your parents and family?"

The Brailack hacker turns, "Good as any visit with family. You sure this is a good idea?"

Before Wil can answer, Maxim turns from his own console, "What he said. This seems risky. Brai isn't exactly a backwater or anything."

Wil smiles, "True, but it's well traveled enough that there are always Multonae, and dozens of other species, on the planet." He ticks off a finger, then another, "Plus thanks to Bennie, Drell has an entirely new identity, and it's easy enough to blend in with other Multonae." He ticks a third finger, "Also he knows it's in his best interest to lie low and avoid discovery."

Bennie chimes in, "Also, he needed a core GC planet, so that his little money siphoning app could work without being traced."

Cynthia purrs, "I can't believe you convinced him to go through with Grythlorian's plan, but to give us the money."

Wil shrugs, "Well he gets some too, enough to live comfortably."

Zephyr says, "That doesn't exactly make it better."

Wil beams, "No, but he tweaked the math so the amount being siphoned is even less, and it's being split in two. He has an incentive to not mess it up, and so do we."

"We're thieves," Zephyr says.

"I'll remind you of that the next time we're low on food and fighting over the last bag of Cheetos." Wil holds up a hand, "Oh wait, that will never happen again now that we have a nice little stream of passive income."

Maxim tuts, "You make it sound like we own real estate and are renting it out. We're stealing from the GC."

"But only a little," Wil replies.

"It doesn't work like that," Maxim says.

"I don't know. The GC has plenty, and I really don't enjoy those Cheeto things," Cynthia offers.

Zephyr shrugs, about to answer when Cynthia's console beeps. Cynthia turns to her console, "It's Gabe."

The main display switches from the view of the stars streaking past to the familiar chrome-plated face of Gabe.

"It is good to see you all. I trust the mission was a success?"

Maxim shrugs, "It went about as expected; shooting, screaming, property damage."

Gabe smiles his not quite right smile, "Indeed."

Wil leans forward in his chair, "You ready to come home buddy? How's your mission going?"

Gabe looks offscreen, "It is a work in progress. My involvement is no longer needed, and I am ready to resume my duties aboard the *Ghost*."

"Uh, when we left you were the figurehead of a GC wide droid rights movement." Zephyr presses, "Now you're not?"

"That is correct. I am on Durbril Two but can arrange transport elsewhere if needed."

Wil waves him off, "No worries pal, we can come to you, we're just leaving Brai." Wil pauses, "You sure you're alright?"

Gabe inclines his head, "I can provide more detail in person, when you arrive."

Maxim looks over at Wil, who shrugs slightly, then looks at the screen, "Ok man, we're on our way. See you in a few days."

When the screen blanks, then resumes its streaky star view, Wil looks around the bridge, "That seem weird to anyone else?"

Bennie nods, "Yeah weirder than normal Gabe weird. Wonder what's up?"

Wil looks at his controls, adjusting their course, "Guess we'll find out in six days."

Cynthia grins, "Movie night?"

EPILOGUE_

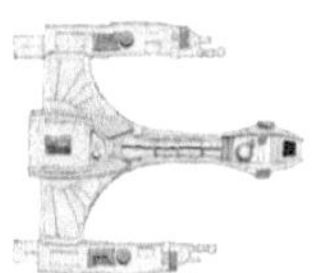

"You're sure you have it, right?"

"Ask me that again, and I will shoot you." Cynthia deadpans.

Bennie looks up from his console, "You're sure about this?"

Wil nods, "Yeah, it's the only way... I think. You good on the data?"

Bennie tuts.

Maxim grunts, *"You think?* This," he gestures toward the display, "is a big step, for *you think.*"

"Would you all shut up, you're freaking me out!" Wil snaps. He turns to the main display, "Do it."

Cynthia turns to her station, tapping a few controls. The main display, previously showing Fury rotating below the *Ghost* shifts to a grid, each with the logo of one of Earth's major national powers.

Wil looks at his friends, "Assuming James did his part—"

"Look!" Bennie whispers, pointing at the screen. Faces appear.

Wil focuses on the main display as more faces join the call.

"Captain Calder." The face in the middle of the screen, the President of the United States, Albert Stiverson says unhappy to be on the call.

"Mister President, thanks for taking this call." Wil leans forward in his chair.

"Wasn't given a lot of choice, was I?" The President says. His drawl making his a's sound soft and drawn out. "Your ultimatum didn't leave much wiggle room."

"No, it did not, and the People's Republic of China resents being dictated too." Chairman Chen says from the lower right of the screen.

Before the rest of the faces on the display can chime in, voicing their displeasure, Wil raises a hand, "Let's get this over with, shall we?"

The nearly forty faces on the primary display nod slowly.

Wil dives in, "Thanks to the aggressive experimentation of the United States, the Earth is at a crossroads it shouldn't have come to for years, decades at least. The Galactic Commonwealth has moved Earth from protected status to more of a warning kind of thing."

"A warning kind of thing?" The head of the European Union asks.

"Yeah like you'd place on a dangerous location."

"Quarantine?" Zephyr whispers

Wil waves her off, "The GC has labeled our solar system as dangerous." President Stiverson nods his approval. "That's not a good thing!" Wil growls, "By losing protected system status, anyone can move in on Earth and the Peacekeepers won't stop them."

"And the one thing that might have protected us is at least eight months from combat effectiveness, thanks to you." President Stiverson growls.

"As if that thing would have made a difference." Maxim said, looking over to Zephyr, his hand up for a high five. Wil snapped his fingers, then flipped his big tactical officer off.

"Ok look. This is getting away from the point." Wil says, trying to steer the conversation back on track.

"And that was what?" The British Prime Minister asked, her tone dry.

Wil inhales, "We're transmitting a data package, a big one, to each of you. You're all also getting a unique pass phrase. The data files are encrypted, and the only way to decrypt them will be for every single one of you to come together as one. Only when the files are together, and you each use your pass phrase will the archive open. Trust me when I say this, nothing you have access to can even come close to decrypting the files."

"And just what are in these files?" The President of the South American Alliance asks.

"Everything; ship designs, weapons tech, bio-tech, engineering that will make your head spin, the works." Wil answers. He continues, "Earth is vulnerable, and the only way to survive is to come together. The data file will solve hunger, power, defense and more. The data in the archive will jumpstart Earth's entry onto the galactic stage by a century or two, at least."

"And if we go it on our own?" President Stiverson asks.

Wil frowns, "Jeez dude. I don't know; the Xelurians roll in and eat everyone. The Partherians show up and start charging you a fee not to nuke the planet from orbit. Any one of the many crime syndicates shows up and loads everyone on the planet into freighters to sell into slavery? Take your damn pick." Several of the world leaders look visibly stricken by Wil's outburst.

"Transfer complete, Wil," Bennie says.

Wil nods, "Ball's in your court, ladies, and gentlemen. Don't fuck it up." He turns his head slightly to Cynthia, nodding. The screen turns black, then returns to the view of Fury below.

Maxim stands and walks over to Wil, placing his large blue-skinned hand on Wil's shoulder, "Think they'll do the right thing?"

Wil shrugs, "Who knows, they're not ready, but once word gets out that the GC has revoked their protected system status, who knows who will show up first."

"Maybe we'll get lucky and you'll stay the only human out here." Bennie offers.

Wil flips him off, then says, "God, I need to get drunk, like now." He stands and leaves the bridge, the others hot on his heels.

THANK YOU_

Thank you so much for reading Space Rogues 5: So This is Earth?

If you enjoyed it I'd love it if you left a review. Seriously, reviews are a big deal. They help readers find authors.

Reviews are social proof and go a long way to encouraging other readers to take a chance on an unknown.

As I get more and more used to being "A Writer" I realize how much work goes into it, that isn't *writing*.

Marketing, sales, networking, promotion, etc. Plus of course, writing, cover designing and editing.

It's a job, one of the most fun jobs I've ever had and I get up every morning excited to sit down and share worlds with you. I hope you enjoy them as much as I do.

OFFER_

As they say, there's no harm in asking, so here we go.

If you can help connect me with someone who can get Space Rogues on
a screen (Big or Little) I'll cut you in for 10% (Up to $10,000) of
whatever advance is paid.

Send me an email and we can discuss.
rights@johnwilker.com

STAY CONNECTED_

Want to stay up to date on the happenings in the Galactic Commonwealth?
Sign up for my newsletter at
johnwilker.com/newsletter
Lots of goodies await you, just sayin'

Visit me online at
johnwilker.com

If you like supporting things you love by sporting merch, well you're in luck! I've launched a Space Rogues Shop, take a look.

Coming Spring 2020
Space Rogues 6: War and Peace
Pre-Order it now!

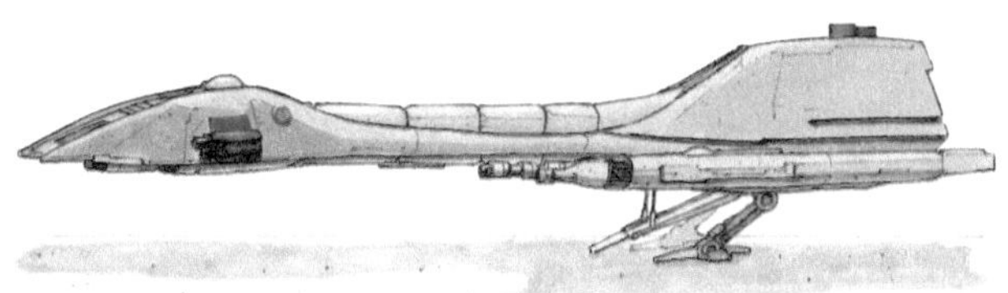